Locked Down

by

Jeanne Selander Miller

BY
JEANNE SELANDER MILLER

For the Tuesday Writers
at the Laura Riding Jackson Foundation
in Vero Beach, Florida
Thank you for your weekly encouragement, kind words,
thoughtful critique, and for keeping me company
via Zoom
throughout the Covid-19 pandemic.

Watch your thoughts;

They become your words.

Watch your words;

They become your actions.

Watch your actions;

They become your habits.

Watch your habits;

They become your character.

Watch your character;

It becomes your destiny.

~ Lao Tzu

Chapter 1

It was late in February when my results arrived. My sister, Becca, had given me one of those genetic testing kits for Christmas. You know the ones where you spit in the tube. They're advertised all over the internet and social media. They had been offering a sixty-nine-dollar special just before the holidays and Becca had bought them for everyone in the family. There must have been some kind of a discount if you bought five or more. This had always been her thing as she had spent years gathering data and filling out the branches of our family tree using information from Ancestry.com and the Latter-day Saints website. Nearly every time we got together she had some tidbit of information to share about some long lost relative she had discovered. Cynical, as I am known to be, I couldn't help but wonder who these gifts were really for, as I wasn't the least bit interested in our family genealogy.

But that was then and this is now, and to say the world has changed would be a gross understatement.

My sibs and I had grown up in a small rural town in the Central Adirondacks. It was unbelievably beautiful with the mountains, rivers and lakes. Every summer our little town filled up with tourists and they had more cash than they knew what to do with. Come autumn the trees on the mountainside displayed a brilliant array of colors when the leaf peepers arrived to bask in the loveliness. The stillness of the winter has a magic all its own where all of life as we know it becomes buried beneath the snow. That is until the snowmobilers arrive en masse creating all kinds of chaos. The home of my childhood was truly nature's playground.

But I had grown up poor, not totally impoverished, but money was tight in our family and we learned to scrimp and save. I wanted things and experiences that we simply couldn't afford. I lived with my two brothers and two sisters and my parents, as unlikely as that was in a town where people changed partners on a fairly regular basis. Maybe it was because Grandma lived with us, and she was just about as no-nonsense as a person could be. She wouldn't put up with anything like that, she just wouldn't.

Our camp and all our land had been in Grandma's family for as long as anyone could remember. There was no question about it, she was the matriarch of our family. After all we were the Earls, and the Earl family had standards, Grandma's standards. And just in case we forgot, as we were continually reminded as children, it was in everyone's best interest if you remembered which side your bread is buttered on.

Like most kids in my town, I'd been working since I was thirteen, and babysitting, yard work, and shoveling snow before that. There were child-labor laws but that didn't apply if you were working in the family business, and besides, nearly everyone was being paid in cash. We were a hard-working, independent lot, and we did our best to keep Uncle Sam's hands out of our wallets.

As beautiful as the Adirondacks are, by the time I was eighteen I'd had just about enough of this small-town living. The summer after I graduated from the Union Free School, my eldest brother, Josiah drove me to the train station in Utica. I was leaving this little burg behind and headed for New York, the city. I had a second cousin on my mother's side who said I could stay with her for a few days until I found a place of my own. I felt pretty flush with over five thousand dollars in the bank. I wasn't naive enough to believe it would go very far in one of the most expensive cities in the world, but it was enough to get me started.

This was just over ten years ago, but it feels like another lifetime.

The phone rings but no one answers and after a few rings it switches over to voicemail.

"This is Edward Earl. Can't come to the phone. You know what to do. Beep." It always grates on me that he still only uses his name on the voicemail for the landline. There are four other people who live there too. But Dad thinks he's something special—king of the castle and heir to the kingdom.

"Hey Mom, it's me, Emma. I don't know if you've been watching the news or not, but Governor Cuomo just ordered all non-essential workers to stay home to keep this virus from spreading. Hard to believe he considers designer lingerie non-essential. Anyway, I'm out of work for the time being and I thought I'd come home. Can someone meet me at the train in Utica? I'll be in at 7:45 tonight. Call me back. I'm on my cell."

"So, you're leaving."

"I guess. There is no way Gabriella is going to do the right thing and stay home. Besides, even if she did, I don't think I could stand it. I can barely stand to be around her when she pops in to change her clothes before heading out to yet another grand gala or tea with the queen. I never was much for playing dress-up or Barbies."

"You're too much. So, you're just going to leave me here with her. I don't think she'll be here very much, she rarely is. Besides how long can this forced furlough actually last?"

"Do you want to come with me?"

"No thanks, I'm a city girl. Besides, I remember how you lovingly refer to March in the Adirondacks as the mud season. I think I'll pass."

"I'm a little concerned that no one will be available to pick me up. The cell service is really spotty once you get up in the mountains."

"I guess you could always call an Uber."

"That's a good one. There's no such thing where I come from, but I think I have a third cousin once removed named Hubert. Maybe if I can hitch a ride to the Walmart and yell really loud he'll be driving back to town from the Tractor Supply, and give me a lift."

"Seriously? It's not as bad as all that."

"Who said anything about it being bad, I'm only givin' you the good stuff. Are you laughing at me? Look I've got to pack and get out of here if I'm going to make my train."

"Don't even try and hug me goodbye," Cassie says as she takes a step back and crosses her arms across her chest.

I laugh. "Don't you look tough."

"First off, for all I know you might already have the beastly bug and be one of those asymptomatic carriers. And besides, I'm not all that happy you're leaving me here with Gabriella." And with that Cassie opens her arms for a hug. "I'm going to miss you."

"Are you sure you don't want to come?"

"'I'm sure. Now get going and be safe."

It didn't take me long to throw a few things into a bag, I didn't need much. I still had some clothing and personal stuff in a room at my parent's house. Besides, I work in the fashion industry and the way I dress in the city isn't exactly what I'll need upstate. I pull on a thermal Henley, then a flannel shirt and my red puffy jacket. It's still raining here and no doubt it will be snowing by the time I get home.

Home— I've lived in the city for over ten years now, and still, I think of the home of my childhood in the Adirondacks as going home. It's really been too long since I have spent any real time with my family. Perhaps, in times of trouble and pervasive fear, going home implies some element of safety and comfort that I no longer feel here in the city. I shake off the notion as I pull on a pair of wool socks and winter boots, not quite hiking boots, but these are warm and should be pretty good in the ice and snow.

I grab the paperback I've been reading, the latest mystery in the series by Louise Penny, and my sewing bag. I'll need something to keep me busy on the train, if all goes well it should take about seven hours. But it never does, God knows what kind of delays we'll encounter today. I check one more time that my e-ticket has downloaded to my phone and that my phone is fully charged before I head out to Penn Station.

I try to get an Uber. No one is available. The drivers must be apprehensive about picking up strangers on the street and putting themselves in harm's way. I hadn't thought this through. I shouldn't be surprised. It's a rainy day in Manhattan. Non-essential businesses are closed. Everyone and their brother, who has any other option, is trying to get the hell out of the city. I stand on the corner and try to hail a cab. A good ten minutes pass as I slowly get soaked in the drizzle, still no luck. All the cabs are engaged and in these days of the Coronavirus nobody wants to take the subway. But I have little choice, I have to get moving or I'll miss my train.

I head for the subway and I get caught up in the throngs of humanity, good luck attempting any social distancing in here. By the time I arrive at Penn Station, the place is mobbed with people trying to get out of the city. New Yorkers are not known for being particularly gentile and mannerly, even on the best of days, at least not when compared with the stereotypical Southerners, bless their hearts. Today those jockeying for position at Penn Station exemplify New Yorkers on steroids— agitated, paranoid, aggressive, and delusional. We are not at our best today. God help us all for common courtesy has blown out the window and the Coronavirus has blown in. I try to limit my exposure and keep to myself. It's a skill I learned at my Mama's knee, we keep strangers at arm's length. This is nothing new to me, and there are plenty of strangers here amongst this frightened collection of God's children.

I'm grateful I had the forethought to buy my ticket online last night. I guess the worry and insomnia that kept me up was good for something. Long lines of people wait impatiently to talk to a ticket agent or to attempt to buy a ticket at the vending machine.

It doesn't make me feel any safer to see armed members of the National Guard roving through the waiting areas. Nearly every guy I know in the Adirondacks has a gun. It's a throwback to another time, as they fancy themselves as our fearless providers when they head out to the woods to hunt during deer or bear season. But what the hell are these guys hunting?

I can't help but wonder if this is what it was like in Europe when masses of people attempted to flee the madness of the encroaching Nazi's during the lead up to World War II.

I watch the board and to my great relief train 233 on the Empire line is on time and is scheduled to begin boarding on track 6-E in a few minutes. Once they post the track, people in this disperse crowd begin to move. I'm lucky not to be trampled in the stampede as people push and shove while grumbling and peppering their displeasure with profanity as they aggregate towards the east gate and encroach on my personal space. Many of these travelers have brought big suitcases and lots of luggage that they inadvertently bang into me and others who wait in this line without any acknowledgement or a word of apology. Do they know something I don't? Looks like wherever they're going, they're planning to stay for a while. Someone behind me begins to cough, a deep rattling cough, as everyone turns their head to see who it is. I offer up a prayer; please God— please don't make me sit next to *that* person. I'm fairly certain every seat on the train has been sold, so I'm pretty sure I'll be sitting next to someone. So much for spreading out and any social distancing.

To my great relief, the man with the cough is not my seat partner and not even seated in my car. Still I wondered why he isn't wearing a mask with a cough like that, and for that matter why am I not wearing one? My anxiety is rising as more and more people find their seats. I have an overwhelming sense of vulnerability and I begin to wonder if this really is a good idea.

An older woman stands in the aisle and looks at her ticket, then takes the seat beside me. I'm at the window and she's on the aisle. I pull my book from my bag and turn away from her, giving her the old cold shoulder. Maybe if she doesn't talk to me, she won't infect me. I'm not above being rude, after all self-preservation is at stake.

When had I become such a New Yorker? I think about my behavior, and feel ashamed. I could at least say hello. Looking over my shoulder, I see her adjust her expensive noise- cancelling headphones. She's not inviting conversation either, I guess I'm off the hook.

I settle in and start to read as we pass through one station after another. Yonkers, Croton-Harmon, Poughkeepsie, Rhinecliff-Kingston, the conductor calls out the stations as passengers arrive at their destinations, awkwardly gathering their cumbersome belongings as they make their way toward the exits while others wait anxiously to board. All I can think about is the number of people who are breathing in this confined space and potentially infecting one another. I might have been safer staying in the city.

By the time the train pulls into Albany-Rensselaer I have already finished my book and I still have at least two hours before we get to Utica, something about changing the engine and track repair. The woman sitting next to me got off at the Rhinecliff station and at least for now no one is seated beside me. I stretch out a little and pull out my sewing. I hadn't thought this through very well as I start to tack some Milanese lace across the bodice of an ivory negligee. The guy across the aisle looks me over. I guess my shit-kicking snow boots and my flannel shirt portray quite a contrast to the image I create by demurely sewing lace on this silky, sexy garment. I want to tell him to stop judging me, and that things are not always as they seem, but decide against it. I don't want to invite any conversation. Besides, my creep meter is going off.

"Hey is that for you?" he asks.

I look his way, straight-faced and shrug before responding, "Je ne parle pas anglais." I return my eyes to my sewing hoping he doesn't speak French.

He turns and looks away muttering to himself but still loud enough for me to hear, "Fuckin' foreigners."

By the time we pull into the station in Utica it's dark and has been for a while. The train is an hour late and I just hope there is someone here to meet me. The snow is falling and there are only a handful of people here. Lucky for me, one of them is my brother.

"Hey Emma," Joe calls to me from the doorway across the empty lobby. His voice echoes resoundingly off the tiled floors, walls, and ceiling.

"I thought you were Fran-chaise," the plump beast with the curly mustache snarls at me as he passes by me on the way to the exit.

I choose to ignore him as I wave to my brother.

"What did you do to that guy?" my brother asks as I approach.

"Why? Did he say something to you?"

"He said you were a bitch and I should teach you some manners."

"He's probably right," I respond and both my brother and I break into laughter as he leans in to hug me.

9

"Hey now, none of that. I might have the cooties."

"Oh, that's right. This is going to take some getting used to," Joe says as we walk to the lot across the street.

It's a lot easier parking in Utica than most other cities in the country. Given there is little public transportation, almost everyone travels by car and very few people take the train anywhere.

"Don't be surprised if you aren't welcomed with open arms up here, everybody and their brother is afraid of this virus and getting infected."

"Great."

I put on my mittens and pull up my hood as I help my brother brush the snow off the car windows. "Wow, it's really coming down."

"You haven't been away that long that you've forgotten all about winter in the Adirondacks, have you? It might still be snowing here on Memorial Day."

"No, but for heaven sake the first day of spring is next week and this is a fricken arctic blast."

"I can't decide if you talk like Grandma or a truck driver. Heaven sake and fricken this and fricken that. You've got fifty miles before we get home to clean up that mouth or Gram will be getting the soap out just like she did in the old days."

I laugh. "You had a little of that Lifebuoy ground between the teeth. I remember the story. Mom said you had a *potty mouth*, and said that was bathroom talk. So, you ran in the bathroom and yelled all the bad words you knew." Now we were both laughing.

"You mean like poop and fart? I know worse words now and sometimes I use them, just not around the *Countess*."

"Oh, my aren't you a brazen-faced fellow, don't let Grandma hear you call her that."

We pass the Citgo in Remsen and Josiah checks the gas gauge before he turns north onto Route 28 as he drives the old Jeep into the park and toward home. The next gas station is a good thirty-five miles away and we don't want to run out of gas tonight. The snow, which had been falling steadily since we left Utica was now coming down fast and furious as we gained altitude moving into the mountains. Thankfully this old truck has four-wheel drive and my brother has grown up driving on these snow-covered roads. Although it's clear the plows have been out, the roads are already covered over again and are slippery. The gleaming eyes of a small herd of deer peer out from beneath the trees hugging both sides of the road. Nearly everyone from these parts has a story or two of someone they know who totaled their car or worse when one of these creatures decided to dart across the road without warning.

And I thought the city streets of New York were dangerous.

By the time we pull into town, it's deserted. This shouldn't come as any surprise, it's a snowy night in March, not exactly the height of the tourist season. Still it's a little disconcerting to see that even the TOW Bar and Tony Harper's are closed. They're always open. "This place is even more desolate than usual, I was kinda hoping we could stop for a quick one before we have to hunker down with the family."

"Did you think when they said all non-essential businesses had to close they would be making an exception for the TOW Bar."

"I'm sure some of the old coots who frequent that place find it absolutely essential."

"Hopefully they stocked up at the liquor store or there will be more than a few old fellas going through alcohol withdrawal. Hopefully Pop isn't one of them."

"Rest assured our old man is well prepared, he probably has enough Budweiser to see him through to Armageddon."

"Hopefully that's a long way off. He won't need to worry about me breaking into his stash, I can't stand that stuff. Do you think he has any wine?"

"Gewürztraminer or some New York Riesling, he picked up a case when he heard you were coming home."

"Oh God, I'd rather drink a Bud. That stuff is so sickly sweet, it tastes like fermented raisins, yuck."

Josiah laughs, "My, haven't you turned into a wine snob, nothing but European wines for you."

"Actually, Gewurztraminer *is* German, I just don't like it. I hope he didn't buy it just for me. How many times must I tell him I don't like it?"

"Oh please, you know he's an old Kraut and he knows what's good for you. So just shut up and drink it. Maybe it will grow on you."

12

"Yeah, like mold on something rotten." I say a bit too snarky. "I know he means well."

"Remember that. You haven't been home in a long time. It'd be nice if you could show a little gratitude and take it easy on Pop."

"I'll try," I mumble. I turn my head to look out the window into the darkness as I wonder if he'll afford me the same courtesy.

We drive through town and then head further into the park towards the even smaller town of Eagle Bay and then pass through the Village of Inlet. Everything is dark.

It is beautiful tonight with the freshly fallen snow. I miss this place, our home, the land, the lakes, and the great outdoors when I'm away and working in the city, but perhaps it's all just a romantic illusion. I'm already beginning to chafe at the notion of being here and doing things just like we've always done them because that's the way Pop wants them done. "I wonder how long this quarantine is going to last."

"Your guess is as good as mine."

"I guess you'll be working from home."

"I keep pretty busy plowing snow in the winter. The ground is already getting too soft for logging. We had a few warm days last week. Besides, Pop thinks this is a good time to work on the property since I won't be needed up at the mountain. There'll be no more skiing this season. How about you? Will you be working while you're here?"

"I will as long as the internet keeps working. I have some design work to do and some sample mock-ups I can finish."

"Well la-di-da, who knew all that sewing and mending that Gram taught you would help you become a big-name fashion designer."

"They may be my designs but it's not my name. I make enough to keep a roof over my head and that's not for nothing in a city like New York."

"Still I'm proud of you."

"Thanks Joe. I just wish Pop didn't think what I do is so frivolous."

"Come on Emma, you make lacy ladies' underwear that costs more than most people in this town spend for groceries every week. You have to admit it's not exactly essential, and kinda bourgeois."

"Since when did you become a card-carrying member of the Communist Party?"

"Don't start with me, I'm just another hard workin' American and I'm not apologizing for that, not now and not ever."

Josiah pulls off onto the long private road back toward our land and the house. He drops the plow on the front of his truck as the snow has made the road impassable. We have over a thousand acres back here in the woods and a couple of small ponds connected by the Moose River. There was a time when there was talk of selling some of it off to a developer but Gram won't hear of it. We need to hold onto all of it, just in case.

Just in case of what?

Chapter 2

The outside lights go on as the truck sets off the motion detector and in no time at all someone has turned on the porch light and Mom can be seen with her face up against the glass of the front door of our old log home. Trigger darts through the dog door barking like mad.

I wait a moment before grabbing my bag and opening the door while my brother calls the dog off. With a click of his tongue, the shepherd sits in the snow beside Josiah. "Impressive," I say. Clearly, he has been working with the dog. "Thanks for picking me up, Joe. I appreciate it."

"No problem. I'm glad you're here and out of that cesspool of humanity."

I decide to let it go. I tell myself, *he means well.* This may well become my mantra.

The snow is already over the tops of my boots as I plow my way towards the front door. Mom opens the door, "Come in, come on in Emma. You haven't been home since Christmas and that is much too long." She wraps me in her arms and kisses my cheek. I can't help but notice how Mom's once blond hair is nearly white now. She wears it long and loose, and it looks good on her. She is still such a beautiful woman, and as understated as always. But she looks tired, living with Pop can do that to a person.

"Mom, you're not supposed to be hugging and kissing me." I give her a squeeze before we disengage.

"Oh, I'm not afraid of you," she says with a smile as she whispers in my ear, "just don't go acting like Pop, he hasn't hugged anyone in years. It might actually serve him well now that we're supposed to be keeping six feet from one another," Mom laughs. "Edward, come out here. Emma's home."

"Hi Pop." I say as I wave across the room to him.

"We waited dinner for you. Your mother made a venison stew but we expected you over an hour ago. So, we ate without you. I've just finished but your mother has a couple of plates warming in the oven for you and Josiah."

I go to set my bags inside the front door, but Mom picks them up before they even hit the floor and carries them down the hall to the bedroom I once shared with my sister, Becca. "Thanks Mom."

I follow my father into the front room where there is a big roaring fire in the fieldstone fireplace. Pop calls out to my brother, "Don't come in here empty handed." So, before Josiah can even get his coat off, he turns around and heads for the woodshed.

"Come warm yourself beside the fire. I'm certain you've had a long day."

"Where's Gram?" I ask.

"She's already gone off to bed. She was tired. She starts her day early, and works hard around here, as you well know."

"Indeed, she does."

"She said to tell you she'll see you in the morning. Can I get you a glass of wine?"

I think about the promise I made to myself— just be nice. "Sure Pop, that would be great."

Joe comes in with an armload of split hardwood which he puts into the old copper boiler next to the fireplace. "Something sure smells good," Josiah says as Mom returns from the bedroom.

"Venison stew, I use the shoulder from that buck you shot last fall."

I take a deep breath but I can't really smell anything at all, not even the fire.

"Are you hungry, Emma?" Mom asks.

"Maybe a little." I should be, I try to remember when I ate last. Nothing really sounds good.

Mom comes in with a glass of white wine for me and a mug of beer for my brother. "To your health," Josiah says as we clink glasses. I take a sip of my wine. It's not as sweet as I had remembered, in fact, it's rather tasteless. In this case, that makes it at least palatable.

"Come join us in the kitchen while your mother gets your supper on." I follow Pop and Josiah into the brightly lit kitchen where Mom has the table set and a large portion of steaming hot brown stew is already heaped up the plates. It looks like something shoveled up from a barnyard.

"Sorry we don't have any salad to go with your dinner tonight," Mom says as she passes me the breadbasket filled with hot homemade rolls. "We're not going into the grocery store these days, besides I heard from Greta Vogel that the shelves have already been picked bare. But we won't starve. We have all we need stashed away in the larder."

"Might not have any fresh veggies until they come up in the garden. Pop has put an extension on the greenhouse and Mom and Grandma planted about a week ago. Most of the seeds have already started to sprout," Josiah says as I pass him the breadbasket.

"Really? It's still snowing up here."

"We've really bumped up the greenhouse operation since last fall. We'll be able to extend the growing season for at least a month on either end with grow lights and the new propane heater we've installed," Pop says with pride as he takes a big gulp of his beer.

"Propane? I thought you didn't want to use propane because you didn't like being dependent on Helmer's to deliver if there's another oil crisis and all that."

"I don't. Your brothers are already working on converting the whole thing over to solar, but we wanted to get the seeds started so we'll have a good harvest come fall. Besides it's always good to have a backup plan. Having a tank full of propane is a good thing, just in case," Pop says.

Just in case. There he goes again. I've been hearing this since the day I was born.

I push the venison stew around on my plate, it's never been one of my favorites. There is something about eating Bambi that has killed my appetite. I grew up eating this way but I have long since abandoned the life of a carnivore. Everyone in my family knows I rarely eat meat, but no one seems to care. In our house, you eat what you are served or you go hungry.

"You're not eating, Emma. Aren't you hungry?" Mom asks. "Can I fix you something else?"

"Since when did you become her short order cook?" Pop barks at Mom.

"I didn't ask for anything." I snap at my father. "I'm just not all that hungry."

"I'll eat it," Josiah pipes up and I slide my uneaten stew across the table to him.

"Waste not, want not," Pop says as he drains the last of his beer and then slams his empty mug on the table.

He lifts his head in Mom's direction as she jumps out of her chair to get him another bottle from the fridge. Mom pulls an old church key from her apron pocket and removes the cap before refilling Pop's old German beer stein. It's some old family heirloom and he's the only one allowed to touch his precious mug. Unless you're on dish duty, then that rule gets set aside.

"Are you sure you're feeling okay?" Mom asks me as she places a cool hand across my forehead. "You feel a little warm."

"That's because it's a million degrees in here." I say as I push her hand away. Immediately I am filled with remorse. Mom is everyone's punching bag. Magda do this and Magda do that. "Sorry Mom," I mutter under my breath and she gives me a small smile in acknowledgment.

"It's hard to control the temperature in the house with a wood burning stove," Mom offers a simple explanation. "Why don't you move to Lucas's chair and away from the fire?"

I do as I am asked. What is it about going home that makes me resort to acting like a sullen fourteen-year-old all over again?

"So, while we are under quarantine, is everyone pretty much staying put?" I ask no one in particular.

"Willa and the children have been coming over during the day. Becca's been here most days to get on the internet and use her computer. She's been helping Willa's girls with their lessons. Everyone is expected to homeschool their children now that the schools have been closed and Becca has more patience with the little ones than their mother seems to be able to muster. Willa is the first to admit she never wanted to be a teacher. Heidi can sit and read for hours, but Tilly is more like you."

"And what is that supposed to mean?"

"She's a restless wonder, that one. Much like you were at her age. No offense intended." Mom is quick to try to smooth things over.

"None taken. Perhaps that wanderlust will serve her well. I don't think it's hurt me."

To which my father adds a loud, "Harrumph."

I shrug and decide to pick my battles, and this will not be one of them. "Besides Heidi is three years older than Tilly. Tilly's only seven and just a little girl." They need to back off on the children. I remember this tone of judgement and endless comparisons.

"What about Lucas and Elias, are they still working?" I inquire about my brother and Willa's husband. "Or have they been laid off?"

"Elias is considered an essential worker but Lucas has been here most days helping Pop and Josiah get those new solar panels up to expand the grid."

"What's so essential about finish carpentry and cabinet making?" I ask a bit too incredulously. "How is his work more essential than mine? We're both creating beautiful things for people with money." I fear I may have just stepped into something, and I already wish I could issue a retraction.

Quickly Josiah comes to my rescue before I can be branded as a useless ne'er-do-well. "Probably just because he can work independently and doesn't need to interact with anyone else on the jobsite. He's at a pretty low risk for infection putting that new kitchen in out at that great camp on Raquette Lake."

"I'm just glad one of you has some real skills and will still be employed and bringing some money home. We don't know how long this quarantine may last," Pop says.

I know his comment about being without skills is directed at me, but I refuse to take the bait. There may be some truth in what he says and I guess that's why it is so hard to take. Lucas had been just eking by since his job at the waterpark ended last September. Now he's been laid off from his grooming job at McCauley Mountain now that skiing has been declared non-essential, too.

There'll be timber to harvest when the State Department of Environmental Quality approves the long-awaited sustainability plan.

Hopefully, the summer folks will be back for the season, bringing their checkbooks with them. This town runs on the tourists' dollars.

It isn't the first time today that I've wondered how I will pay my rent if I'm furloughed for very long. I make pretty good money in the city, but most of my inflated salary barely covers my rent. I doubt I could command half as much as I make in most other cities, let alone here in rural America.

I try to push the thought from my head. "May I be excused?" I ask, just as I did as a child.

"Of course, Emma. Are you sure I can't get you anything else to eat? You hardly touched your food."

"No thanks, Mom. Can I help you with the dishes before I turn in?"

"That would be great," Mom smiles.

We both stand and begin to clear as my father and brother take their beers and slip out to sit in front of the fire. There isn't much to clean up as my parents and my grandmother ate before we got here. I fill the sink with some hot water and add a squeeze of dish soap. "Okay if I wash?" I ask, hoping to get my hands in the hot soapy water to chase away this chill that has just come over me.

"Sure," Mom replies as she grabs a sponge to wipe down the table.

Before she can finish, Pop beckons her from the other room, "Magda, bring your son and me another beer." He never says please or thank you. I'd have been slapped from here until tomorrow if I ever tried to order anyone around as he does. I learned long ago that the rules of life don't apply to Pop.

I count the empties on the countertop, as I put them into the recycling bin. There are ten. Pop and Joe had three each since we got here, therefore Pop must have had the other four beforehand. I wonder how many more he will have tonight before things get really ugly. I think about Josiah saying that Pop had enough Budweiser to last him through to Armageddon. If he keeps drinking like this, then perhaps the end of the world is a lot closer than I'd thought. Or at least the end of the world as we know it.

Chapter 3

I can't even fathom getting into the shower tonight and going to bed with wet hair. The bathroom and my bedroom are a long way from the wood stove in the kitchen. It gets chilly down at this end of the house. Pop says a cool house is better for sleep. Besides Grandma has been in bed for hours and I know she doesn't always sleep well. I don't want to risk waking her by drying my hair given that her room is across the hall from the bathroom. Instead, I do my best to wash up in the bathroom sink attempting to remove whatever urban grime still clings to me with a sliver of what's left of grandma's lavender soap and an old worn washcloth.

Mom has turned the bed down for me, just like she did when I was a kid. She's put clean flannel sheets on the bed, beneath the old down comforter, and a woolen blanket. I climb in and cover up. I won't be cold for long. I had planned to read before going to sleep but I can hardly keep my eyes open so instead turn over to take one last look out my bedroom window. It has finally stopped snowing and the grow lights from the greenhouse cause the newly fallen snow to sparkle. It would be considered beautiful if it were Christmastime, but it loses its appeal in the last few weeks of March. I'm just over it.

I fall asleep easily, but in the early morning hours I begin to toss and turn, covers off, covers on. I have a rough night of interrupted sleep and even get up about four a.m. to get a drink of water and look for some Advil. As I leave my bedroom, Josiah's Alsatian shepherd greets me in the hallway with low growl. I speak to him softly, "It's okay Trigger. It's only me." I wait for him to give me a sniff. Once he's convinced he knows me, he wags his tail and then lets me pass. I find the bottle of Advil in the medicine cabinet above the sink in the bathroom. There isn't a glass so I cup my hands beneath the faucet and take a camp drink to wash down the tablets.

Once back in bed it isn't long before I'm sound asleep. It's not even light out when someone raps loudly on my door, "Emma, are you awake?"

It takes me a moment to figure out where I am and who is knocking on my door. It's my sister, Willa. "I am now," I grumble. "What time is it?"

"Time for breakfast. See you in the kitchen. You may be furloughed but you're not on vacation."

"How is this my life?" I ask myself out loud as I pull out my cell phone to check the time. Oh, for the love of God, it's only six thirty. We only went on daylight savings time a little over a week ago. The mornings are dark again and I haven't adjusted to the time change. It seems like the middle of the night.

Welcome to life at this outpost of the civilized world. I find an old fleece robe in a red and black buffalo plaid hanging in the closet. This thing must be left over from when I was in high school. Grumbling under my breath to no one but myself, "I work in the garment industry for God's sake, in lingerie no less." Still I pull it on. Who cares, at least it's warm. A pair of old fur lined moccasins from the back of the closet complete my ensemble. Looks like one of the dogs has been chewing on the left one. I push my feet inside.

"Emma, come on. Breakfast is on the table and it's getting cold," someone bellows down the hall. No one is sleeping now. Once Pop is up, everybody damn well better get up.

I open the door to venture out for breakfast when both Trigger and his larger and more aggressive liter mate, Bullet, come bounding down the hallway. I stand stock still while they both smell me. Heidi, their little taskmaster gives a whistle and they both return to her.

"Hi Auntie Emma," Heidi says as she wraps her arms around my waist.

"Good morning sweetheart. Those two are quite the dynamic duo this early in the morning. I'm glad you were here to call them off or I might have looked even worse than this old slipper." I kick my left leg out from beneath the robe to show her the toe of my chewed-up slipper.

"Sorry about that. I think Trigger got in your closet when someone left the bedroom door open. If Bullet had found it, there wouldn't be anything left of it," she says as she reaches down to pet the heads of both of these beasts.

"Better my slipper than my foot," I say with a laugh as I ruffle my niece's pretty blonde hair.

"I didn't see Bullet when I arrived, was he over at your house last night?"

"Bullet was on guard duty."

"Guard duty? What on earth do we have that needs to be protected by these two German Shepherds?"

"There Alsatians, Auntie Emma," Heidi corrects me with an air of superiority that is real unattractive on a ten-year-old.

"You didn't answer my question."

"Bullet and Trigger take turns guarding the supply house, we haven't scrimped and saved for a rainy day only to have the lazy and the spendthrifts come lookin' for a handout now that times are tough."

"Whatever are you talking about?" I can't believe my own ears; what kind of bullshit are they filling the children's heads with? I give my niece a look portraying my disappointment.

"Come on girls, breakfast is on the table," Grandma calls from the kitchen.

"What happened to all of that talk from the pastor about being our brother's keeper?"

"How about God helps those who help themselves," she quips back with impertinence.

I put my hand on Heidi's shoulder, "You and I are going to talk about this later." She shrugs it off as she and the dogs enter the kitchen.

"Good morning, sleepyhead," Grandma says as she reaches around to hug me while still holding a spatula. Grandma is already dressed for the day in a sweater and wool pants beneath her linen apron. "I thought the smell of the bacon would have drawn you out of the sack an hour ago. How about some pancakes?"

"That sounds great. How about a cup of coffee, too?"

"M'dear I thought you'd given up the coffee and were a tea drinker now," Grandma says as she pours me a cup from the old blue and white spatterware pot that sits warming on the woodstove.

"I guess I need a little extra kick to get going this morning, I didn't sleep very well last night and you folks are early risers." With that Grandma turns back to the stove and continues flipping the pancakes off of the griddle and onto a large stoneware platter. I don't know how she does it, as she still cooks breakfast for the family every day, even at ninety-one years old.

The table is already completely set as I take my cup of coffee and find my seat at the table. It's the same seat I have used all my life.

The front door slams as my brothers arrive. One by one the others begin helping themselves to the coffee, and taking their seats around the old farm table. The silence of the morning is broken as everyone is talking all at once. It's enough to make my head hurt. It's hard to believe they all saw each other only yesterday. Everyone chatters amiably until Pop announces gruffly, "Let's thank the Lord for the food."

Everyone stops talking and folds their hands as my father offers the usual blessing over the food.

"Come, Lord Jesus, be our guest,

and let these gifts to us be blessed."

In unison we all respond, "Amen."

We pass the bowl of scrambled eggs and the plate of bacon while waiting for Grandma to deliver that heaping pile of hot pancakes to the table.

"Auntie Emma's here," Tilly squeals with delight as she rounds the table to give me a squeeze.

"Your cheeks are nice and rosy this chilly morning," I say as I hold her little face close to mine.

"Yours are hot," she says as she takes the chair next to mine.

I pour her a glass of apple juice, then pass her the bacon and eggs. "Would you like me to put some on your plate?" I ask.

She nods, "Three bacons please."

"You must be hungry."

She leans in and whispers in my ear, "One is for Bullet, one is for Trigger and one is for me."

I fill her plate as requested and give her a conspiratorial wink. Apparently, this isn't the first-time Tilly has shared her breakfast with the dogs as they both lie in wait beneath the table.

Once we've finished breakfast, I help Gram with the dishes as we both enjoy another cup of coffee. Becca settles our nieces in with their lessons in the lower level, before logging on to her computer to begin her own work. Josiah is busy plowing after last night's snowfall, and Willa and Mom head out to the greenhouse while Lucas and Pop attend to some business in Pop's office. I know better than to ask what they are up to, sometimes ignorance is bliss.

Once the dishes are washed and put away, Gram suggests, "Why don't you go grab your sewing and then come on back over here and we can sit a spell while you focus on your work."

"Sure, I'd like that," I say as I go to retrieve my sewing bag and sketch pad. It has been a while since I've had any real time with my grandmother. I haven't been home since the holidays and there was a house full of people then with everyone talking at the same time.

When I get back Gram is sitting in her chair by the fireplace and has already begun knitting. I take a seat on the couch and pull out the mock up for one of my new designs. One of the good things about a line of expensive lingerie is that it really has no season, unlike men's wear and women's wear. Gram looks over at the silky lace negligee and says nothing, she doesn't need to for even without comment I can sense her disapproval. It's okay, I'm not really seeking her approval. My ninety-one-year-old grandmother is not exactly the target market for my designs anyway. We both sit and stitch in silence for a few minutes.

"Good thing I never went to bed dressed in something like that, or I would have given your poor Grand Pappa a heart attack," Gram says with a laugh.

"Oh, I bet there was a time when you made his heart race plenty, " I say conspiratorially, hoping she'll open up and talk about her life.

"Times were different then. Your Grand Pappa was always quite conservative and reserved, even as a young man. He always said his parents were quite strict with him and his brothers."

"How old were you when you met Grand Pappa?"

"Let's see it was 1947, so I was only eighteen. But your grandfather was twelve years older than I was. He was thirty when we first met. He was still a young man, at least that's how it seems when you get to be my age. We met just after the war," Grandma says as a wistful look passes over her face and she turns her gaze back to her knitting.

I look away, not wanting to intrude on a private memory.

After a moment she continues, "Your Grand Pappa was war weary and an immigrant to boot when he first came to the Adirondacks. We met when I was clerking at the Cohen's Dry Goods store. It was a general store much like it is today. Back then we sold a little bit of everything. Winfield came into the store, he was tall, and strong, and blond. But it was his twinkling blue eyes that I remember." For a moment, Gram gets that far-away look in her eyes and a sweet smile crosses her lips. Then she shakes her head as if to dislodge a private memory of her husband. "He was looking to buy some parts for a washing machine he was repairing. I couldn't understand what he was looking for as he kept asking about vashers for the vashing machine."

I had heard some of this before, but Gram would only go so far. I always felt that there was more to the story, that for some reason, she was reluctant to share. She was ninety-one years old for heaven sake, if I didn't get the story now, I might never hear it.

"Even after all the years, his Ws still sounded like Vs and he always had difficulty saying thank-you and other words with a th sound. They always came out as a *s* or *z*, like *sank you* or *zis* and *zhat*. Pappa retained elements of his German accent all of his life, no matter how hard he tried to cover it." Gram returns to her knitting as she remembers her husband.

"Why would he need to cover it?" I asked. "I know lots of people with accents that are far harder to decipher than Grand Pappa's ever was."

"He wanted to fit in, to be a real American. You have to remember, we didn't live in the city like you do. It was just after the war, and people were still holdin' a grudge against everything and everyone German. A lot of folks lost loved ones during the war— husbands, brothers, and sons. They didn't take too kindly to foreign nationals, either Germans or the Japs, moving into our little mountain town. There were a lot of folks still lookin' for someone to blame for their heartache."

"I guess some things haven't changed very much," I murmur under my breath. Gram either chooses to ignore me or perhaps she just didn't hear.

"Pappa fought on the side of the Germans during World War II, but he never really wanted to talk about the war. I suppose that is because the Allies were victorious."

I find this more than a little odd. He didn't want to talk about it not because what he saw and experienced was so horrific or because of a sense of shame that Germany had been in the wrong, but rather because they lost. "Do you know what Grand Pappa did in the war?" I ask the question but I'm not sure I really want to know the answer.

"Winfield was a private man. He never wanted to talk about it. But I do know he suffered from night terrors, particularly as he grew older.

Poor man, we called it battle weary, back then. Today, I think it's called post-traumatic stress."

"Did he ever want to go back to Germany?"

"No, my dear, he lost most of his family during the Allied bombing of Dresden. When the war was finally over he immigrated here. He just wanted to start over."

"Just like that, a German soldier can immigrate to the United States. I guess it was easier to get in under Harry Truman than it is now, during the reign of Donald Trump."

"Well, Pappa was a hard-working, English speaking, European, and a Christian. Other than his accent, he fit right in. Besides, there were other German families up here in the north country and Winfield had some shirttail relations on his mother's side up in the mountains near Long Lake." Gram sets down her knitting and gives me a stern disapproving look.

"I'm not saying he shouldn't have been let in, I'm just a little surprised that's all. One moment they're shooting at each other and the next thing you know they're moving in down the street." My grandmother holds my gaze for just another moment and sets her jaw warning me that if I continue this line of inquiry things could get ugly, so I back off deciding not to press the issue.

"My family loved him. Once we were married, my father took him in like he was his own son. There was a huge housing boom and an unmet demand for lumber with all the GI's coming home and wanting to start families. My father owned all this land and we had over a thousand acres in uncut timber. Father needed some help with the logging, but the truth is I

34

think my father always preferred Winfield to me. I suppose after the war there were a lot of men of his generation who preferred the company of other men— both sons and sons-in-law."

Oh God, truly some things haven't changed, I take a deep breath and change the subject. "I've always thought Winfield Earl sounded like an English name, it doesn't sound very German to me."

"Pappa changed his surname to Earl." Grandma says matter-a-fact and I wonder why I've never heard this.

"What was it before?"

"Winfield Graf. Graf is German for Earl."

So, if Grand Pappa hadn't changed his name, my name would have been Emma Graf instead of Emma Earl. I think I prefer Emma Earl."

The door from the lower level opens as Becca comes up to join us, her long blond hair has been pulled back into a braid that falls midway down her back. "Finally got those two little darlings started on their school work, I don't know what their teachers have been doing since the start of the school year but both of the girls could benefit greatly if they were homeschooled. They are smart enough but could use a little discipline to say nothin' of that whack-a-doodle curriculum they've been subjected to.

"Are you offering to be their teacher?" Gram pipes up.

"I could do a better job than whoever it is that has been put in charge of their education. You should see what they're filling their heads with: global warming propaganda, evolution, saving the rainforest, stories filled with pictures of black fathers and white mothers and little mulatto children where the boys are wearing aprons and doing the dishes while the

35

girls are being scientists and astronauts. It's not right I tell you, it's just not right." Becca is a force to be reckoned with, standing tall at five foot eleven in her stocking feet while her pale blue eyes flash with righteous indignation.

"By mulatto children are you referring to mixed race children? God-forbid. And what exactly would you propose exposing the next generation of adults to?"

"Don't start with me. I've been filling in with their schoolin' for the last two weeks. There is truth to what *they* say about today's public schools," Becca calls into us from the kitchen as she fixes herself another cup of coffee.

"And just what are *they* saying about today's public schools?" I ask as I stir the bubbling cauldron of my sister's fears and malcontent.

"Oh, come on now, surely you know that the curriculum is about an inch deep and a mile wide. It's no wonder American kids are falling behind in reading and failing math. Parents have totally lost the ability to direct the upbringing and education of their own children. The whole system has a liberal bias, a stinkin' liberal bias."

"Where did you hear this? Fox News?"

"*Girls*," Gram says sternly, exerting her authority as the matriarch of our family and putting a stop to any further discussion of the state of the public-school system.

I haven't been home for twenty-four hours and already I'm at odds with my younger sister. I know there are people who think like her, just not anyone I choose to hang out with. Becca's face is flushed red and she looks like she wants to explode as she tries her best not to give me a piece of her mind.

I take a deep breath.

Gram has put the kibosh on anymore petty bickering. This feels like old times when we'd be sent to opposite corners of the room and be told to mind our tongues and just stop talking. I've never been very good at that, and neither has Becca.

Gram finishes a row of her knitting then takes her needles and pushes them into a ball of navy-blue yarn before putting everything into her wicker knitting basket. "I think you two could use a little sister time. So, if you'll both excuse me, I think I'm going to head down to the cellar and get some meat out of the freezer for supper. Then I may take a little rest before your mother and sister come in from the greenhouse."

"You feeling okay, Gram?" I ask.

"Just a little tired. I was up early getting the breakfast on and I just can't run all day like I used to. I'm fine sweetheart. Don't you worry about me."

Becca and I sit in silence as Gram heads down the stairs. Sister time—some sisters are best friends but Becca and I have always been like two cats in a bag, ready to claw each other's eyes out if it could give us an advantage or better yet, if it would allow us to escape. "So, Becca," I say as I look down at my stitching, "I understand that you've got a new job and are telecommuting while we're all under quarantine. Mom said something about you working with the media, but she didn't elaborate about what you're doing."

"I was recruited to write short articles and opinion pieces, editorials really."

"No kidding? Have you been hired as a journalist, per se?"

"I'm freelancing for a couple of conservative political platforms that are geared towards women and responding to people on social media like Facebook and Twitter."

It's hard for me to believe that someone is actually paying my sister for her opinions, not that Becca isn't smart enough because she's plenty smart. It's just hard to believe that any thinking woman would willingly embrace the anti-feminist ideology and deeply ingrained misogyny of the alt-right. And Becca has bought into all of it. She did say it was a job. So, I ask a question that is really none of my business. "How are you being compensated?"

"With money, the same as you are." Becca is snarky and getting irritated, I can hear it in her voice. She stands to leave the room. She doesn't want to spend any quality *sister time* with me any more than I want to spend it with her.

"Don't go," I plead. "That's not what I meant. Do they pay you by the word or by the piece? I'm just curious how this whole thing works."

Reluctantly, Becca lowers herself back down in Gram's chair as she indulges my curiosity. "The more people who react to my posts, or when one of my posts is shared or retweeted, the more money I make. It's kind of like YouTube. The more people who watch your videos the more money you make."

"And you're making money doing this?"

"Way more than I ever made waiting tables at Slickers," she says with a laugh. "And

I don't have to worry about being followed home by some drunken snowmobiler either."

"Who pays you?"

"People who share my concerns about the state of the world and our country. There are some people with pretty deep pockets and the money is good. And so far, it keeps coming in. We're supposed to be really ramping things up as the November election gets closer."

"Are you one of those trolls?"

"Trolls? You really have no idea how this whole thing works, do you? We have a very elaborate and sophisticated operation. We are well funded and our influence runs both wide and deep, I've met with some pretty powerful people doing this. It would make your little liberal head spin."

"No shit. You've met them personally?"

"No, but virtually and online. They've even commented on some of my posts and some of my memes on 4chan and Reddit. They've liked my stuff and shared it. I'm getting noticed for the work I'm putting out there."

"And you think you're in the *right* and doing good things for the country?"

"I don't doubt it for a minute. I'm doing good things for the *right* and the *right people*. Just doing my part to try to combat all the fake news and the lies spread by the leftist media who want to sell our country down the river."

"Wow, you really drank the Kool-Aid, didn't you?"

"What are you talking about?"

"You've never heard that expression before? How about Jonestown, Guyana? Maybe you should look it up." And with that we hear Gram starting back up the stairs.

"I need to get online and get to work before the girls need me to help them with their schoolwork."

"Will you show me some of your *work*?"

"Maybe later," Becca says as she heads off towards the study.

I follow her and before she can close the door and close me out, I see she has a brand-new iMac Pro sitting on the desk. I ask, "How did you get into all of this?"

"While you and Gram were sittin' and stitchin', I was spending my time gaming and learning to program. What can I say? It just comes easy to me."

"Does Pop know what you're doing?"

"Who do you think set me up?" she laughs as she closes the door and I'm left standing dumbfounded in the hallway.

I head back to the family room to resume my sewing. I can't help but wonder how two sisters raised in the same household by the same parents could come to see the world so differently. I say a small prayer of gratitude that somehow, I have been able to escape the shackles of this small-minded thinking that afflicts my sister and so many of her compatriots. No sooner do the words take shape in my mind than I am absolutely convinced that no doubt my sister is also feeling overwhelmingly blessed that she has not been completely brainwashed by the *Libtards* or more accurately put— by people who think as I do.

I pick up the ivory silk gown and finish tacking the lace overlay onto the bodice, before retrieving my sketch pad to work up some ideas for a new collection. It isn't long before I'm lost in the rendering of a new design when Mom comes in from the greenhouse.

"It truly is a beautiful morning," Mom says as she stomps the snow from her boots. "Emma, you should really get off the couch and go outside and get some fresh air while the sun is out. More snow is forecast for tonight."

I think about telling her that although it may look like I'm only lounging about, I am actually working. I decide to let it pass.

"I thought I might do a little cross-country skiing down near the camp road later this afternoon. Are Sandy and Pierre still grooming the trails?"

"As far as I know, but they might be waiting until the next storm blows through before they head out. It's not like it's the beginning of the season, people around here have pretty much had their fill of winter and winter sports. Most folks were all thinking about getting out of town before the summer tourists arrive. You know how April is in the mountains.

Everyone was planning on heading to Florida or somewhere warmer for the mud season. All I've heard is lots of grumbling in town. The locals are hunkering down, staying home, and trying to figure out how to make ends meet now that everything is closed because of the virus and all."

Willa, my eldest sister, comes in and the wind catches the door as it slams behind her, "Have you seen the girls?"

"Becca got them started on their school work a little while ago, but I haven't heard a peep out of either of them and they haven't come upstairs," I answer.

"Ooh, that doesn't sound good. I'd better go check on them," she says as she pulls off her boots and slips into a pair of moccasins.

Mom takes my sister's coat before she can even set it down and hangs it in the closet beside her own. Mom is excessively tidy. There is a place for everything and everything is in its place. This is nothing new. We've all grown up like this, but it's only today that I've given it any thought. Why is this so important to her? Perhaps she is trying to control what little she can. It can't be easy for Mom— living here with Pop. God knows he is a force to be reckoned with and living here in a house that belongs to your mother-in-law. And just in case anyone forgets that fact, Gram is always here to remind you. This is her house and therefore her rules. I swear if this was my reality, I think I'd lose my freakin' mind.

While Willa is downstairs checking on her daughters, Mom heads into the kitchen to see about lunch. Mom looks tired, it can't be easy with all of us back living here, looking to be fed, and attended to, just like when we were children.

Pop and Lucas emerge from Pop's study. "Is lunch ready?" Pop calls to me as he looks at his wristwatch and the old grandfather clock strikes twelve.

"Mom just came in, she's in the kitchen." I close my sketch pad and go to give my mother a hand. I can tell by the way Pop is pacing and grumbling that he's irritated. For as long as I can remember, Pop has expected to have his lunch on the table precisely at noon.

Mom has one place set at the head of the table with a plate of knockwurst and sauerkraut along with a jar of hot mustard and Pop's beer tankard and a can of Budweiser ready for him. In the meantime, she is standing over the stove cooking up a pan of bacon for everyone else.

"BLTs today?" I ask.

"Yes, and I'm warming up a kettle of vegetable soup. Could you slice the tomatoes, dear?"

I help Mom get the lunch on the table when Pop comes into the kitchen. He takes his seat and begins to eat even before anyone else is seated or anyone else's lunch is served. One by one the others arrive and take their seats, just waiting for mom to serve them. Someone shoot me if I ever sign on for a gig like this.

Willa's voice can be heard as she ascends the stairs from the lower level where her children have been doing their school work, "That is enough Heidi, I don't care where you heard it, you know the difference between right and wrong. I don't want to ever hear that kind of talk again."

As they enter the kitchen it is clear that something is up, Willa is steamed and ten-year-old Heidi hangs her head in shame as she murmurs

43

under her breath, "Loony liberal."

"What did you call me?" Willa says as she grasps her daughter by the upper arm and draws her in so they are face-to-face.

"Auntie Becca said," Heidi stammers as if this justifies her insolent behavior.

"We will talk about this later," Willa says as she shoots a look at Becca. Heidi pulls her arm free of her mother's hand and snarls as she goes to sit in her seat beside Becca, while little Tilly climbs silently into her chair with the booster seat beside me.

"Come on Willa, don't be such a snowflake. You haven't forgotten— *sticks and stones may break some bones but words will never hurt you.*" Becca smirks.

"Is this how it is going to be? You're going to start calling me names, in front of my own children?" Willa glares and directs her words towards Becca.

Tilly pipes up, "Words can hurt. They can hurt people's feelings." Then she bursts into tears as I reach down to take her hand beneath the table as she leans into me and whispers in my ear, "I hate it when they fight."

"Maybe the truth hurts," Pop says as Lucas and Becca nod their heads in agreement. "If you don't feel any pride in being a snowflake or a loony liberal maybe you should do something about it. And that goes for you too, Emma."

"Would anyone like another sandwich, or some more soup?" Mom asks as she tries to change the subject. God bless her, she's always trying to keep the peace.

Rather than take the bait and drag this family luncheon any further down the rat hole, I ask, "Do you want me to go and wake Gram for lunch? She went to lie down about an hour ago."

"No," Mom says, "let her sleep if she's tired. She's an early riser and I'll save her something."

Everyone has stopped talking and turned their attention towards their food as if vegetable soup and a bacon, lettuce and tomato sandwich is the most interesting thing in the world.

Still I think about the name calling and how defensive Willa became, not that I blame her. And then Pop just painted both of us with that same broad brush. I always thought Willa and I didn't have very much in common. Perhaps I don't know any more about Willa than she knows about me. Time and distance can do that.

"I thought Josiah would be home for lunch as everything is closed in town." I say to no one in particular, just trying my best to stay away from this minefield that could explode at any moment if any one of us is not careful with our words.

"Joe will be home when the roads are cleared and not before. He has important work to do," Pop says. Although he does not say it, he doesn't need to, the message is clear— Josiah's work is important, unlike mine.

Fuck him. Again, I try my best to let this unspoken animosity that hovers between us pass.

"Hey, I almost forgot to tell you, just before I left the city I got my results back from that genetic testing. You know the *23 and Me* thing that Becca got us all for Christmas." I say and these simple words bring a total change to the ambiance to the room. Becca's demeanor lightens and the pervasive hostility seems to dissipate. "Did anyone else get their results yet?"

Chapter 4

Becca stands, "Give me a minute, I got mine back last week. I haven't had a chance to look at them yet."

"Must we do this now?" Mom asks and appears agitated.

"Did you do it, Willa?" I ask.

"I did, but my results are at home."

With this Becca returns to the table with a few pages of computer printout in her hand.

"Did you get yours back Pop?" she asks.

"Ya, no surprises. I'm German, through and through, and you kids are too. But, I don't have time for this foolishness. Lucas and I have to meet some folks up in Indian Lake this afternoon. We're making a delivery. If we don't get going we might get caught in that storm they're callin' for." Pop turns to look at Lucas, "Go on, get a move-on, boy. Pull the truck around, we've got things to do."

Lucas stands leaving his dirty dishes and a crumpled napkin on the table.

Again, Becca looks down at the papers she holds, she looks a little confused.

"Do you want me to get mine? They're just in my suitcase. We could go over them together, if you like." I suggest, but Becca shakes her head as she continues to look at her own results.

"No, I don't think so. I have a deadline to meet. Why don't we look at them after dinner when all of us can have our results in front of us, then we can determine what pieces of our genetic code came from Mom's side of the family and what came from Pop's. Maybe we can finally fill out some of the branches of the old family tree," she says, still looking a bit perplexed.

I've only glanced at my results so I doubt I can say anything to alleviate my sister's obvious concerns. It isn't as straightforward as I had expected, and I took a genetics class when I was in college. Albeit, Genetics 101 for non-science majors, I did learn the basics. Besides this whole thing was Becca's idea. She was the one who wanted to do this family genealogy project, not me. And after the quarrel Becca and I had this morning, I don't want to press the issue. Instead, I opt to follow her lead on this. Becca takes her papers and walks out of the kitchen leaving Mom, Willa, and I to clean up.

The little girls can be heard talking in high squeaky voices as they play with their dolls in front of the fireplace.

"I've got this Mom. I'm sure you and Willa have plenty of things you need to do this afternoon," I say.

"Are you sure, Emma? I need to throw in a load of wash and fold some of the laundry in the dryer."

"No problem," I assure her. "What do you want me to save for Gram?"

"How about some of the soup. She doesn't seem to have much of an appetite these days."

"My girls seem to have made up and are playing nicely, at least for now. How about you wash and I'll dry. You can help me decide what I'm going to do about our narrow-minded sister."

"Okay. Anyway, I'm glad to know I'm not the only *snowflake* up here in the mountains."

Willa laughs. "We're few in number, that's for sure. I love Becca, but I don't always like her. And I can't abide with her filling my girls' heads with her hatred and bigotry. Since I've been helping Mom out in the new greenhouse, the girls have been spending more time with Becca. Heidi thinks her Auntie Becca has hung the moon. She tries on that attitude of superiority along with airs of entitlement just like she is playing dress up, trying on a costume, and playing a character in a play. But then she bullies Tilly until she has her in tears and I want to wring her neck. I can only imagine how this attitude must play out if she behaves like this at school. Her teacher has implied that Heidi thinks she's all that, and more."

"When did all this start? She was always such a sweet girl."

"Becca has a new friend who sometimes works with Pop and Lucas, and he has shared custody of his ten-year-old daughter. Ivy spends quite a bit of time over here playing with my daughters."

"Hold on. Becca has a new *friend*, as in a boyfriend?"

"She would like him to be."

"Wow, I didn't see this coming. It's kind of slim pickins for eligible men up here in the north woods."

"Oh, there plenty of men up here, but you know what they say..." Willa pauses, as if she expects me to complete her thought. But all I can do is give her a quizzical look. So, she breaks into a smile and continues, "The odds are good, but the goods are odd. And Rolfe Teufel is certainly an odd one."

"Odder than the usual cast of characters?" I grimace, "Because that would really be saying something."

"I'm afraid so. To say I don't think either of them is a good influence on my children is a gross understatement. Rolfe makes Steve Bannon look like prince charming."

"Steve Bannon as in that overweight, slovenly, racist force behind Breitbart News? The Steve Bannon who used to be The Donald's White House Chief Strategist, that Steve Bannon?"

"Yeah, that's the one. Maybe Rolfe is Bannon's younger brother, but unlike Bannon, all evidence points to that fact that poor Rolfe may have been dropped on his head a few times. Although Bannon is no prize in any estimation, at least he is smart— devious, underhanded, evil, and smart. Rolfe is just devious, underhanded, and evil."

"Oh, dear God, poor Becca, she can't be that desperate that she's set the bar so low that she'll date any slimy snake that crawls in on its belly." For the first time in a long time I begin to feel the stirrings of compassion for my younger sister.

"Like it or not, she is an adult and she should know better, but I will not have her exposing my girls to this neo-Nazi propaganda. There is something extremely unattractive and downright frightening when a ten-year-old child spouts that hate-filled rhetoric as if she's a budding white supremacist."

"Good God," is all I can say. I hand Willa the last of the clean dishes to dry and put away while I wipe down the kitchen table. Mom emerges from the lower level with a basketful of clean laundry that she has already folded. I take the basket from Mom and set it on the kitchen table.

"Would you like me to put the laundry away?" Willa asks Mom.

"Maybe you could put the towels in the linen closet," Mom says. "And could you peek in on Gram while you're down there? She doesn't usually nap this long in the afternoon."

Watching from the kitchen I see Willa flick the hallway lights on before putting the towels away, then she knocks gently on the door to Gram's bedroom. Before waiting for a response, she enters the darkened bedroom. It only takes another moment before Willa is shouting, "Mom! Emma!" We can hear the panic in her voice and we both start to run as she continues to call to us, "Come quick, I think Gram is sick."

Willa sits beside her on the bed as I turn on the lamp on Gram's bedside table, and I hear my grandmother moan as she moves her hand to cover her eyes. The pale, frail woman lying there in the bed, looks nothing like my robust grandmother who cooked our breakfast only a few hours ago.

Willa stands as Mom takes her place and sits on the edge of the bed. She speaks softly to Gram as Willa and I stand silently in the shadows and hold our collective breath. "Kathrine, it's me, Magda." Gram groans something incomprehensible as Mom places the back of her hand against Gram's forehead. "She's burning up with fever," Mom says as she pulls all the blankets back and hangs them over the footboard and then begins to undress our grandmother in an effort to cool her. "Emma, bring me a pan of cool water and a washcloth, and the thermometer. It's in the medicine cabinet. Willa try to get a hold of your father and tell him we need him to come home."

I'm glad to leave the room, I can't bear the thought of seeing my grandmother's ancient naked body. She is such a proud and private woman. It just seems wrong. When I return, Mom has covered Gram's now naked body with a clean sheet.

Then Mom shakes the mercury down in the old glass thermometer and I wonder why they haven't purchased a digital one. They are available in every drugstore across the country and have been for as long as I can remember.

But if it isn't broken, why in the world would we get a new one when this one is good enough.

Another example of our family philosophy being played out right before my very eyes.

Mom places the thermometer underneath Gram's arm. "Emma, just hold this here. It needs to stay in place for a full five minutes. I don't want it to slip if Gram should get restless."

I do as I am asked, but in truth I'd rather she'd asked me to call Pop and left this job to Willa. I'm not good around sick people, and Gram looks really sick. Her face is flushed red and she is sweating and shivering at the same time. Her body shakes and her teeth clatter. Although she is moaning like she is in pain, nothing she says is understandable. I'm afraid.

Mom wets and folds the old wash cloth and gently places it across Gram's brow, then she sponges her body down with the cool water, all the while offering gentle words of reassurance. I watch in awe as Mom tends to the needs of her mother-in-law with such proficiency. It is as if she has been doing this all of her life, but it is more than that. She is loving and compassionate to a woman who has gone out of her way on a daily basis to make my mother feel as if she is unworthy and never quite measures up.

After five minutes, Mom nods to me and I know what she wants. I remove the thermometer from under my grandmother's arm and hand it to my mother. Her reading glasses are perched on the end of her nose as she purses her lips and she turns the thermometer between her fingers trying to read it. Just then Willa re-enters the room, she quickly grasps the situation and we wait in silence for Mom to let us know, "102 degrees, and you add a degree to an underarm reading in order to estimate the body's core temperature."

Mom continues sponging. Gram begins to cough relentlessly and appears to be having difficulty catching her breath. In this light, Gram's lips look a shade of gray or maybe a light blue.

"We need to bring her fever down," Mom says softly as her brow is furrowed and her careworn face is filled with worry.

"Do you want to give her some aspirin or Tylenol?" I ask, trying to be helpful.

"I'm afraid she is becoming delirious with fever and may not be alert enough to swallow any pills. She might choke it we try," Mom says and now she seems worried too. "Did you get a hold of your father?" Mom asks, turning her attention towards Willa.

"No, he said they were headed up to Indian Lake and the cell service is very spotty between here and there. What time do you expect them to be back?" Willa asks, knowing full well that Pop never gives anyone an accounting of his whereabouts.

"Probably before dinner, but another storm is coming so it's hard to say. I think we should get Gram to the hospital and neither of the trucks with four-wheel drive is here. Has anyone heard from Josiah? Is he still out plowing?" Mom asks as she tries to process her limited options.

"I can try to call him," Willa says as she leaves the bedroom to go out near the front porch where the cell reception is usually a little bit better.

Willa returns and finds Becca and her daughters now standing in the hallway. We all turn our attention to Willa who shakes her head, "Josiah didn't pick up."

Mom sighs deeply as Gram appears to have settled a little. She is no longer shivering and appears a little more comfortable. "I do wish your father was here."

For the love of God, the woman has never been allowed to make an independent decision in her whole life and now time is of the essence, all the hale and hearty menfolk are gone leaving only the women and children. "Good God, why are we debating this. We need to call 911 and get Gram to St. E's."

Inviting no discussion, I leave the bedroom and head to the kitchen to use the landline. From the kitchen, I can hear my sisters' forced whispers as they discuss whether this is really necessary as they concern themselves with how much it will cost to take an ambulance all the way into Utica while my mother worries and ruminates over Gram. Then the backroom conversation shifts and is fraught with agitation and speculation as to whether or not I have exposed my entire family to the potentially deadly Coronavirus.

Before I am even off the phone with the local fire department and an emergency medical technician, Willa has both of her girls dressed in their snowsuits and boots. She has packed up the girls and all three of them are headed for home. If this is what she thinks it is, she doesn't want to expose her children. I can't blame her. Fortunately, they live on property and it is only a short walk to their home through the newly fallen snow.

"They are sending two trucks. One to plow us out, since we're snowed in again and the second to transport Gram to St. E's." I fill Becca and my mother in on what I've just learned. "Do you think one of us should ride down to Utica in the ambulance?" I ask tentatively as it appears that neither Becca or my mom are speaking to me. This was not really a question that needs an answer as it is obvious that Gram is in no condition to go alone and we don't have a vehicle that is safe on these snow-covered mountain roads.

I help my mother pull together a few things as we pack an overnight bag for Gram with a clean nightgown, undergarments, some toiletries, and a change of clothes. In the interim, no one speaks as we wait for the ambulance.

It isn't long before we hear the sirens and see the lights as both trucks make their way down the road. While our long tree-lined driveway is being plowed, both EMT's approach the house carrying a stretcher. They're local guys that I recognize but I can't recall their names. People look familiar but also different after ten years of being away.

One of the men starts an IV and puts Gram on oxygen. She rouses slightly but is unable to answer any of their questions in a coherent way. She has no idea why they are here or where she is going or even what year it is. She has even forgotten that Donald Trump is the President of the United States. "Maybe that's a good thing," I quip to the paramedic, but he doesn't seem to think I'm funny.

"Who will be riding with us, Mrs. Earl?" the younger of the two men asks my mother.

"Oh, is that necessary?" she asks.

"I'll go," I say, and my mother gives me a nod of approval as I go to get my coat and put on my boots.

Becca follows me out to the foyer as I sit down to tie my boots. Becca snarls, "And get yourself tested while you're down there. It would be nice to know if you're infected and contagious, before you come back and give *it* to the rest of the family."

"You're a real peach," I say.

"Our own little Typhoid Mary," she says just loud enough for me to hear.

I grab my purse, and a book to read while in the waiting room, along with Gram's identification and the bag we've packed for her.

I follow the EMTs as they carry my grandmother out on the stretcher to the ambulance. "Do you have your phone?" Mom yells after me.

I nod.

"Call me on the landline and let me know how she's doing," Mom shouts out.

"I'll call you when we arrive."

"Thank you, Emma." Mom waves and I can see her wipe the tears from her eyes. Becca stands on the wrap around porch with her arms folded across her chest, looking like she'd like nothing better than to beat the shit out of me.

Chapter 5

I ride in the front passenger's seat of the ambulance while one of the paramedics drives and the other attends to my grandmother and hooks her up to a cardiac monitor. He takes another set of vital signs then readjusts the oxygen and her IV. As we pull out onto State Route 28 and turn towards Utica, the driver turns on both the emergency lights and the siren. The plow has been out recently and thank goodness, the main road is relatively clear, especially considering how much snow has already fallen this afternoon. I turn my gaze out the window where the glow from the red and white lights can be seen reflecting on the six-foot high snow banks that line the highway like a tunnel. It has been a cold and snowy winter. We pass through the town of Old Forge where all the cars and trucks that are out on the road this afternoon can be seen slipping and sliding toward the snow-covered shoulder attempting to get out of our way. The closest hospital is at least an hour away, even with the lights and sirens.

It isn't until we've passed the town and are making our way through the Adirondack Park that one of the paramedics turns his attention towards me. "My name is Ernie Muller and that's Gerald Thomas driving." The driver takes one hand off the steering wheel to wave to me but he doesn't take his eyes off the road. "In our haste and all of the commotion of getting your grandmother loaded up to go, I don't think any introductions were made. If it's okay with you, we'd like to get a little more information."

"Of course," I say. I reach into Gram's bag for her insurance card and identification so they can get her registered and secure some assurance they'll get paid.

Next they begin with all the usual questions I've come to expect when someone is sick: "When did her symptoms start? Is anyone else in the family ill? Has she recently traveled

outside of the country or been exposed to someone who has been out of the country? Has she been in contact with anyone who may have been in contact with someone exposed to Covid-19?"

"Covid-19?" I ask.

"Yes, that's what they've started calling the Coronavirus. Apparently, there are a lot of different strains of the virus, but we are particularly interested in the strain that was first identified in December," the paramedic in the back with Gram says.

"December 2019, that's why they're now calling it Covid-19. We just watched a training video on it this morning, down at the fire station. There is an international committee that is responsible for the naming of viruses," the driver adds his two cents.

"I guess I'm a little out of the loop up here, I just got into town last night."

"From where?" the driver asks.

"I took the train into the Utica Station from Manhattan after Governor Cuomo decided my work was non-essential," I say with a chuckle as I try to lighten the mood.

The driver makes eye contact with his partner in the rear-view mirror as he pulls over on to the side of the road before we're even in Forestport. "You could have told us this before now," the paramedic in the back says rather snappishly. They both put on medical masks and gloves before they put a mask on Gram, then they hand another one to me.

"I'm sorry, I guess I was just so worried about my grandmother. I didn't think..." I stammer out an apology that we all know is grossly inadequate as the driver shakes his head and gives me a look filled with contempt. "I'm sorry," I try again.

Gram is clearly agitated by the mask as she tries to pull it off of her face. The paramedic in the back attempts to restrain her as he ties her hands down with leather belts strapping them to the metal bars on either side of the stretcher. Gram calls out for help. I feel so frustrated that there is nothing I can do to ease her suffering. She is so sick and she doesn't understand what is being done to her or why.

The driver initiates a call on the speaker phone.

"St. Elizabeth's Emergency, this is Dr. Tolia who am I speaking with?"

"This is EMT Gerry Thomas, Old Forge Fire Department Rig 323. We are inbound with a ninety-one-year-old woman. She is febrile, with an altered level of consciousness and agitation."

"Is this markedly different from her usual state of being?" The doctor's voice fills the truck as she tries to determine my grandmother's condition. "Yes, according to the family she was awake, alert, and oriented early today. We've started an IV and have her on oxygen. Her respiratory rate is a little tachy and O2 sat is at ninety percent, even on the oxygen. Blood pressure and heart rate are stable at this time. There has been a possible Covid-19 exposure as her granddaughter came into the home last night from New York City. She is in the rig with us and is asymptomatic at this time. We'd like to give the patient something for the agitation."

"How far out are you?"

"At least another forty minutes."

"How much does she weigh?" Dr. Tolia asks. The driver looks over at me for an answer.

"Probably about 140 pounds," I guess as the tears start to come to my eyes.

"140," he says into the phone.

"Give her one milligram on Ativan IV and watch her respirations. And all of you are now considered exposed and will need to go directly into an isolation room. Call us from the ambulance bay and someone will escort you to isolation."

"Thanks Doc, see you in a little bit," the driver says as he signs off. "Shit," he says under his breath but loud enough for me to hear his fear and his displeasure with me, and this entire situation.

"Do you want me to sit beside her and see if I can calm her down? I could hold her hand and sing to her like she used to do for me when I was little and afraid," I ask.

"No. I think you've done enough already. Don't you?" The paramedic in the back says from behind his mask. I watch as he fills the syringe with the medication and injects it into the port on Gram's IV. It isn't long before her breathing slows and she appears to be sleeping.

What in God's name have I done? If I've exposed my Grandmother to the Coronavirus I'll never forgive myself. We ride in silence the rest of the way into the hospital as the snow continues to fall and the winds blow the drifts across the road.

When at last we pull into the ambulance bay, EMT Muller announces our arrival over the speaker phone in the rig. We are met beneath the bright lights of the overhanging roof by three people dressed in modified hazmat suits. Dear God, I don't know what I had expected, but believe me it was not this. Two men pull the gurney from the back of the ambulance. The wheels drop down to the ground as I watch my sleeping grandmother being taken away from me. A woman in the hazmat suit, completely masked and gloved beckons to the paramedics and me to follow her. Through the mask her muffled and disembodied voice commands, "Don't touch anything."

Just inside the emergency department we are separated into two isolation rooms, the paramedics go into one and I go alone into the other. The room is stripped bare of everything but a single plastic chair as the masked woman points at it and gestures for me to sit before she closes the door behind me without further explanation. I am overwhelmed by the smell of disinfectant, bleach I think. I can't help feeling a huge sense of shame as if I am a pariah for bringing a deadly virus into my home and my community.

But I don't know if this is true, I don't feel sick.

I sit in the sterile room for over an hour before someone comes in to see me. They, too, are dressed in the modified hazmat suits. Introductions are made as one woman gets me registered and the other, a nurse, begins to ask me the same kinds of questions that the paramedics asked about my grandmother and her condition. Then she takes my temperature, swiping a digital probe across my forehead and asks me to place my finger in a little plastic finger casing, "This is to determine the oxygen saturation of your blood." She looks perplexed.

"Is anything wrong?" I ask. "I'm really feeling fine."

She doesn't answer, but walks around behind me and listens to my lungs through my flannel shirt. "Just breathe normally," she commands.

I thought I was.

"You don't have any symptoms," she says and I'm not sure if this is a question or a statement.

"No, like I said I feel fine. I had a restless night's sleep last night. First, I was hot, and then I was cold but I took some Advil in the early morning and now I feel okay."

She types something on her iPad for the electronic medical record. "Given that your grandmother is gravely ill and you've just come from Manhattan, we'll have to test you for the virus."

"I thought the tests were in short supply," I say.

"They are. We've been told to be judicious about who gets tested, but since you've just come from the emerging epi-center, you qualify."

"Have you tested many people?" I ask.

"Actually, you're the first." She smiles apologetically.

Okay, I guess someone has to be first. "What's involved?"

"I need to swab the inside of your nose."

"Okay, let's get on with it." So, with that she probes my right nostril with a long-handled Q-tip, it is more than a little uncomfortable but not painful. Still I'm glad when she is done. "Can I go now?" I ask.

"I don't know. Dr. La Croix, the head of infectious diseases, has been called in to consult on your case and to see your grandmother."

"Can you tell me how my grandmother is doing?"

"It's too soon to say. We're still waiting for her lab work. Just make yourself comfortable, the doctor should be in fairly soon."

"Comfortable?" I say as I look around the stripped-down isolation room. There isn't a bed, a pillow, or even a blanket. There's just one orange plastic chair, in a room with a linoleum floor and overhead fluorescent lights that glare down too brightly. The thermostat feels like it is set to about 60, which clicks on intermittently blowing the smell of bleach around the room. "I'm freezing."

She raises one shoulder and smirks indifferently as she leaves the room closing the door behind her.

Perhaps her indifference is well founded. I just hope my grandmother is getting better care and greater kindness than is being bestowed upon me.

I pull my new book from my bag and attempt to read. Although I am turning the pages, in truth, my mind is elsewhere. I am retracing my steps, wondering where and how I might have been exposed. It doesn't take long for me to conclude it could have been anywhere and by just about anyone. How am I to know?

I close the book and close my eyes and for the first time in a very long time I try to pray. When had I abandoned the practice, one that was so deeply ingrained in me at my mother's knee? When I was a child we always prayed before meals, and every night before bed when Mom would come to our bedsides to tuck us in. Now my prayers seem stilted and awkward like I'm trying to make polite conversation with an old friend, one I've so callously ignored but now need a favor from. I feel like such a phony. Tears run down my face.

There was so much I wanted to leave behind when I left home for the city but I fear now, in my arrogance, I have also left behind much of what my mother so patiently tried to instill within me. Did she know there would be times like these, when all the skills and knowledge that I have so diligently acquired and carefully cultivated would simply be inadequate? Did she know the time would come when all that I can do is call upon God for mercy? Shivering and alone in the isolation room I have never felt such an abject poverty of spirit. Yet somewhere within the depth of my soul I call out for help, help for my grandmother and forgiveness for me, forgiveness for so many things.

Time passes slowly and no one even opens the door or peeks in to see if I might need something. But the time comes and I need to use the restroom so I push a call bell that hangs on a metal IV pole. I can hear the high-pitched beeping calling for a nurse from outside my door, when at last a masked woman wearing a surgical gown appears in the doorway. She does not come in.

"I need to use the ladies' room," I tell her.

A momentary look of panic flashes in her dark eyes as if it never occurred to her that this might be a possibility. "I'll need to check and see where we can send you. I'll be back in a minute," she says as she closes the door behind her.

I cross my legs and wait. Please don't bring me a bedpan. How ironic, if I have to use a bedpan when I haven't even been given a bed.

It isn't long before she's back and has located a restroom at the end of the corridor for me to use. I wear my mask and follow her down the hall remembering how I'd been admonished not to touch anything when I first arrived. There's a single stall restroom where someone has taped a sign on the door— Covid-19 Patients Only.

I hesitate before going in. "We don't know for certain that I've been exposed to the virus," I say. "I don't know if I want to use *this* bathroom if other people who are known to be infected have been using it."

"You and your grandmother are the first cases here at St. E's. We just put the sign on the door. It's to warn other people that *you* have been using this restroom. It's for their protection, not yours." She says as she stands back to let me pass.

Before entering, I ask, "Does my grandmother have the virus? I was told that you won't have the results back until the end of the week."

"We are operating under the assumption that she is infected, and therefore, we are taking every precaution. She is going to be admitted as soon as we have a bed."

"Can I see her before she goes up to her room?" I ask.

The nurse just stands there and looks at me, as if trying to decide how to respond. Instead of answering the question I've asked she says, "Someone will be in to talk with you once you've returned from the bathroom."

"Okay," I say. I don't want to miss the opportunity to see my grandmother if that is even possible. I use the bathroom, scour my hands with the antibacterial soap, and return to my isolation chamber.

Again, I wait for someone, anyone to tell me what is going on. I'm starting to have some sympathy for prisoners in solitary confinement, I've only been here a few hours and I'm ready to jump out of my skin. My anxiety mounts as I check my cell phone for the umpteenth time, but still there is no reception within the hospital and the Wi-Fi is password protected. The boredom and the worry threaten to overwhelm me.

Thirty or forty minutes pass and still no one comes. I think about using the call bell again to see if they've forgotten me, when at last the door opens. My father and mother walk in, both of them are masked but I can read the fear in their eyes.

"What's going on?" I ask.

"Lucas is sick too," my mother says as she begins to cry and my tough, old father enfolds her in his arms.

Chapter 6

"What happened?" I ask as a nurse wearing a mask, gown, and gloves carries in two metal folding chairs for my parents. My father settles my sobbing mother into one before he sits himself down.

He looks at me and just shakes his head, and I can feel his revulsion as if I am some kind of odious creature or vermin in need of extermination rather than a beloved daughter. A sense of shame threatens to overcome me as once again tears fill my eyes. "I'm so sorry, I never intended to infect anyone, I thought I'd left the city in time. I didn't know or I never would have come home."

Grasping the depth of my sorrow and regret, my mother comes to my side to offer me some comfort.

"For the love of God, Magda, what are you thinking? Get away from her. We can't have you getting infected, too."

My mother holds me gently with her eyes before retreating back beside my father and onto her cold metal folding chair. "It will be alright, Emma. The doctor says that Lucas will be okay, he is young and strong. Young people often fare better than us old folks."

Somehow, I don't find my mother's words all that reassuring as my Grandmother is ninety-one and everyone seems to believe that I've infected them both.

"Jesus, Magda, don't you go puttin' too much stock in what that Chinaman says. Send those goddamn foreigners back where they came from, we need to find a good ole American doctor, one who speaks English. Or that one'll be practicin' some of that Chinese medicine and stickin' needles in my son and my mother like they're some kinda pin-cushions." Pop reaches over and touches Mom's arm as a sign of solidarity.

Good ole racist Pop, offering an opinion about something he knows nothing about.

Mom folds her hands in her lap as if she is at prayer. She just looks down at her shoes and doesn't dignify Pop's bigoted rantings with a response. She sits in silence, keeping her own counsel as she so often has.

Pop stands and paces like he is some kind of a caged animal, restless and ready to pounce on anyone who comes near him. I once thought my mother's silence was a sign of weakness. I see things differently now, perhaps her silence is a sign of her inner strength and wisdom. I can still learn a thing or two from her.

At last Mom speaks, directing a look of concern towards me, "Forgive me Emma, but I didn't even ask, how are you feeling my dear?"

"I'm fine Mom, please don't worry about me."

My father gives a loud, "Harrumph," and continues pacing.

Then the same nurse, who brought the chairs in, returns with a laptop and a couple of long handled nasal swabs. "Mr. and Mrs. Earl, we need to get you tested since two members of your household are showing symptoms of Covid-19." She directs her comments to my parents.

"What about *her*?" My father says as he points at me. "*She's* the one you should be testing. *She's* the one who is passing this thing around."

He won't even speak my name or acknowledge that I am his daughter. I don't know why I should care. He has nothing but disdain for me and it's been that way for a long time. But it still hurts.

"We've already taken a nasal swab from your daughter, Emma. We won't have any definitive results back for a couple of days. But the county health department is requiring that anyone who may have been exposed will need to be quarantined for fourteen days. And that means all of you."

Good luck getting the king of the forest to comply with the quarantine and stay home.

Then the nurse obtains a nasal swab from both of my parents. My mother grimaces a little, but my father acts as if he is being given open-heart surgery without anesthesia.

He's not only a big bully, he's also a big baby.

Once she's obtained the swabs and taken their vital signs, she tells us, "You can all go home now. Your mother has already been taken to room and your son is set to go up to his room any time now. Right now, both of them are stable and resting. I know you would love to see them, but I'm certain you can understand why that is not possible when we don't know if any of you have been infected or are contagious. Someone from the Herkimer County Health Department will be in touch tomorrow and they will advise you on what to do next."

I hang my head in shame, as my mother cries silently and Pop broods.

Once we've signed the discharge papers and the instructions to stay home have been reiterated, we are free to go. Somehow it just doesn't feel right to be leaving my brother and my grandmother here at the hospital, particularly when they are both so ill. I feel like one of us should be staying at their bedsides, just in case they need something in the night and no one is there to hear them or look out for them. I look at my mother and I know she is also feeling torn apart by leaving. But Pop is already in the truck and he blasts the horn for us to hurry up. He is impatient and wants to get going.

Mom goes to get in the jump seat in the back of the pickup, but I refuse to let her. I climb in the back behind my mother and extend my legs behind the driver's seat. Without saying a word, Pop adjusts his own seat, pushing it back a little further pinning my legs between the seats, then opens his window and inhales deeply of the cold night air.

"And leave that goddamn mask on," Pop barks an order to no one in particular. My mother catches my eye in the makeup mirror in her visor and I can see the apology in her eyes. But what does she have to apologize for? Except maybe for marrying this asshole. "Not you, Magda," he says. "Take that thing off, you look like a goddamn Arab. You're not the one spreading diseases and threatening the lives of the family."

Pop's words sting. I don't know if that is his intent or if he just doesn't care. Either way, his words wound me. This is not the first time, I should be used to him by now. I'm not surprised but still his words strike me in a tender spot.

The cold wind blows in through Pop's open window, whipping my long hair around my face and causing a painful vibration on my eardrums until at last, my mother says, "Edward, I'm chilly. Could you please put up the window?"

Wordlessly, he complies with her request.

The snow has stopped falling and plows have been out. Thankfully the roads are clear. No one says anything for almost an hour until we cross over the McKeever Bridge and Pop announces, "Emma will stay in the guest cabin while she is under quarantine. We can't have her infecting anyone else."

"But Edward, it isn't winterized and the water can't be turned on yet or the pipes will freeze."

"Magda, that's enough. She is not a child. The old outhouse is still functional and there is plenty of wood for the fireplace."

"I suppose she can warm a kettle over the fire for wash water. There's a hot plate, and a coffee pot. I'll send food over," Mom begins to plan aloud.

They talk about me as if I'm not even here.

~ ~ ~

Pop pulls the truck up to the guest cabin. "Get out," he says. "Your mother will pull together your things."

Mom jumps out of the truck and opens the back door so I can untangle myself and get out. "I'll fix you something to eat and bring your things over in an hour or so. Is there anything in particular you want or need?" she asks.

"Just my sewing bag and my computer. I guess I'll need my suitcase and toiletries, too. Will you let me know if you hear anything about Gram or Lucas?" I ask my mother.

"Of course, my dear. I'll be praying for them and for you, too. Are you sure you are feeling alright?" Mom asks.

"Magda, get in the truck right now or you can walk home. I haven't had anything to eat since lunch."

"Okay, dear, I'm coming," Mom says as she reaches over to place a reassuring hand on my shoulder.

"And you're gonna need to sanitize the back seat, I have a delivery to make in the morning," Pop says.

"The nurse said we all needed to stay home and self-isolate for fourteen days, so we don't expose other people," Mom says as she opens the car door, but she receives no reply or acknowledgment from my father that she has even spoken. Mom climbs back into the front seat.

Without waiting to see that I'm even in the cabin, Pop's truck pulls away down the long tree-lined driveway towards the main house. Again, the driveway is covered over with drifts of snow. I hear the shepherds start to bark and carry-on. You'd think Osama bin Laden had just been resurrected from the dead and was traveling in the truck rather than my parents.

Thankfully the cabin was electrified a few years back. Lucas had gone to trade school to learn to be an electrician and then had apprenticed for a year with a local guy, but apparently, Pop needed him around the compound so he never completed his training. Still Lucas had been able to bring some light and power to this old cabin, as well as a connection for the internet and tonight I'm grateful for it.

I flip on the light switch beside the door. I don't think anyone has been in here since last fall when it was closed down for the winter. The cabin smells dusty and stale. I think about getting a fire started and warming the place up, but decide I'd better head out to the outhouse. First things first, I sure won't want to get dressed to venture out there once I get settled in. I grab the flashlight sitting on the butcher-block table and as luck would have it the batteries are dead. Fortunately, the snow has stopped for now and the night sky is illuminated by a nearly full moon. I won't have difficulty finding my way down the snow-covered path tonight. I take the snow shovel from the porch and clear the path. It is one thing to have to use an outhouse during a beautiful Adirondack summer, it is quite another in the cold snow-covered months of winter. At least it doesn't stink in the winter, that's one consolation.

Once I get back to the cabin I can see that someone has already dropped off my belongings and a picnic basket that Mom has lovingly packed for me. I carry my things inside. Before I put anything away, I'll need to get a fire going in the fireplace.

The fire has already been laid, no doubt someone did this last fall as part of the closing routine. When I was growing up, I always thought it was just another burdensome task we were required to do. Now I see the wisdom behind it. Getting down on my knees, I reach up into the chimney and open the flue. My hands are covered with soot and I feel the rush of cold air. The wood is dry and the kindling and shredded tinder have been carefully set beneath the large pieces of aged hardwood. It takes just one matchstick to set the whole thing ablaze.

I fill the fire bucket with snow and set it near the fireplace. I'll have water to wash up with fairly soon. I sit in the old rocker, careful not to touch anything with my dirty hands until I can wash up.

Once my hands are clean, I unpack my things and settle in. If the circumstances had been different, I really wouldn't mind waiting out the quarantine over here by myself. But the circumstances are not different, and a sense of guilt and shame threaten to overwhelm me, to say nothing of my worry for my brother and Gram. And what about me, I felt a little under the weather yesterday, but today I feel fine. This whole thing is so new, even though I've done a fair amount of reading online about the virus, I don't think anyone really has a very good idea of how it is spread or how to treat it.

The cabin is warming up but it is far from warm. I make a pot of coffee and try to warm myself from the inside out. Sitting in front of the fire, I eat the turkey sandwich that Mom made for me. The only sound I hear is the crackling of the fire and the shifting of the burning wood in the fireplace. Any other night, I could justify going to bed early, but not tonight. The litany of worries plays on and on in my head and the second cup of coffee has only added to my anxiety. There is no way I can sleep. So instead of retiring to the comfort of bed, I pull out my computer bag and retrieve my results of the genetic study and the corresponding genealogy reports I received a few days ago. Then, as recommended, I open my computer, and attempt to connect to the internet.

Out here in the great north woods the power can go out if someone sneezes in town, to say nothing of the kind of winter storm we've endured the last two days. If the power goes out it can be out for days. I say a quick prayer of thanksgiving as my laptop boots up and connects. I write my roommate, Cassie, a short email to fill her in on my grandmother, my brother, and to inquire about her health.

I'd feel just terrible if I infected her too.

Then I pull up the *23 and Me* website and login to see if I can determine what any of this even means.

Chapter 7

The results are fascinating as there are a multitude of reports, including an overview of my ancestry, the composition of my ancestry, and a list of DNA relatives, and a map of where these people currently reside.

Earlier today, while we were having lunch, Pop had said he was German through and through. Where my report indicates: I am 44.2 % French and German, 17.7 % Scandinavian, as well as 24.8 % British and Irish. That only adds up to 86.7%. What about the other 13.3 %? Maybe Mom is right, we're all a little bit of this and a little bit of that. What did she say? *'She's a Heinz 57.'* I can't help but wonder how my Aryan father likes having his German heritage indistinguishably linked with the French. How many times have I heard him make one remark or another disparaging the French as weak and frivolous? Maybe Pop isn't actually the pure-bred Aryan that he proclaims he is.

Still if Pop is indeed one hundred percent German, wouldn't it only stand to reason that I would be at least fifty percent German? But according to my results, I am not.

Mom has always claimed she neither knows nor cares about this kind of thing, that the only thing that really matters is how we treat one another in this lifetime. I can't say I disagree with her. Still, it is curious.

Next, I click on the list of DNA relatives and I can see that I share fifty percent of my DNA with Pop. He is listed as my father.

There is no reference to my mother at all. Is it possible that Mom has not received her results yet? Or perhaps she hasn't even done the test or submitted her saliva sample. I know she wasn't too keen on the whole prospect.

I read further on my profile page, and I have to get up and walk away. This cannot be saying what I think it says.

This can't be right.

I feel as if I have been struck by lightning or touched the hot stove as the shockwaves and the pain course through every cell of my being.

I slam shut the cover of my laptop.

I want to unsee what I have just seen, but the images and the accompanying words are burned into my brain.

I step out onto the porch and breathe deeply of the cold night air.

This cannot be true.

I try to rationalize.

There must be some mistake.

Our understanding of DNA is really only in its infancy.

But if it is true, then heaven help us.

Dear God, have we just opened Pandora's box and unleashed information that will wreak havoc within my own family?

I look up to the moon, and pray for an escape.

There are some things that can rock the very foundation I have built my entire life on, and this is one of them. I feel the winds of change shifting and things could be about to get really ugly.

Returning to my laptop, I cannot bear to look at it, but neither can I bear to look away. And there it is again. My eyes have not betrayed me. Willa, Luca, and Josiah are listed as my full siblings and Becca is listed as my half-sibling. How can this be? I take a deep breath before I continue, I cannot just let this go. My hands tremble as I click on Pop's profile, Willa, Luca, Josiah and I are listed as his children each of us carrying half of Pop's DNA, albeit a totally randomized distribution of genetic material and traits, still fifty percent of each of our genetic code has been inherited from Pop, as he is our father. But Becca is listed as Pop's half-sibling.

Does this mean that she is not his daughter?

I grab a sheet of paper and start to sketch out a pedigree, a genetic family tree, just as I did at least a hundred times in my college genetics class. I use a square for the males and a circle for the females, drawing lines between couples that share children. I need to sort this out. I must be missing something, for the conclusion that looks back at me is abhorrent and unthinkable.

If Becca is our half-sister and Pop is not Becca's biological father, then Josiah, Lucas and I must have the same mother as Becca.

If Becca is also Pop's half-sister, then who is her father? Dear God, please tell me I have this wrong. Is my Grand Pappa, and Pop's father, and Gram's husband and beloved, Winfield Earl, also Becca's biological father?

Did my Grand Pappa have sex and father a child with my mother twenty-four years ago?

I pull out my phone and open the calculator app. Mom is sixty now, which means she was thirty-six when Becca was born. Gram told me that her Winfield was twelve years older than she is, and she is ninety-one. That would make Grand Pappa one hundred and three if he was alive today. He would have been seventy-nine when Becca was born.

Good God, no thirty-six-year-old woman in her right mind would *willingly* have sex with a seventy-nine year-old-man, particularly her husband's father. I take a deep breath as I begin to taste bile. I fear I might get ill.

I suppose it is possible that some woman might willingly have an affair with a man who is forty-three years older than her, but not my mother. No, Mom has way too much integrity and would never have *willingly* consented to such an arrangement. This I am absolutely certain of. So, what does this mean? I shudder at the implications. I have seen the photos, my mother was a beautiful young woman, and she is still beautiful.

I remember the look on Becca's face as she looked at the printouts of her results. Was that really only at lunchtime today? No wonder she looked confused. My heart swells with compassion for my younger sister. She has always been Pop's favorite. Everyone in the family acknowledges this as a fact. I can only imagine how Pop will react if he learns he is not Becca's father.

I click over to Becca's profile. On *23 and Me*, over nine million people have submitted their saliva samples for testing. And here, there is a list compiled of those who have been tested who share pieces of her genetic code and their relationship to Becca. Of her DNA relations, Becca has eight half-siblings: me, Willa, Lucas, Josiah and Pop, plus three other women that I have never heard of. One by one I click on their profiles, one of these women Margrit Wolfram is living outside of Munich, Germany and is eighty-five years old, the second Julia Jaeger is living in Oslo, Norway and is seventy-eight, and the third woman is Ruth David and she is living in Haifa, Israel and she is seventy-five. Each of these women's profiles also have both Becca and Pop listed as their half-sibling. Clicking back to Becca's profile, I see Becca's profile also lists numerous first through fifth cousins, and multiple nieces and nephews that I have never heard of.

Holy shit.

How much of this does my grandmother know about? I have never heard even a whisper about my grandfather having another family before coming to the United States.

I check my own profile and some of these people are on my profile, too. But the relationships are generally more distant and removed, meaning these women are not of my generation. I've always been confused about exactly what once or twice removed even meant.

I click back and forth between the profiles on the older women who are listed as Becca's half-siblings, these women are also half-siblings of one another, so none of them have the same mother, either.

I add them to the pedigree I've sketched out on a piece of printer paper from my computer bag.

From all appearances, Gram's beloved Winfield was not as honorable as she has led us to believe. But if the story we've always been told is not the truth, then what is the truth and why all the lies?

I close my laptop. Before going to bed, I make another trip out to the privy. I start to understand where the expression, freezing my ass off, may have come from. I put another couple of logs on the fire before pouring some hot water from the kettle hanging over the fire into a basin and attempt to wash away all the stress and strain of the day. Feeling reasonably clean I change into an old flannel nightgown before crawling into bed and under the covers. I'm bone tired and emotionally burdened.

Is this what it feels like to carry the weight of the world? The very notion feels like a gross exaggeration but it is burdensome to me. If I have brought this virus into my family I'll never forgive myself and there are those who will never forgive me either. And what about this information that my grandfather and my mother had a child together, my sister Becca? I can't even fathom how that took place, did he rape her? Does Mom know that her father-in-law is Becca's biological father? Has anyone else even read these reports? Does anyone else know this? Or maybe everyone knows and it's all just a big secret that has been kept from me and my sibs? My mind races as question after question takes shape in my mind and once I get to the bottom of the list I start all over again with all the unanswered questions.

Trying to clear my head, I decide to pray for my grandmother and my youngest brother Lucas. I beg God for mercy and ask him to spare my family the fate that has befallen so many other poor souls. It seems almost absurd to ask for divine intervention. Why should my loved ones be spared when so many others have already been taken? Do I really believe that we have been so *good and holy* that the Almighty would spare my family? It is almost laughable to believe that we, *The Earl Family*, should have this kind of grace and mercy bestowed upon us. I can't help but think of the comments that were thrown about so freely around our dinner table when we were growing up. *Good and holy* is not how anyone in their right mind would describe my family. Except, perhaps, the arrogant among us who think we are so much better than everyone else, and therefore God must prefer us to all other lesser human beings. Oh, dear God, help us.

And then the questions start all over again. How could I possibly have infected Lucas? I only sat across the table from him at breakfast this morning, perhaps that was enough. I sat next to Gram while we were sewing. We do share a bathroom, I suppose it's possible I infected her. I didn't feel great last night, but I wasn't really sick. At least I didn't think I was. Lucas is only twenty-six years old and a big strong guy. I didn't think the young were supposed to get very sick, but he's sick enough to be hospitalized. I guess there's much I don't know about this virus.

Gram is the one I'm really worried about. She's always been so hale and hearty even for ninety-one years old, but she is ninety-one. If the virus doesn't get her, the heartbreak of her husband's infidelity just might do her in.

I toss and turn for hours, cursing myself for having a cup of coffee so late in the day. Somewhere in the predawn hours my fears and anxieties at last give way to sleep.

Chapter 8

I wake to the familiar sound of Pop barking orders at my mother, "Magda, I told you last night I wanted the truck cleaned and disinfected. I have to make a delivery this morning."

"Sorry Edward, it was so late when we got home last night," I hear her call from inside the house.

I reach over to the nightstand and look at my phone. Good God, it's only 5:30. The old rule still applies: if Pop isn't sleeping then no one should be sleeping.

He starts the truck and revs the engine to be certain it will be warmed up when he's ready to leave. The exhaust billows out the tailpipe in the cold morning air.

Looking out the window I see my mother, she still wears her plaid bathrobe with knee high winter boots. Carrying a red plastic bucket filled with her household cleaning supplies, she trudges through the snow towards Pop's big ass truck as her long white hair wisps behind her like cirrus clouds dispersing in the wind. She looks ethereal, and otherworldly, like an angel trapped in human form.

"Hurry up," he snarls impatiently. "I still have to get the truck loaded before I can get on the road." He paces back and forth as she climbs in the back to clean. "Is breakfast ready?" Pop asks. He leaves my mother cleaning and heads back into the house. The door slams loudly behind him and the dogs bark aggressively waking everyone who may still have been sleeping.

This is not the first time I want to whack him in the head with Mom's cast iron frying pan. If it's filled with his bacon and eggs, all the better. The notion of sending my father heading out the door to his *very important meeting* with egg on his face and clothes and smelling of bacon grease brings a smile to my face. I shake the notion from my imagination as I realize how much animosity I hold for the man.

Laying back down within the still warm flannel sheets, I cover myself with the scratchy, old Hudson Bay woolen blanket with its green, red, yellow, and indigo stripes. The memory of all of yesterday's drama comes rushing back to me with all the ferocity of a Nor'easter. I am in quarantine and isolation. But where is Pop going? He's supposed to be staying home. He's in quarantine, too.

I pull the covers up around my shoulders, it's cold in here. Looking over at the fireplace, there are still some embers glowing beneath the grate. I start the day with a quick prayer of thanksgiving, as in— Thank God, I don't have to start a fire from nothing. I climb out of bed and find a copy of the Adirondack Express, the local weekly paper. I check the date— August 27, 2019. It's from last summer. Crumpling it up I stuff it beneath the grate and gently blow on it. It doesn't take long before the paper is engulfed in flames and I am feeding the fire with some small dry twigs from

90

the tinder box and then a few larger ones and lastly a couple of small logs. There is a sense of independence and self-reliance that a girl gains by growing up in the Adirondacks. At the very least, I know how to build a fire and I won't freeze to death out here.

Nature calls and I head out to the outhouse. Mom hears the door open and looks in my direction. "Good morning Emma, how are you feeling?"

"I'm fine Mom. Any news on Gram or Lucas?" I call back.

"I talked with the night nurse about thirty minutes ago, both of them are resting quietly. Thank heavens. Would you like some coffee this morning? Maybe a little breakfast?" she asks as if taking care of me is the most important thing she has to do today.

I should offer to give her a hand, God knows she has enough to do, but I know that my presence rarely seems to make anything any easier, at least not when Pop is around. My very being is like bringing gasoline to the match as far as my father is concerned. Together we are incendiary.

"I'm good Mom. No hurry at all. I may go back to bed for a little while."

"Just let me get Pop and Josiah on their way, then I'll bring you over a basket. Anything in particular you'd like or need this morning?"

Before I can answer Pop is out the door with Josiah. "Get those *ghosties* loaded in the back, cover 'em with those old moving blankets. Make sure the cap on the truck is secure and locked. I don't need anybody minding my business this morning. We're leaving in forty-five minutes, so get going." Pop turns his attention from Josiah and towards our mother,

"Good God woman, are you done yet?"

Whatever is he up to now? And what the hell is a *ghostie* that he doesn't want anyone to see?

I plug in the electric kettle and make myself a cup of tea before taking a seat beside the window in this one room cabin. I sit there watching my eldest brother from behind the sheer curtains that Mom has hung in here to insure a little privacy. I can't help but notice how the windows are clean and the sills wear a coat of new white paint. In the midst of all this craziness, Mom has attempted to make the old cabin as comfortable and homey as possible.

Josiah disappears into the old barn as I fire up my laptop. Thank goodness, the internet is up and running this morning. I Google *ghostie*. Nothing relevant comes up. Is this a term that's code for something else? I wonder. My attention is drawn to the window again, where Josiah emerges from the garage under the cover of darkness. The sun won't be up for another ninety minutes or so. Only the light from inside the garage silhouettes my brother as he heads towards the back of the truck carrying a rectangular box which appears to be constructed from rough sawn lumber. It must be heavy as he carries it across his two arms before bending his knees to hoist it into the back of the pickup.

A shiver goes up my spine and I sense something nefarious is going on. The shape of the box reminds me of something I have seen before in a movie or maybe on television. This time I Google *ghost guns*.

Wikipedia has an entry. "A ghost gun is a term for a privately-made firearm that lacks commercial serial numbers or other identifying marks.

The term is used mostly in the United States by gun control advocates, gun rights advocates, law enforcement, and some in the firearm industry. By making guns themselves, owners are not usually subject to federal or state commercial background checks and regulation. Under U.S. federal law, the creation and possession of firearms for non-commercial purposes has always been legal. In contrast, firearms for sale or distribution requires a federal license for their manufacture, and must bear unique serial numbers. The firearm receiver, the part that integrates the components by providing the housing for internal action components such as the hammer, bolt, or firing pin, if left unfinished may be sold without the requirement of federal and state background checks."

Good Lord. I can't even fathom what *he* is into now?

Last night Pop said he needed to make a delivery this morning to an important client. Is that old goat selling illegal firearms? Is this what he referred to as *ghosties*? I can guarantee my father doesn't give a rat's ass about what the law says, either federal or state as long as he is making money and doesn't get caught. The questions keep coming as I try to put this all together.

And furthermore, who the hell are these important clients?

A moving shadow outside my window catches my attention as one of the dogs runs back towards the garage, where my brother reappears with another wooden box. Again, he loads the box into the back of the truck.

I return to read on my laptop. "More recently it has become popular to produce receivers from plastic with a 3D-printer. The most popular tool for finishing the AR-15 weapons is made by Defense Distributed and is called the Ghost Gunner. They also make pistols and semi-automatic weapons as ghost guns. These weapons do not have any identifying serial numbers and therefore are virtually untraceable."

Good God, the pieces of this puzzle begin to take shape in my mind. Since I was here at Christmastime, Pop has had Lucas upgrade the entire compound, including all the outbuildings, to high speed internet with a VPN, or virtual private network. Is this why my father and brothers are so intent on security and have been aggressively training their dogs?

The Wikipedia article goes on to indicate that the Department of Alcohol, Tobacco and Firearms or ATF says there are tens of thousands of ghost guns in California alone.

Well, it looks like my father is ensuring there will be plenty of firepower here in upstate New York as well. As long as I can remember Pop has been bad mouthing liberals about coming for his guns, yammering on about his right to bear arms, and his constitutionally protected sacred second amendment. He needs re-schooling. The second amendment refers to a well-regulated militia's right to keep and bear arms but there is nothing well-regulated about what Pop is doing. I just never dreamed it would come to this, where he and my brothers would be trading in illegal firearms.

I guess I have been safely tucked away in my own world in the middle of New York City and haven't been paying close enough attention to what is going on right here at home. Or for that matter, anywhere else in rural America.

Watching out the window I see Josiah load another box and then another for a total of four. How many guns are in each box? I can't even hazard a guess. But it looks like they are arming a small militia with untraceable weapons. Are they prepping for Armageddon and the end of days?

I need to check this out.

I rationalize, maybe this is just my imagination off and running.

Maybe this is not at all what it appears to be.

The door slams again and Pop is outside yelling, "Josiah, get going. It's already 6:15 and we need to be in Indian Lake before sunrise and it's at least an hour's drive."

"Just one more box and I'll be ready. Can you ask Mom to fill a thermos of coffee, for me?" Josiah calls to Pop who is standing on the front porch.

"Get it yourself." Pop shouts as he pulls on his old Carhartt coat. "Bullet, Trigger," he calls, then gives two short whistles in quick succession. The two German shepherds come bolting out of the woods. Pop opens the door to the truck as both dogs jump into the back seat that Mom has just cleaned. Pop climbs into the driver's seat of his truck to wait for my brother.

Thank goodness, my mother was out there before the crack of dawn scrubbing down Pop's truck to accommodate his dirty dogs.

Chapter 9

I don't know how long they will be gone. Nor when, or if, anyone else in the family will be arriving for breakfast before they begin their daily chores, work or school. If I want to know what's going on, and I do, I'd better get on it while I have a chance. Pulling on a pair of thermal long johns, I struggle into my skinny jeans until I feel like a stuffed sausage. Who cares. I finish dressing and grab my coat and a black watch cap. I feel like a spy in some overwritten Hollywood movie. I leave the cabin, careful not to slam the door, I step into the shadows of the snow-covered pines and wait. Standing in the darkness I take a deep breath and then another as I try to calm my racing heart. Reigning in my anxiety, I stay in the shadows of the trees as I head towards the back door of the detached garage. This building has never been used as a garage, or at least never to store any car or truck as far as I know, although it could easily house three vehicles. In truth, it has always functioned more as Pop's workshop and his man cave, and as such, I have never felt welcomed here. To even cross the threshold without permission feels like a grave trespass and a serious transgression.

I reach the back door and find it locked. Damn it, I should have expected this. I look over to the main house and lights burn in the kitchen, Mom is probably cooking breakfast. This is usually Gram's job, but not today. Gram is in the hospital. My eyes fill with tears as I wipe them away with the back of my mitten. I don't have time to indulge my grief or my fears right now. So, I swallow hard to get past the lump in my throat then stuff my emotions back down. I've been doing that my entire life. Why should today be any different?

Keeping to the shadows, I move towards the driveway where Lucas' snow-covered truck is parked. I approach the vehicle and open the driver's side door. There on the seat I find my brother's key ring. Surely, he will have a key to the man cave.

By the time I try all the keys, it is already starting to get light. I open the door and slip inside as I hear my nieces' high-pitched, little voices as they chatter to one another on their way through the snow towards the main house for breakfast. I turn off the flashlight on my cell phone, hoping they will just keep walking. My eyes begin to adjust to the light as I feel my way around the room, but it is not light enough to see in here. I pull the heavy drape completely closed across the only window making the room pitch black. Feeling safely hidden inside I turn the light on my flashlight back on and scan the room.

Holy shit!

The first thing I see is a black banner which bears a red shield with a large medieval knight's helmet in profile at the top and the words, *National Resistance Revival,* in big, bold letters in gold across the shield. There is something eerily familiar about the shield and the crest.

There are boxes stacked up from floor to ceiling on metal racks along two of the three walls. Some of the boxes are open beside a workbench. This is where Pop used to keep his ordinary household tools, tools for fixing things, common everyday tools but those have been replaced with metal drills and a sophisticated piece of electronic technology. I don't know what it is, but I suspect it may be a 3-D printer that I read about this morning. Some of the guns on the workbench appear to be in various stages of completion.

Still wearing my mittens, I carefully turn over a pistol that rests on a wooden tray on the corner of the workbench. An order form can be seen beneath the hand gun. The form is embossed with the same image of the shield that hangs on the banner, but the words are missing from the logo. The handgun looks to be complete or nearly complete. Not that I've ever held a pistol or have any idea what I'm looking for. I shine the light from my cell phone over the gun. There are no identifying numbers or any kind of a logo or trademark on the gun, at least none that I can see.

I shift the gun in the box to get a better look at the order form. Instead of a name or address, the purchaser is indicated by a seven-digit identification code composed of both letters and numbers, much like a computer password or username.

There is a clipboard on Pop's old desk with a stack of order forms. The form looks to be computer generated, and there is a list of military or paramilitary equipment in a bold type-face with categories including: body armor, stun guns, hand guns, automatics, holsters, casings, and ammo. Beneath each category are sub-categories with lists of things I've never heard of and certainly can't identify, except perhaps the AK-47s, AR-15s, which are listed under the automatic weapons category.

I shudder as I have read about so many massacres in this country that have occurred where military assault weapons have been used to kill thousands of innocent people every year and even small children.

Not only are my father and my brothers illegally selling and distributing weapons, but it appears that they are also manufacturing ghost guns without any serial numbers on them, right here in the garage.

Oh God, now what do I do? My hands are shaking and my heart races as I'm caught in an ethical quandary that I don't know how to resolve. My conscience is acting up; if this were anywhere else and anyone else, there is no doubt in my mind what I would do. I'd call the police and turn them in. But this is my family and I'm having a full-blown moral crisis.

I don't know where I got the idea, but I thought the manufacture and sale of weapons was a big business run by major corporations. Didn't some of the guys I went to high school with go to work at the Remington Arms plant in the Village of Ilion? I think the plant is only about an hour from here. Anyway, I never expected to see something like this, not in my own home.

Who the hell is Pop arming and why?

Are both of my brothers involved?

I take my mittens off and stuff them in my coat pockets. Using the light on my cell phone, I start to look through the few random papers filed neatly in manila folders on my father's desk, when a message bar flashes across the top of his laptop. It appears to be an email with another order. I take a moment to click around on Pop's laptop to see if I can find it, but everything is password protected. I stop abruptly and start to hyperventilate. It dawns on me that he may have some kind of program installed on his computer that would let him know that I am onto him. I start to tremble just thinking of the repercussions if Pop even thought I was snooping about in his business, let alone if he ever caught me. My heart is racing and I feel sick to my stomach.

I nearly jump out of my skin when I hear a car pull into the driveway. Again, I turn off the cell phone light and freeze in place. Alone in the darkness, I realize I'm holding my breath. God-forbid someone will know I am in here. Standing in the silence of the early morning my heart is pounding so loudly I am certain it can be heard by whoever it is that just arrived.

Then I hear my mother call out, "Becca, will you take this thermos of coffee and basket of scones over to Emma? She's staying in the guest cabin."

"Sure Mom, let me drop this stuff off in the house first," she says.

I slip out the back door of the garage, the door locks behind me with a click. I slip my hand into my coat pocket to find my mittens. Lucas' keys are still there. I debate locking the deadbolt and decide against it. It's too risky. Dawn is just breaking as I skulk around the back of the building and then scurry beneath the low hanging branches of the snow-laden evergreens, hoping to avoid detection and to get back to the cabin before my sister arrives.

Chapter 10

I close the cabin door behind me and lean the weight of my body up against it. I am shaking with fear and the cold. The fire has burned through the logs I put on an hour ago and I hustle to restart it from the dying embers, just as it ignites there is a knock on the door. I slip out of my coat and toss it in the corner before opening the door.

"Hi," I say as Becca stands outside with Mom's old picnic basket and a thermos. "Want to come in?" I ask.

"No thanks," she says as she hands me the goods. "It's not that I don't want to, it's just that it's probably not a good idea, given that both Gram and Lucas are sick and all."

"I'm really feeling fine. I'm not the least bit sick," I say.

Becca hesitates. She stands there on the snow-covered porch shifting her weight from one foot to the other, I have a sense she needs to talk. Perhaps she, too, has looked at the genetic reports on *23 and Me*.

"Have you already been out this morning?" she asks. It is only then that I realize in my haste to get back to the cabin and deal with the dying fire that I have forgotten to remove my snow laden boots. I look down at my feet. I am standing in a puddle.

"Only to the outhouse," I say. I am amazed at how quickly and effortlessly I can come up with a plausible explanation—albeit a blatant lie.

"Oh, well I guess I should get going. Mom already has breakfast started, and I need to get Willa's girls started on their schoolwork." Becca starts down the steps.

"Any more news on Gram or Lucas? I know Mom called the hospital about an hour ago," I say.

"Not since then, I guess they both got through the night okay." Becca takes another step off the porch and into the eight inches of new snow.

"Thanks for bringing this over," I say lifting the basket in her direction.

"No problem, I'll bring you some lunch over around noon." She is ready to go, then she hesitates a moment before turning back to me, "Oh, I forgot to tell you, I have a new boyfriend, Rolfe Teufel."

"Willa mentioned that," I say.

"Oh, *she* did. Well, don't believe everything she says, I don't think she likes him very much. But Pop and Lucas do. In fact, he should be here shortly. He's helping Pop out with a few things. He has a ten-year-old daughter, Ivy, who has been coming over with him. Sometimes Ivy sits in on my lessons with Heidi and Tilly."

"That's nice." I try to think of something else to say that doesn't sound too disingenuous as I try to mend our fractured relationship. I think Becca is going to need some support when, and if, all of the family saga comes to light. "I'd like to meet them. Not today, of course, but when I'm out of quarantine."

"Sure. I didn't want you to be afraid if you see some guy coming and going from the garage when Pop and Josiah aren't here."

"Okay, thanks." *Afraid*, hmm, is there something about him that is scary? Interesting, word choice. Whatever is going on in this family and in the garage, is already frightening enough.

"They should be here pretty soon. See you at lunch," Becca says as she turns and heads back towards the main house.

I bring the basketful of food into the house. I take off my boots and set them by the fire to dry, before I pour myself a coffee from the thermos. I pull up the news on my computer to get the latest update on the virus.

Governor Cuomo has ordered all New Yorkers to stay at home and shelter-in-place, I guess he means all New Yorkers except for Pop and his entourage, while the governor of Florida has yet to close the public beaches in the sunshine state. Too bad there isn't a unified, science-driven protocol on how best to handle this pandemic. Still, it kind of makes me wish I was sheltering in Florida. It sounds positively delightful, I could self-isolate on a beach with periodic dips in the ocean to cool off. Instead, I'm alone in this drafty old cabin without running water or even a functional toilet. I've only been here less than ten hours and I know this is going to get old pretty quick. At least I have electricity and a solid internet connection.

After an hour of perusing the internet in search of any good news at all on the pandemic, I decide to click over and log into my *23 and Me* profile. To my surprise, there is a notification on my page indicating that a relative has sent me a message.

The message begins—PERSONAL AND PRIVATE.

I click to the note:

Dear Emma,

I have been looking for members of my biological family nearly all of my life. And now I have found you and it appears that we are related. My name is Julia Jaeger. I am 78 years old and I live in Oslo, Norway.

According to the algorithm you and I are cousins and related on my father's side. It appears that we both share a half-sister, although I am a little confused about your relationship with my half-brother Edward. Somehow, we are all related.

Rebecca Earl, our sister, has not completed her profile in as much detail as you have. Given that you live in the same town in New York, share the same last name, and are only four years older than Rebecca, I assume that you know one another and may know how to get in touch with her.

I am looking for information about my father. I was a war child born in 1942 near Trondheim, Norway during the German occupation of Norway. I have come to understand that my birth was part of the Lebensborn Kinder program where my mother was a young Norwegian woman and my father was most likely a German officer in the Waffen-Schutzstaffel. I was adopted at the end of the war when I was six years old and have no memory of my biological parents.

This may all come as a shock to you and your family, if you have no previous knowledge of this, and now to have a long-lost relative reaching out across the globe. This information may be difficult for our sister to hear, so I will leave it to your discretion how much of this you want to share with her. I would love to meet you and your family when we are all free to travel again. But for now, I am getting on in years and know nothing of my father or my siblings or my cousins. If you would be so kind to write me back you would help heal an old woman's heart.

Julia Jaeger

Good God, what the hell does any of this even mean. There are a couple of words in her letter that I am not familiar with, the context sheds some light but I am not certain. And I need to be. I pray I am wrong. With some hesitation, I type *waffen-schutzstaffel* into Google. I pause a moment before hitting enter on my keyboard. Again, an overwhelming sense that I am opening Pandora's box threatens me. If this means what I think it means, there will be no going back and undoing the evil or fixing what is at risk of being broken. I can't help myself, I take a deep breath and hit enter.

"Waffen-Schutzstaffel was an armed major paramilitary organization under Adolf Hitler and the Nazi Party. Otherwise known as *the SS*," according to Wikipedia.

Oh God, not Grand Pappa. The taste of bile fills my mouth and I rush outside. I'm going to be sick. I hear the door slam behind me as I fall to my knees and vomit in the snow beneath the trees. I stay there on my hands and knees trying to get my breathing back under control when I realize I am wearing my now wet long underwear and socks, and no pants and no boots.

A rusty old truck pulls in the driveway and a man and a child get out of the front. This must be Rolfe and his daughter. What did Becca say her name is? I can't remember.

He wears a red baseball cap with his Carhartt overalls. His overalls are about the color of wet mud or maybe peanut butter. There is something so unsavory about the color. Again, I gag as he heads around the back of the garage.

I jump to conclusions based on everything else that seems to be encircling this whole stinkin' swamp, he's probably a Trumpster out there Makin' America Great Again.

I spit out the last remnants of vomit and bile and then rinse my mouth with a handful of pristine snow.

I watch as the little blonde girl heads towards the house and her father calls to her, "Be a good girl, Ivy. Pay attention to Miss Becca, and make yourself useful. And don't go orderin' Heidi's granny around like she's an ole black mammy."

"I won't Papa," the little girl says with a laugh.

I cringe at the racist banter and the use of the old stereotype. I have little doubt that my dear mother dotes on this little girl just like she does with her own grandchildren. Still, this little girl takes no note of her father's offensive words and makes no objection. Clearly, she is used to this kind of talk, even if I am not. It grates my soul.

Her father shakes his head as if this is a battle with his ten-year-old he has already lost. He turns toward the garage.

Ivy enters the house without stopping to knock on the door or be invited inside. She clearly is comfortable at my parents' home. I wonder how Mom feels about people coming and going when our family is supposed to be quarantined due to the Covid exposure.

Once I'm fairly certain that Rolfe and his daughter have gone, I come out from under the trees. Using my stockinged foot, I cover the remains of last night's dinner with snow then walk back to the cabin. By now my socks and thermal underwear are soaking wet. I take them off and hang the underwear on a hook beside the fireplace and place the socks on the granite hearth. I put on my old moccasins and wrap the wool blanket around me as I settle back in. I swipe my finger across the mousepad and the computer comes back to life.

No wonder no one in our family has ever talked about this. I feel sick as I have read a great deal about the war crimes and atrocities committed by the SS during World War II. There was never any doubt in my mind that my grandfather and my father, for that matter, were sexist, racist, and anti-Semitic. But somehow, I was able to create a distinction between people who acted on their prejudices and those who just espoused the beliefs. I was deluding myself and I can no longer do that. I have no doubt the seeds of hatred that my father embraces were planted long ago by his father and are now being sown within my brothers and sister and even in my sister Willa's little girls, or at least in Heidi.

I open a new tab in my browser and type in the words—*lebensborn kinder.* I brace myself for whatever else I am about to learn about my grandfather. I hit the enter key. There are many options. I start on Wikipedia to get an overview.

"Lebensborn—literally translates to *Fount of Life.*"

"It was SS-initiated, state-supported program in Nazi Germany with the goal of raising the declining birth rate of Aryan children by persons classified as racially pure and healthy. It was used to promote Nazi eugenics. The Lebensborn program was in operation from 1935 to 1945 and provided welfare to its mostly young, unmarried Aryan women who were systematically bred with and impregnated by members of the SS. The program encouraged anonymous births at their maternity homes and most of the children were put up for adoption after the war."

I can hardly believe my eyes. How come I have never heard of this? My heart races as I begin to skim, reading as rapidly as possible. Good God, tell me this did not really happen.

"The first Lebensborn home was located outside of Munich, however the program was expanded to several occupied countries including Austria, Poland, Norway, Denmark, France, Belgium, The Netherlands, and Luxembourg. There were nine Lebensborn homes in Norway. It is estimated that over 8,000 children were born in this breeding program in Germany and as many as 12,000 children in occupied Norway. It has been estimated that hundreds of thousands of war children were fathered by Nazi soldiers in occupied countries during World War II.

"After the war these children were frequently discriminated against, socially isolated, and bullied by other children. These children were often called *tyskerunger* or "Kraut kids," which was a derogatory term. The mothers of these children were often arrested in Norway on suspicion of collaboration with the Germans leaving their children abandoned."

I gently close the cover on my computer. I need some fresh air. I need to think. I pull on my jeans and a dry pair of socks. I pour myself another cup of coffee from the thermos. It's still hot. There is no cream or sugar so I down it quickly before putting on my boots and outerwear. Without further thought I head out for a morning walk, stopping briefly to replace Lucas' keys on the front seat of his truck, just where I found them.

Chapter 11

I decide to walk out towards Otter Pond. Leaving the driveway and can hear the roar of snowmobiles out on the trails. It sounds like an extra-large herd are out enjoying the latest snowfall. They must be heading up towards Big Moose as the sound of their engines grows weaker with each passing moment and soon I am encompassed by the silence of the morning. The sun is out causing the snow to sparkle, in spite of all the mayhem and personal pandemonium that I can't escape, Mother Nature carries on undisturbed.

I do my best just to breathe as I try to restore a sense of equanimity. I walk for over an hour, when I can no longer keep thoughts of the ensuing chaos at bay I decide to turn and start back towards home. I don't know what I will do when I get there, but I turn towards home just the same.

Making my way up the long driveway, I'm surprised to see we've been plowed out in my absence and that Pop's truck is back. Pop said they were making a delivery up in Long Lake and that's at least an hour's drive from here. I check the time on my phone, it's almost ten o'clock. I didn't expect them back so soon.

As I approach the cabin I see my brother and Becca's boyfriend carrying those wooden crates around to the back of the garage. "Yo Joe," I call out to him using a greeting I have used since we were kids. Fear flashes in my brother's eyes as they both turn in my direction. Josiah does not answer. Instantly, I regret my decision to make my presence known as Josiah attempts to hide the box he carries with his body as he hurries behind the garage towards the other door. Rolfe Teufel stands his ground, narrows his eyes, and stares me down.

How is it that this *Johnny-come-lately*, whom I've never even met, is giving me the distinct impression that I am persona non-grata within my own family and in my own home?

I stare back.

A moment later, Pop storms out of the house and starts shouting in my direction, breaking the stalemate between Rolfe and I. Pop is yelling at me. It takes me a moment to figure out what he is saying. "What are you doing sneaking around here?"

"What are you talking about?" I'm dumbfounded. "I just got back from a walk, I haven't been sneaking around anywhere?" No sooner are the words out of my mouth then it dawns on me that he might know that I've been in the garage, and that I was trespassing in his white supremacist's gun factory while he was away.

"Don't play dumb with me, *Missy*." He's raging now, he's red-faced and I can almost see the spittle flying as he screams at me. "I saw the footprints in the snow leading from the cabin to *my* garage and back again. I know they belong to you and you've been poking your nose into things that are none of your business."

Now Mom and Becca have come out on the porch to see what all of the shouting is about.

"Why are you making such a big deal about this. I was just looking for some snowshoes, I thought there might be a pair in the garage. That's where we used to keep that kind of stuff."

His face eases slightly as his temper begins to cool.

So instead of running from him while I have the chance, just as I would have as a child, I continue adding details to my fabricated story. "The door was locked, and since I couldn't find any snowshoes, I decided to go for a walk. They'd just plowed the road." I point with my arm indicating the direction I've just come from and give a big huff like I'm terribly insulted by the insinuation that I would sneak into his secret space that everyone else in the family seems to have unrestricted access to. I take a deep breath as he appears to be satisfied with my answer. I am surprised and more than a little concerned at how I am rapidly becoming such a proficient liar.

I walk up near the main house and stand on the freshly shoveled front walk. I stand just off the porch so we don't have to shout at one another.

Pop stands there glowering at me with his hands on his hips. Any respect I once had for him has become so diminished. He's such a big bully. I shake my head at him, my heart is breaking to think that my family has come to this. I'm filled with both pity and contempt while he stands there overtly trying to position himself to appear bigger, stronger, and more powerful. But more powerful than what or who? Just what is he trying to prove?

I don't know why but I can never seem to leave well enough alone. Instead of silently congratulating myself on a hand well played and exiting with my dignity intact, I decide to shift the attention back towards my father and his crack of dawn delivery of illegal firearms. "I didn't expect you to be home so soon," I say, trying to appear nonchalant and not tipping my hand indicating what I already know.

"Mitch was a no-show— no call and no show. That sonofabitch, I don't know what went wrong." Then Pop lowers his voice and mutters, "We saw him last week and again yesterday, he was so gung-ho to finalize the deal. We hauled all that hardware up there for nothing. It just doesn't make sense." He shakes his head appearing perplexed by something he can't quite grasp.

Does he think I can't hear him or am I so inconsequential that what I hear doesn't even matter? I don't know who he is addressing his comments to. I have no idea who Mitch even is. Instead of asking him about Mitch, I say, "*Hardware?*" Inquiring as innocently as I am capable of.

"Mind your own business, Emma," Josiah says as he comes up the walk in my direction. "Mitch has taken ill, and that's all you need to know."

"Mitch who?" I ask, in spite of the fact I've just been told to mind my own business.

"He's sick?" Pop ignores my question and directs his question to Josiah.

"Yep, I just got a text from his ole lady. She's taken him to the ER in Saranac Lake. He has a high fever and a cough. She said he's been feelin' poorly for the last couple days. The doc thinks it may be that virus," Josiah says.

A look of alarm crosses Pop's face. "Get away from your sister," Pop bellows at Josiah. "I can't afford to have you getting sick, too." Then he turns his attention back towards me, "And you're supposed to be in quarantine."

"So are you," I bark back. I turn to head back toward the cabin. He makes me feel like a leper. He'd like nothing better than to have me locked far away from the rest of my family, and the rest of humanity while he's at it. I am that thorn in his side. I always have been and that certainly hasn't changed. If anything, our relationship has grown even more contentious over the years. I don't know why I always have to have the last word, but I do. He just pisses me off.

And with that Pop is off the porch and coming after me, just as he did so many times when I was a kid and didn't know when to shut up. He lunges at me and grabs me by the arm.

"Take your hands off of me," I demand in a slow deep voice that I don't even recognize as my own.

"Or what?" he snarls.

"Or I'll breathe on you and infect you too."

He gives me a shove and I land in a snow drift like a bag of discarded garbage.

I pick myself up and brush the snow from my coat. Looking back over my shoulder, I see that no one has moved. Everyone is just standing there, watching my humiliation. No one says anything, not one word. Not now and not ever. Again, the bully is triumphant.

I turn to walk back to the cabin. Attempting to offer comfort, Mom calls after me. "I've just made a fresh pot of coffee and some coffee cake. It's just come out of the oven and is still warm. I'll bring you some."

Still raging from this latest indignity, I turn and wave to my mother. "No thanks, not now," I try to say but my voice breaks before I can get the words out. I'm sure everyone knows I'm about to cry. But the tears don't come. Not this time, I'm too filled with fury.

"Put your thermos out on the porch," Mom calls out just as I reach the cabin door.

I'm twenty-eight years old, and yet I still feel like the same angry and frightened little girl, left to fight my own battles all alone for there isn't now and never has been anyone who ever had my back, or came to my defense. Why do I always excuse my family for their lack of compassion and lack of courage? I know the answer. They fear for their own safety and security if they should cross him.

It is not that I feel unloved, for I know that people show love in different ways. My mother is the very best of our family, but what in heaven's name did she ever see in *him*?

I re-enter the cabin, leaving my boots by the door and hanging my coat on the old hickory coat rack. Heading over to the fireplace I stir the dying embers with the old iron poker before throwing another log on the fire. Then I change out of my damp yoga pants where the snow has crept in over the tops of my boots.

Sitting by the fire I take a moment and try to regain my composure. I watch the flames in the fireplace and focus on my breathing. Time passes as I rock back and forth in the old rocking chair as the all-consuming rage begins to dissipate.

I decide to focus on something else.

I bring my laptop over and attempt to write back to Julia Jaeger using the messenger program on the *23 and Me* website. After several false starts I finally pull something together.

Dear Julia,

Thank you so much for reaching out and writing to me. To say your letter came as a surprise is indeed an understatement, for nothing has *ever* been said to me about my grandfather having any other children.

Our sister Becca was the one who was curious about the family genealogy and purchased the *23 and Me* testing kits for all of us at Christmastime. I must say, I'm personally having a great deal of difficulty with much that I have learned about my family in the last few days. Many things I've believed to be true, I find have been built upon misconceptions at best, and more likely, lies. Either lies of omission or the bold-faced lies that may have been perpetuated as a cover-up for horrific depravity and unspeakable evil. At this point I do not have enough information to discern which is which.

It was only a day ago that I learned that Becca is my half-sister and not my full-sister as I'd previously believed. I am going to ask that you not reach out to Rebecca or Becca as we call her until I get a little of this sorted out on my end, as it will come as a crushing blow to her, to my father, and my grandmother to learn of her paternity. I do not believe my father knows that Becca was fathered by his own father, as the results of this genealogical study seem to indicate. Becca is my father's favorite child. To learn she is his half-sister and not his daughter could create unbridled rage in the man, as I have seen him behave this way in the past.

Reviewing the information that is listed on your *23 and Me* profile, I assume that you still don't know your biological father's name. And I believe you have every right to know. If this is correct, his name is Winfield Earl. I understand from my 91-year-old grandmother that he changed his last name when he came to the United States from Germany after the Second World War from Graf to Earl.

I must admit I had never heard of the Lebensborn Kinder program until yesterday and did not know anything about it. Nor did I know about my grandfather's military service during Nazi Germany, that was something he refused to talk about, at least to me. In the next few days, I will be reading and researching more about the Lebensborn Kinder as well as the role of the SS in occupied Norway. I would like your perspective and any relevant information you have would be greatly appreciated.

I would like to know more about you, Julia, and more about your childhood and your life. Please feel free to write back to me. I have plenty of questions for you and I am sure you have questions for me which I would be happy to answer if I can. Perhaps it would be better for us to correspond directly through email. If you agree, please send me your email address and I will write to you there.

I am curious to know what you have learned about your mother and if you have you reached out to your other half-siblings: Margrit Wolfram and Ruth David?

> Your Niece,
> Emma Earl
> EEElacythings@gmail.com

I hit send and almost immediately regret my decision. I feel so vulnerable. Perhaps, I have said too much. Without waiting for a response, I decide to compose two other letters of introduction to both Margit Wolfram and Ruth David, my grandfather's other daughters. I will use the *23 and Me* messenger service for these letters as well. This time I will exercise more caution. After all, I don't know any of these people. There is way more to this story than I have been told. Family or not, sordid or not, I want some answers. Everyone in my immediate family already sees me as the outlier, the one who doesn't belong. What the hell do I have to lose?

Chapter 12

Sitting there in front of my laptop trying to decide how I should begin, there is a knock on the door. "Hi honey, it's me," Mom calls as she opens the door.

"Oh, I forgot to set out the thermos!" I exclaim as I jump up out of my chair. "I'm sorry. Give me a minute to pour out the old coffee and rinse it out."

Mom steps in through the doorway.

"You're not supposed to be in here," I say.

Mom smiles and takes a step closer to me, "I'm not afraid of you." She smiles, "We just heard from the health department, they left a message on the answering machine."

"So much for HIPAA and the protection of our privacy," I say.

"Anyway, the good news is— we both tested negative for the virus. You are not the carrier and neither am I."

"What about Pop?" I ask.

"Positive for a bad temper, but negative for the virus." She smiles.

I laugh, "Is it curable? His temper tantrums, I mean."

"If you can find a cure for those, be sure and let me know." Mom opens her arms and offers me a long-awaited embrace. "I've brought the coffee and some coffee cake. Let's sit a minute by the fire." Mom pulls another thermos of coffee and two ceramic mugs from her basket and pours us each a cup. I throw another log on the fire as Mom sets the coffee table with a freshly pressed linen towel, the coffee mugs, and two slices of cinnamon-streusel coffee cake.

We sit in the old hickory rockers adjacent to one another and sip our coffee. "Ahh, it's delicious and fixed just the way I like it with both cream and sugar."

"I'm glad you like it," Mom says. "Simple pleasures, that all." She smiles and gazes off into the fire as the skin around her pale blue eyes crinkles. She is still so beautiful but showing her age. Her long white hair cascades down her back and the joints in her fingers are gnarled with age and arthritis. Her life here in the mountains has never been easy, and made all the more difficult now with this craziness and chaos of Pop's very own creation. I want to ask her about so many things, but she keeps her own secrets and her own counsel. It can't be easy for a woman with Mom's gentle disposition. We sit in the quiet for a moment rocking back and forth just sipping our coffee and having a bite of cake.

"It's very curious that both Gram and Lucas are infected but no one else, I wonder who infected them."

"We might never know for certain. Gram hasn't left the property in

122

weeks but Lucas has been out with your father making deliveries almost every day. I suppose he could have been exposed and picked it up almost anywhere and brought it home with him. Gram is the oldest among us, and perhaps just more vulnerable. Maybe the rest of us were able to fight it off better than she was."

"Have you heard anymore from their doctors?"

"Pop called again when he got home. He talked to both of their nurses. Gram was moved to another floor so they could put her on a heart monitor. Gram and Lucas have different nurses taking care of them now. She's still on oxygen and they're giving her some experimental antiviral medication. Pop asked if he could talk with her but the nurse said that wouldn't be possible. She is medicated and sleeping most of the time. He did get to talk with Lucas, but not for long. I guess Lucas started coughing pretty hard and was having trouble catching his breath, but at least his fever is down. All the rooms at St. E's are private now, so patients who are infected with the virus don't give it to any of the other patients. One of the nurses told your father that the hospital is already at full capacity. All ambulances are being diverted to Syracuse, if the patient is stable enough for transport."

"Just because we tested negative a couple of days ago, doesn't mean we might not be infected now. I might not have infected Gram, but I did ride down to the hospital in the ambulance with her. She could have given it to me, for all we know."

"I suppose that's possible."

"This could get really bad. Do you think Pop will stay home now?"

"Good luck getting that man to think about anyone, but himself and his agenda. I can't control him, I never could," she says.

I just nod as I take another sip of my coffee. I can't remember my mother ever being so forthcoming with me. Perhaps that was because I was so much younger the last time I really spent any time here at home with her or perhaps she, too, is at the end of her rope with him and all of his ill-fated and reckless endeavors that put our whole family at risk.

"Well, if it's all the same to you, I think I'll stay over here and out of harm's way if Pop has no intention of abiding by the quarantine."

"Do you really think that's necessary?" Mom asks.

"I do, and I worry about the rest of you too. If Pop and Josiah are coming and going and not sheltering at home, their behavior puts you all in jeopardy. And what about Becca's boyfriend, Rolfe and his little girl? Do you know if they're being careful or if the other people they are coming in contact with have been exposed? We need to rethink this whole thing. People are dying from this virus, more and more every day.

"What are Pop and Josiah doing that is so important? What is so critical that they are making personal deliveries during a global pandemic?" I ask, yet not expecting her to answer.

Mom just looks at me. She holds my gaze and says nothing. No doubt she has been sworn to secrecy and is keeping her promise. This shouldn't surprise me, she is both loyal and trustworthy, even to those who deserve neither. I decide not to push her. I already know what they're up to and don't need her to confirm it.

"Someone has already exposed two members of our immediate

family. Maybe it was that Mitch guy that Pop and Josiah were supposed to meet this morning. Josiah said his doctor thought he might have the virus."

"Hmm," Mom says as she turns her gaze to the fire. "Let me think about this, maybe Pop and Josiah can stay out in the bunker until this dark cloud passes over."

"What bunker?" I ask.

"There's been a few changes takin' place up here since you were here last, quite a few changes." She nods her head but doesn't say anything more.

I want to press her to tell me what is going on, but that has never been a good strategy with Mom. She'll only tell me what she wants to tell me and all in good time. Maybe she is protecting me as much as she is protecting them.

"I should be going, I need to water those seedlings that are sprouting in the greenhouse. It's supposed to be sunny and, in the forties, tomorrow."

"A virtual heat wave," I say.

"It's nice and warm in the greenhouse," Mom smiles then stands and collects the dirty cups and plates. She refolds the linen towel, and returns everything to her picnic basket. I stand up, too.

"Pop's gone out again, but I'll talk with him about the quarantine again when he gets home tonight. He can be a bit of a bully, but he doesn't want to endanger his family. This I know for sure. Have a nice afternoon, honey." She moves towards the door and lets herself out, without giving me a kiss or a hug.

I guess she took to heart what I said about the possibility that we could still be infected. Although we tested negative a few days ago, we could have been infected since then, either at the hospital or by one of Pop's contacts or one of the myriads of people who've been coming and going from the house.

This damn virus, I really could use a hug and I think Mom could use one too.

Chapter 13

I stir the fire as Mom's words linger in my head. She said, *'they could live in the bunker.'*

When I asked her what she was talking about, she was evasive, changed the subject, and now she has gone leaving my questions unanswered. She may know more about what's going on around here than she lets on, way more. For a moment more, I think about her loyalty. Unlike so many people I know, she does not trade in the currency of idle gossip. She never has. She is both loyal and trustworthy.

Or is she?

My mind comes back around to what I've learned about Becca's parentage?

Mom has secrets of her own.

I need more information before this whole thing explodes and people say things they may regret and cannot take back.

I put another log on the fire before I sit back down at the computer. I need to write to my two other long-lost aunts that I've never met and I didn't even know existed before yesterday.

Dear Margit,

I am writing to you as it appears we are related. I believe my paternal grandfather may have been your father. Prior to joining *23 and Me*, I didn't realize I had any close relatives living in Germany. My grandfather, Winfield Earl, formerly Winfield Graf, immigrated to the United States just after WWII. I don't believe anyone in my immediate family had any idea that Winfield had other children prior to coming to the United States.

I have been contacted by one of your half-sisters, Julia Jaeger, who lives in Oslo, Norway and she has had an interesting life. She was adopted at the age of 6 and has no memory of either of her parents.

I hope you will write to me so I can fill in the missing pieces of *our* family story.

> Your Niece,
> Emma Earl

I read it over and over, editing and revising, then editing and revising again. There is so much I want to ask her, but I fear being too intrusive. I don't want to frighten this eighty-five-year-old woman with my unwelcome inquiry. Before hitting the send key, I copy the letter into another document so I can change the name and location from Margrit to Ruth and from Germany to Israel.

Oh, what the hell. Within the next minute, I have flung both letters out into cyberspace. I have no idea if they will even reach their intended recipients and if they do, will I get a response?

I close my computer.

The pants I'd worn earlier this morning are still a little damp but my mittens are dry. I dig through my suitcase for another pair of yoga pants. Mom has washed them and folded them neatly in the bottom of my bag. It looks like I may be here for a while so I decide to unpack, putting my few things away in the old walnut dresser that has been here in the cabin as long as I can remember. The drawers are lined with a pretty floral paper and there is a lavender sachet made from an old hand-embroidered handkerchief in the top drawer. I bring the sachet to my nose. It hasn't been here all that long as it is still fragrant. Mom has always grown lavender in her garden. Maybe she has some growing in the new greenhouse.

I put my lingerie in the top drawer and inhale deeply before tucking the sachet back inside. While attempting to open the bottom drawer of the dresser to put my jeans and sweaters inside, the drawer sticks so I can't open it all the way. Getting down on my knees I reach my hand up inside the partially opened drawer to see if I can figure out what the problem is, when I pull out a fabric pouch about the size of a paperback book that was caught up underneath the drawer above it. The drawstring bag is made of an old blue and white striped remnant, it reminds me of pillow ticking. What the heck? I untie the old shoelace that has been pulled tight and knotted to hold the bag closed. The bag is filled with hundred-dollar bills.

Good Lord—who does this belong to?

I take a quick look out the window to be certain no one is coming my way. Sitting on the edge of the bed, I pull out the wad of bills. There are bills that are old and wrinkled, as well as crisp new ones with the color changing holograms. They all bear the face of Benjamin Franklin and are one hundred-dollar bills.

I count quickly. I am nervous I might get caught holding this money. I lose count and need to start over. My palms are sweating and my heart races. There are over ninety hundred dollar bills here, over nine thousand dollars, give or take. Someone has been saving these for a while, but why? And why have they hidden them over here? I'm sure whoever this bag belongs to is feeling very uncomfortable with the fact that I've taken up residence here.

And I'm very uncomfortable with all the freaking guns.

I close up the bag and quickly put everything back just where I found it. I close the bottom drawer and decide to put my clothes in a different drawer.

I pull on my boots. Ugh—they're still wet from my morning walk. I don't care, I'm going out anyway. It's hard to imagine being any more uncomfortable than I feel right now. I have a pervasive sense of danger and mounting anxiety which is combined with cabin fever and isolation. I'm about ready to jump out of my own skin.

I have to get out of here.

So out I go, wet socks and all.

~ ~ ~

Someone has taken the snowmobile and they've cut a path out through the woods heading up towards Stillwater. My feet are already freezing so I decide to follow the snowmobile tracks rather than forge my own trail.

It isn't long before the snowmobile path I've been following connects with another road at the north end of our property. I'm surprised that someone has been out plowing this far away from the house and all the out buildings. I go around a bend in the road and see the same snowmobile parked at the base of a hill, beneath a grove of old growth hardwoods. There are two other snowmobiles parked there, too.

What's going on?

It is then that a ray of golden sunlight streams through the trees and catches on something. A flash of light draws my attention towards something shiny in the hill. What is it? I walk a little closer trying to stay hidden beneath the dark shadows of the trees.

There is a dark wooden door with a metal handle embedded in the side of the hill. The clouds part and again the sunlight hits the door handle.

I'd explored every inch of this property as a child, given that was well over a decade ago, still I think I would have known if something had been built in these woods. Good Lord, could this be the entrance to an underground bunker that Mom was talking about?

Although my feet are freezing I walk several hundred feet around the base of the hill, staying beneath the cover of the trees towards the north side of this elevation. I need to get a better look. I wonder how big it is and how they heat it. It can't be very comfortable in there on a day like today. The view opens up and I stand there surveilling the landscape. This side appears a bit deforested. Did they bring construction equipment in over here to hollow out the earth? If they did, they've been building this thing for quite some time. The old growth trees are gone, but the low-lying scrub pines and undergrowth are thick and obscure any entrance, if there is one, on this side. But there is a six-foot metal exhaust pipe protruding skyward from the side of the mountain. It looks to be emitting something, probably either steam or smoke.

Lost in my own thoughts, I start back towards my cabin under the cover of the heavily snow-laden branches of the evergreens when I hear the door open. Rolfe and Becca emerge from somewhere deep within this earthen dwelling. The door closes behind them and Rolfe grabs my youngest sister's long blonde ponytail and pulls her towards him. I watch as he grabs her ass with both hands and rubs his crotch up against her body. I fear he may defile her right here and now. I feel like a voyeur as I watch him push her up against a tree while he kisses her aggressively and paws at her. I may be disgusted, but it looks like she's into him.

Once I'm fairly certain she's a willing participant, I turn further into the shadows and head back towards the cabin as silently as I can.

There is no accounting for taste. Willa was right, that guy's a creep. I wouldn't let him get within ten feet of me. I shudder with a sense of revulsion. There is something off about him. I don't know what it is, but my gut tells me he's not a good person. And I've learned long ago, not to disregard my intuition. Come on Becca, you can do better than *him*.

Chapter 14

By the time I get back to the cabin my feet are absolutely freezing, I'd like nothing better than to have a hot bath. But that option is off the table as there is no running water here and won't be until the winter is over and the ongoing threat of frozen pipes is behind us. I pull off my wet socks and go to the dresser to see if I can find a dry pair. Alas, there is a pair of carefully mended woolen ski socks tucked into the back of the top drawer. It looks like Mom has been here. My laundry has been returned, all washed and folded. When did she have time to do all this? Or maybe Willa brought my laundry over, I did see her car in the driveway.

I look around the room, the whole place has been tidied up, dry wood has been carried in and stacked beside the fireplace, and the refrigerator has been stocked with some fruit and cheese, and cream for my coffee. This kindness and consideration have Mom's name all over it.

My curiosity gets the best of me and I just have to know. I get down on my hands and knees to look underneath the third drawer in the old walnut dresser. The drawstring bag of hundreds is no longer there. Only an hour ago, I had replaced it—just where I'd found it. Now someone has come and retrieved it. I suppose it could have been Willa, but I don't think so. Elias makes pretty good money as a finish carpenter, and he seems generous with Willa and the girls. I think that money has been saved by Mom. Pop is as tight as they come and the only nice things Mom has ever had are those she has made for herself. It's long been said that Mom can make a silk purse from a sow's ear.

But what is she planning to do with the money? And why hide it? I don't know the answers to the questions, but I do know that she must have her reasons and no doubt they are good ones.

I add another log to the fire before sitting down to my laptop. Where should I begin? I Google *National Resistance Revival*, the name on the flag hanging in the man cave. Nothing comes up. Nothing at all. This seems so unlikely, how else would they be taking orders and selling all those weapons if not by using the internet?

I try another tact and attempt to Google my sister's boyfriend, except I'm not certain how to spell his name. Using the keyboard, I try to spell it phonetically—R-A-L-P-H space T-O-O-F-E-L-L. Again, nothing comes up. Not ready to give this up, I go to Becca's Facebook page and begin scrolling through her friends. She has over a thousand friends. I click on her posts and then start to look at her Facebook friends. Some of these profile pictures show men carrying Confederate flags, others are tattooed with swastikas, and still others have been photographed carrying automatic weapons. Or at least that's what I think they are.

I click onto some of their pages to look at their posts. Some of their pages are private and I can't get very far, but not all of them. There are skinheads screaming, guys in all-leather looking like bikers, others dressed like they're in some kind of militia, and those who look like they could be cast as pirates—dirty, unshaven, with bad teeth, and visibly angry. Some look really rough and scary. But then there are others who like any other *ordinary Joe* who might be stocking shelves at Home Depot or working as a cashier at the grocery store. There is something overwhelmingly disconcerting and frightening when I think about regular guys buying into this and embracing this hate-filled rhetoric. And then there he is—Rolfe Teufel.

I cringe as I click on his page. I try to rationalize that I'm not passing judgement on someone I've never met. I'm not being prejudiced or biased against a stranger. I've met this guy and I just saw him getting handsy with my sister. He's a nasty piece of work who gives me the creeps.

I scroll through his friends. He's Facebook friends with Donald J. Trump and Marine Le Pen, the right-wing French politician. I don't know why this should surprise me, still it does. Next, I click around on his profile to see who and what he likes and who he is following. This is very revealing, what pops up in his feed is vile and disgusting. One link leads me to another and then another and before long I am deeply entrenched in the world of white supremacy and the alt-right, and I'm filling my head with so much bullshit I can almost smell the stink.

I grab a pen and pad of paper from my computer bag and begin to take some notes. Looking over the photographs, some of these guys can be seen raising their straightened right arms with an extended hand as if they are giving a Nazi salute. Others are heavily tattooed and some carry signs. Some of their tattoos and signs bear the numbers 14, 18 and 88. I take a moment to look up what these numbers might mean.

Apparently, the number 14 stands for the number of words in one of their mottos. *We must secure the existence of our race and the future of white children.* I shudder to think where this kind of fear and animosity comes from. Is this something that has been taught in their homes?

Something just below my consciousness is nudging me to explore this idea further, but I can't quite grasp what it is, so I ignore it and return to my research.

I read a little further, 18 stands for Adolf Hitler. The number 1 is for A the first letter of the alphabet and the number 8 is the eighth letter of the alphabet, H. I would scoff at this as childish nonsense if it wasn't so scary. And then there is the number 88 that is emblazoned on some of these guys' bodies, again the eighth letter of the alphabet is H and 88 is code for Heil Hitler.

My mind spins in horror as the implications of living in a world where this mindset has again taken root and is proliferating like some uncontrolled cancer.

Who are all these disaffected white males who are rebranding all their old hatreds and blaming anyone and everyone who they feel is ascending to a place they thought they were entitled to. From one Facebook page to the next the posts are filled with extremism of the vilest varieties, some clearly objectifying women to others that advocate for violence against women, others who refers to themselves as *Incels*.

I've heard of this before, still I switch screens to look it up, just to be sure. *Incel*—it's an acronym for those who are involuntarily celibate. It started as an inclusive community of both men and women who were socially shy and hadn't had much success in relationships as a forum to discuss their loneliness but it has since been co-opted by a growing group of misogynistic white males.

Okay, I understand that frustration, I don't have a boyfriend or a partner right now. But I can't imagine blaming this on someone who is not interested in dating me, let alone advocating violence against people who choose to be with someone else. But these yahoos are advocating brutality against lesbians, feminists who are not interested in a traditional relationship, women who are career oriented, and women who are not interested in having children and staying home.

Good God, these assholes need to get a life, preferably a life where they are not intent on dismantling the lives and rights of others! How is it that they've come to believe they can dictate what someone else does with their own God-given life? These men are part of this online subculture that believe they are entitled to sex, and they resent other men and women who do have a partner, particularly non-white men who are in relationships with white women.

I've lived in New York for the past decade, so I haven't been living under a rock. I know this mindset exists, I just didn't realize it was so prevalent. This one Facebook page has thousands of followers and the posts are darn right scary. One guy posts that "Rape is a property crime and nothing more. The slapping and beating of women are a necessity in every household."

Maybe his inability to be in a loving relationship has everything to do with the way he views women and isn't anyone's fault but his own.

Incel communities have become increasingly extremist and more violent over the years and their numbers are growing as this kind of talk finds a wider and wider audience in anonymous online communities.

Hmm—anonymous. I guess anyone can be anonymous.

Another guy is advocating *white sharia*. I have no idea what that even is. I open a new tab so I can look it up.

One of the key philosophical components is their fear that Western civilization and the white race is dying out because of increased immigration and falling birth rates among white families. One of their members is quoted as saying, "Our men need harems and the members of our harems must be baby factories."

Good God, these white supremacists are advocating eugenics to build up a white race. This man who is hanging out around our house is an active member of more than one of these groups, they are involved in building and distributing untraceable guns out of our garage, and my youngest sister Becca has described him as her boyfriend.

What am I supposed to do with this information? Does she have any idea what this guy is into? Does anyone in my family realize who this guy is and what he believes?

My conversation with Willa replays in my head. 'He's like Steve Bannon. Although Bannon is no prize in any estimation, at least he is smart— devious, underhanded, evil, and smart. Rolfe is just devious, underhanded, and evil.'

My heart is racing as I go to the bed and lie down and try to quell the rising panic that threatens to overwhelm me. I take a long slow deep breath. There are so many moving parts and things are getting more and more complicated with every twist and turn.

I need to clear my head so I can think this through.

I need to come up with a plan. I grab my laptop and begin to list my concerns. I look at the date and time that flashes across the screen, it's already well past midnight and I've only been here less than a week, five days actually. Although I'm exhausted, there is no way I can sleep. I open up my electronic journal and begin to write. I write and write, page after page until it all spills out, including every excruciating little detail I can remember. I may not know what to do with all of this. I don't have anything that even resembles a plan, but I feel, at least, I have begun to identify the issues, and that's *not fer nothin'* as we say up here in the north woods.

The words in one of their mottos spills out on the page. *We must secure the existence of our race and the future of white children.* Where does this kind of fear and animosity come from? Is this something that has been taught in *their* homes? No sooner do the words form in my head, then I think about all the subtle bits of racism and sexism that have been tossed out as truths in my own home for as long as I can remember. Throughout my childhood, Pop was always talking about the immigrants that were stealing American jobs, and the not so occasional racial or ethnic slur, to say nothing of how he treated my mother, my sisters and me as if our only purpose was to make life easier for the men in our family. I'm damn lucky I got out of here before more damage was done.

But how did I escape it when my brothers and sisters clearly did not? I think about conversations with my mother, and all the times Pop excluded me in favor of my brothers and made derogatory comments about women. I remember feeling so hurt. Mom would try to comfort me as she asked me to excuse my father, 'He doesn't really mean it. He's just repeating the things he heard his father say.'

Even as a young girl I was often sent to my room for being sassy and giving him some lip, in the hours of isolation that followed I remember questioning if what he said about me wasn't true, then maybe what he says about others isn't true either.

I have long seen him for who he is, an insecure man who tries to make himself feel better by putting others down. I had so much animosity for him growing up that I have never wanted to be anything like him. I've never wanted to hurt anyone like he hurt me. Even as an adult, the pain endured in my childhood remains. I wipe away a tear with the sleeve of my nightgown.

Maybe my sibs embraced Pop and have emulated his egotistical world view, that they are better than everyone else, out of fear that they might become Pop's next target. Maybe they went to school on the way he treated me, and still treats me. Bullies do that, they strike fear in the hearts of others.

And so, just like Pop was indoctrinated by Grand Pappa with hatred towards his fellow man, the seeds of white supremacy are sown again from one generation to the next.

God help them.

God help us all.

I take a deep breath and exhale slowly. There is something about the simple act of writing, that seems to release some of my anxiety. With each breath, my mind begins to let go of the fear. Just before dawn my vision begins to blur, at last, I am drifting off towards sleep

Chapter 15

I wake to the sound of the dogs barking and snarling as if we are under siege. I look out the window while still in bed to see that two unfamiliar pickup trucks have pulled into the driveway. The men in the trucks do not get out of the cabs and I can hardly blame them, those dogs act like they could tear your leg off. I do know this, those men are not here to see me and I have no intention of going out there to see what they want, not with Bullet and Trigger on full-alert and in guard dog mode.

It isn't long before I hear the roar of the snowmobiles coming through the woods. One of these men must have called them or maybe they heard the dogs or perhaps the whole place is under some electronic surveillance system. I don't know if my imagination is running away with me or if any or all of this might be true. I pull the blanket up around me as the fire has nearly burnt out. I want to keep watch to see who is out there. It's nearly dawn and it will be getting light very soon but I need to rekindle the fire or I'll have to start a new one. I slip away from the window and stir the still glowing embers and put another log on the fire.

The snowmobiles are quiet now and someone has called the dogs off as the barking has stopped. Josiah must be there as he is the one who has trained the shepherds. I can hear men's voices, but I cannot make out what they are saying. By the time I get back to the window I can see that the men have left their trucks. But where have they gone and with whom?

I get up and straighten up the bed and fluff the pillows. Just another nervous habit, the whole world could be falling apart and I decide it would be a good time to sweep the floors or alphabetize the soup cans in my pantry.

Okay, now what? I decide to check my email, as if there might be anything there that might lessen my burgeoning anxiety. There's a note from my roommate, Cassie. It simply says, *Call Me.* It was sent about an hour ago. I guess I'm not the only one who can't sleep.

I pick up my cell phone and send her a text in case she has fallen asleep in the last hour. It doesn't go through. I have no signal out here. So instead, I decide to send her an email.

Hey Cassie,

Sorry I can't call, we have terrible cell service out here. What's up? —E

Almost immediately I get a response.

I thought you were going to download Signal on your phone. The encrypted service that uses WI-F that I told you about. If you haven't got it, get it at the App Store and call me back. I'll be waiting. —C

Oh yeah. I remember her going on and on about the dangers of everyone spying on everyone else, and the misuse of our personal data for nefarious purposes. Cassie's in tech, so I thought she was making a big deal about nothing. I didn't take her concerns seriously. These last few days have allowed me to see the dark underbelly of things I know nothing about. My naiveté clearly does not serve me.

I find the app and download it. Cassie's name shows up as one of my contacts who is also using *Signal.* I place the call and click on the video camera icon. In no time at all, there she is on the screen of my laptop.

She throws me a kiss. "Good God girl, you look like shit," she says with a laugh.

"Well you are nothing short of a vision from heaven," I say as I break down and begin to cry. I hadn't realized just how much I was holding onto until I begin to tell my dear friend the stories that have unfolded over the last few days.

I'm afraid she's going to lose it when I tell her about being exiled to the cabin and the lack of running water and having to use the outhouse in the midst of a snowstorm, but she becomes silent as I lay before her the real horrors of this last week.

It's such a relief to be able to tell someone and to process some of this nightmare aloud. "Get a piece of paper, we need to come up with a plan." Cassie, the systems engineer, is doing what she does best, cutting through the crap and seeing the big picture.

I reach into my computer bag and pull out my notepad, the same one I'd been using when researching what Rolfe Teufel might be up to. "Got it," I say.

"Number one. Take a shower and wash your goddamn hair. You look a fright."

I laugh. "Glad to see there will be something on my list that I'll be capable of accomplishing. What is number two?"

"Can you get yourself out of there? You're not safe Em."

"I don't think I can. I don't have a car, there isn't any public transportation anywhere even close, and all the roads are iced over. It's a good fifteen-mile walk into the closest town."

"That's what I figured. Okay, let me think. Do you trust the police?"

Again, I laugh. "Let's just say that around here the officers in our illustrious police department are referred to as Barney Fife, Robo-Cop, and Tom Terrific."

"Incompetent or corrupt?"

"I don't know. I went to high school with two of the three. They weren't exactly the sharpest tools in the shed, but they weren't bad guys. But that was a decade ago, sometimes life has a way of changing people. I wouldn't feel comfortable relying on either Barney or Tom to act with discretion, read the nuance of this scenario, or have the ability to assure my personal safety. Call it my intuition."

"I see. Let's trust your intuition. What about the other cop?"

"The other guy, the one they call Robo-Cop is highly officious. Rumor has it that he's on a power trip and is known to be just plain mean."

"Okay, let me think on this a little bit more. Just one more question."

"What?" I ask.

"His real name isn't Barney Fife, is it?"

I laugh, "No, it's Bernie Finn, but close enough. Everyone just calls him Barney Fife, not to his face, of course. But Old Forge is similar enough to Mayberry, at least in the off season, except our little burg has a northern twist. So then, what's number two?"

"You said, you were unable to find anything on the internet for the National Resistance Revival. That's the name on the flag in the garage and on the business letterhead for their gun manufacturing business, do I have that right?"

"That's right, they're calling themselves the National Resistance Revival. Still, I know they are on the internet, I was in the office when an order flashed on Pop's laptop and it was sent directly to the printer."

"They are probably communicating via an encrypted server, like TOR."

"What's Tor? I feel like you're speaking another language that I don't understand."

"It allows you to freely explore the internet and defend yourself against tracking and surveillance. It's a multilayered encryption program. You'll need to download it so you can gather information safely."

"How do I go about finding this Tor?"

"Just Google it. It will show up. Just be aware that you're going to come across some pretty dark and scary things. Prepare to have your innocence shattered."

"I think I'd rather go back to sewing my pretty lacy lingerie."

"I don't blame you. But like it or not, you're already in way too deep to just walk away. Better to know what and who you're dealing with then to stumble about in ignorance. Ignorance is dangerous and the people involved in this stuff are anything but ignorant."

"Okay, get a Tor account. What's number three?"

"Number three— you need to set up a false electronic identity before you do any more snooping around. You're not exactly tech savvy. Did I mention that these people are dangerous?"

"By these people, you mean my family?" I ask the question, but I already know the answer.

"Come on Emma, it's time for the red pill."

"The red pill?"

"You know, from *The Matrix*?"

"I think I fell asleep halfway through."

"That's funny, only you could sleep through *that* movie. In the movie, the red pill reveals the unpleasant truth about a situation."

"Okay, I get it. No more delusions about my family. I need to come to terms with the grim reality I find myself in."

"I think it's time, sweetheart."

"Okay, what's number four?"

"I think three is enough for now, don't you?"

"More than enough."

"Okay, go take a shower and for pity's sake wash your freakin' hair."

I catch my reflection in the window, my hair is sticking up all over. I try to smooth it down with the palm of my hand. "Okay, I guess you're right. I do have a pretty bad case of hat hair."

"Call me anytime but use *Signal*. God only knows who is monitoring your calls or watching your house."

"I'm sorry, this whole conversation has been all about me. I didn't even ask how you're holding up during the quarantine. Things look really bad in New York, at least according to Governor Cuomo."

"I've been watching the daily death count but I'm staying home and hopefully out of harm's way. I've been getting my groceries delivered, working from home, and binge-watching Netflix."

"What about Gabrielle?"

"Well, there is a silver lining to this dark cloud, Gabrielle has found herself a rich boyfriend and has moved into his posh apartment on the upper east side. So now I have this palatial estate all to myself." Cassie turns her laptop around so I can get a panoramic view of the inside of our tiny apartment.

"Lucky you, all that *and* running water."

"Go get yourself a shower and call me later."

"Thanks Cassie. Love you."

"Love you, too. And Em ..."

"Yeah?"

"Please be careful, Em."

And with that the screen goes dark.

Chapter 16

My initial inclination is to download *Tor* and get started on this research. I need to know what my father and his despicable companions are up to, but I look at my carefully constructed *to do* list.

Number 1—Take a shower.

I laugh, I'm not exactly dirty as I have been washing up in a basin of water but the hat hair would lead most anyone who saw me to believe that I have been living on the streets for days if not weeks. I close my laptop and pull on my boots.

I guess I can just go over and use the bathroom. I have been cleared as the carrier of the Coronavirus that infected my brother and my grandmother. However, after the altercation in the front yard with Pop yesterday afternoon where he physically threw me down on the ground, I'd like to avoid him if I can. My right wrist still hurts.

I pull on my hat and coat and head over to the main house. The pickup trucks are still in the driveway and half a dozen snowmobiles are parked out front. I go to the front door and knock and before I know it the dogs have charged the door and are barking ferociously. Thank God, I didn't just walk right in as had been my initial inclination.

Josiah turns on the porch light and gives two short whistles. The dogs sit quietly on either side of his feet. They are at full alert just in case my brother decides I'm some kind of a threat. "Emma, what are you doing here?"

"I thought I'd take a shower. My Covid test was negative, so I'm not a danger to you or anyone else." I look down at the larger of the two dogs and in response he bares his teeth and snarls at me. "Unlike my old pal, Bullet."

"I'll need to check with Pop," he says as he closes the door in my face. I hear the dead bolt engage as my brother walks away. However, the dogs remain at attention just in case I try to break in.

How in God's name is this my life?

I hear raised voices and then my mother comes to the door. Before opening it, I hear her call to my brother, "Josiah, for heaven's sake, please call off your dogs. They scare me."

Almost immediately the dogs scamper back towards the kitchen.

"I just thought I'd take a shower, Mom." I can't believe I have to beg for this simple human kindness.

"Of course, darling. It's just that your father has some company here this morning. They are business associates, really."

I wait there in the dark and hold my mother's gaze. Unlike the rest of us, she is a terrible liar. My father has been retired for almost a decade and before that he drove a truck and delivered propane and heating oil. Now he manages the land and financial assets that have been in my grandmother's family for well over a hundred years. What kind of legitimate business associates could my father possibly have? And who has a business meeting before the crack of dawn? I look at my wrist watch. It's just after seven.

"May I come in?" I ask. The pause between us grows as my mother attempts to find some kind of legitimate reason to refuse my request.

"Oh, my dearest Emma ... why don't you go around back to the walk out and I'll meet you downstairs. You can shower in the downstairs bathroom." She holds my gaze a moment longer and all I can read in her face is fear.

I tromp through the snow that is well over the tops of my boots. I make my way through the wet snow and around to the back of the house and under the deck to the French doors that open onto a snow-covered patio. This part of the house was excavated, renovated, and opened up a couple years ago. It is only now that I wonder where the money for such an extravagant project came from. Maybe my dad and brothers have been running guns a lot longer than I thought.

Mom stands in the doorway. She has a couple of freshly laundered towels and a small stack of my clean clothes that she took from the cabin and washed while I was out yesterday. She opens the door and lets me in. "What in the world is going on?" I ask in a low whisper.

She shakes her head, but gives no response.

I feel a sense of rage begin to bubble up from within. I struggle to keep quiet as she puts one finger to her lips. Why won't she tell me what is going on?

I take the towels from her hands and notice she is trembling. I won't push this now. I try to reassure myself that she would tell me if she could.

I walk down the hall to the newly renovated bathroom and close the door behind me.

I let the hot water from the shower wash over me. Mom has made her own lavender soap and the same hair tonic that I used as a girl. I lather up and breathe deeply of the fragrance from her garden. This whole thing feels like I've walked into a chapter from someone else's life. I hate to see my dear sweet mother so trapped by all of this that is so far beyond her control.

Once I've rinsed off, dried off, and towel dried my hair I exit the bathroom, where I find my mother has set up a card table for me with a hot breakfast of oatmeal with brown sugar and raisins and a hot blueberry muffin and butter. I sit and eat alone. Clearly, I am not welcome upstairs with the other members of my family or my father's *business associates*.

Before I've finished Mom comes back down carrying a teapot and a cup, "Can I bring you anything else?" she asks.

I shake my head no, not trusting myself to speak. I swallow hard and try to force the words out. In a low whisper I say, "I don't know what is going on, and I know that you would tell me if you could, so I'm not going to ask."

She nods and tears fill her eyes as she reaches over and takes my hand.

"What have you heard about Gram and Lucas?" I ask trying to stick to safer topics, if not any less emotional.

"Gram is struggling and they are talking about putting her on a ventilator. The nurse said, if she is intubated and goes on the vent there is very little chance she will ever breathe on her own again. So, your father has decided it is best to wait. I have to agree with him, I don't think Gram would want to live her life like that."

My eyes fill with tears and I wipe them away with my napkin.

"And Lucas?" I ask.

"Lucas is improving and he may be released early next week if he continues to do well."

"That is good news," I say, but I feel no joy. I'm just too overwhelmed with the chaos and the fear of losing Gram. "Gram's had a good life. I just thought we'd have more time."

"She has indeed," my mother says as she reaches out to hold me.

"Does everyone else know what's going on?" I ask.

"Everyone but the little girls," Mom says.

"How's Pop?" I ask.

"Stoic, as you would expect. He never shows much emotion."

"Except anger," I murmur and Mom nods in agreement.

And then almost on cue, "Magda! Get up here!" Pop bellows down the staircase.

"I should get back upstairs. The men may need something more or perhaps another pot of coffee." She reaches for my hand and gives it a squeeze before she stands to go.

I cringe at the thought that my mother is the handmaiden to this group of ungrateful men who are so unworthy of her generosity and the gifts she lovingly bestows upon them. But I decide to let it go. There are just too many other important things that need to be addressed right now.

Chapter 17

I leave the way I came, through the back door. I head back toward the cabin, stopping momentarily to glance into the kitchen window. From this distance, I can see Pop's *pals* are still here. I'd like to sneak over and peek in but I don't want to alert the dogs. I've already seen them in action this morning. They looked like they like nothing better than to tear into me.

Instead, I pull out my cell phone and take a couple of pictures of the trucks and license plates belonging to Pop's *business associates*. All three of the vehicles have bright gold New York plates. I don't know what I'll do with these photos, it's not like I have access to the DMV records and can track them down by their plate numbers. Maybe I watched a few too many cop shows as a kid. Still, the photos might come in handy.

The snowmobilers must be locals.

By the time I get back to the cabin it is almost eight o'clock. It's eerily quiet and another unstructured day all by myself looms before me.

I pull open my laptop and open my *23 and Me* app, just to see if I have any messages. Nothing yet. I click over and check my email. Nothing very interesting here either. Just a note from my boss checking in and asking me to send her the prototype of the negligée and robe I've been working on and then there are a few emails from my good friends at

Anthropologie and Zara letting me know about their chance of a lifetime sales events.

I still have things to do. My conversation with Cassie replays in my head as I remember what I have agreed to do. Number two—download Tor, and number three—create a false online identity. There is something about using Tor and searching the dark web that frightens me. I can be plenty bold and brave when discussing my political views and my disgust for the man in the White House among those who think like me. But I'm afraid of whom I might encounter on the dark web. I can only imagine that some of these people are into some pretty frightening and dangerous stuff and that includes the white supremacist who raised me.

My mind wanders and before long I am trying to imagine the lives and the hardships of my unknown and now elderly aunts. Do I really want to know what my grandfather did during World War II? I have read some awful, gut wrenching stories about the crimes committed by the SS. It disgusts me and still I can't help but wonder how much of who we are is inscribed in our genetic code and beyond our control? Do I also carry the same propensity for self-aggrandizement or hatred and violence towards others that must have been in my grandfather and that I have seen played out by my own father? Or is who we are ultimately influenced to become a product of our environment, our family life, and the way we've been raised? It's the old nature vs nurture argument.

Either way I'm screwed.

Refocusing on the tasks at hand, I decide to start with the easy stuff first. I'll make myself a new Facebook page under a different name and see if I can get Rolfe and his despicable pals to accept my friend requests. I have read enough to know that these yahoos are targeting white teenage boys to join their ranks. I grew up with guys like this. I know all too well how they think and how they talk. Maybe I can be their *bro*. No problem. Pulling off this masquerade should be a piece of cake.

I go to Facebook.com and click on the button marked *create new account*. Oh, they want to link my new account to my phone number or an email address. I guess I'd forgotten that. I've already linked my real account to my phone number, so that will never do. I'll just open a new email, but not with Gmail, as I use that for my real legitimate life. This one must be different. I Google *secure email* and find something called *Hushmail*. It even sounds sinister. These goons might think this makes me sound cool, like I'm one of them already. If Saint Joan of Arc could pretend to be a man in real life, then I should be able to pull off the deception in the online world of social media.

At first, I decide to call myself *Blade* because it sounds kind of macho and tough, but after a little more research I decide against it. Apparently, there is an African-American superhero who uses that name. No doubt these white boys would already know that. Hmm, this may be more difficult than I initially thought.

Eventually, I decide to call myself Quest, simply Quest18. Using the numbers associated with Adolf Hitler. God help me. I work up my new Facebook profile making myself an eighteen-year-old boy from Poughkeepsie, New York. I've never been to Poughkeepsie but I think it's a big enough city. I'm pretty sure it's not one of those towns where everybody knows everybody else. I decide to keep the rest of the profile blank for now. I'll add more details later. But what will I do about a profile picture? I find a picture of some white kid in a red MAGA hat holding a gun, then copy and paste it and voila—I have a new Facebook identity.

Now who should I send a friend request to? I never accept friend requests from people I don't know. I'm always afraid they might be someone trying to scam me, just like I'm doing right now. So instead of sending friend requests I decide to follow some of the same people and groups that my old pal Rolfe is following like: Donald J. Trump, Breitbart News, Proud Boys and a dozen more Alt-Right pages. It isn't long before the Facebook algorithm is suggesting all kinds of people and organizations that might be interested in the same things that I appear to be, right wing propaganda, the white supremacy movement, and other forums promoting misogynistic, nationalistic elitism.

Once all of this is in place, I send friend requests to all the good old boys on Rolfe's friend list. Then I begin perusing both Josiah and Lucas' friend lists and sending friend requests to only those who appear to be of the same ilk.

Just before I get ready to hit send, I pause. My hands are trembling and sweating. What does my body know that I feel compelled to disregard? A nebulous fear runs through me, that I can't seem to ignore. If I do this I will be stepping into a world I know nothing about. My anxiety is mounting. Something tells me this could go badly for me, and then, against my better judgement—I hit send.

And at that very moment there is a knock on the cabin door.

Chapter 18

The door opens before I can answer it, and there is Willa.

"Willa, my God you scared me."

She laughs. "You look like you've seen a ghost." She holds up a wine bottle in one hand and two wine glasses in the other. "Want to get drunk?"

Now I laugh, too. "What time is it?"

"It's five o'clock somewhere," Willa offers a snappy retort from an old Jimmy Buffet song. It's only then that I realize I've been sitting at my computer all-day long.

"I think after the last few days you've had a glass or two might be in order," she steps inside not waiting for an invitation.

"Oh, I guess you heard about my little altercation with Pop."

"Tilly told me all about it, and Heidi, my darling perfectionist, corrected her sister on every detail, so between the two of them I have a pretty good idea what went down. Pop can be such an asshole, but this is nothing new. Now that I know you're not going to infect me with a deadly virus, it is time for you and I to have a talk. But first we need to have a drink or we'll never get through the chaos and mayhem that threatens us all."

Before I can even answer she is in the cabin, taking off her coat and boots and opening the wine with a corkscrew she had tucked in her coat pocket.

"Do you always carry one of those?" I laugh.

"Absolutely, it's an essential tool for every north country woman. Do you have any food over here?"

"I think I can put together some crackers and cheese, will that do?"

Willa nods as I start to rummage through the fridge for some of the snacks Mom has brought over. It only takes a minute before I put together a tray of red grapes, cheese and crackers, and some sausage and hot mustard.

"Where are the girls?" I ask.

"Home with Elias, he volunteered to feed them, do the dishes, and get them off to bed tonight."

"How positively progressive of him," I laugh as my older sister hands me a glass with a hefty pour.

"Yep, he's all that. You'd never know it because the man is a lot smarter than either of us, he knows when to keep his opinions to himself." We clink glasses.

"I don't see you jumping into the fray," I say and we both take a drink of our wine.

"Okay, I said either of us, but I really meant you."

I snort with laughter and just barely keep my last swallow of sauvignon blanc from coming up and out of my nose like a leaky faucet.

Willa and I take our wine and go to sit in the old hickory rockers in front of the fireplace. "So, how much do you know?" Willa asks.

"About what?" I answer her question with a question as I'm not sure what she is talking about. A notion crosses my mind, that in spite of her obvious kindness accompanied by this moment of transparency and recent criticism of our father, perhaps *he* is the one who has sent her over here on some kind of reconnaissance mission.

"Well let's see, from the myriad of topics, which one should we begin with?"

I take another sip of my wine and wait, not trusting myself to speak.

"Perhaps you'd like to discuss that fact that our brother and grandmother are infected with a deadly virus, and it is unlikely that Gram will survive. Or maybe it's better to start with the real elephant in the room— that our father has turned our family home into a node in a network of gun running white supremacists. Your choice."

"I thought maybe we'd just get drunk and talk about the latest fashion trends in Manhattan?" Now it's Willa's turn to snort and choke on her drink.

Once she's recovered, I ask, "Is Pop holding up okay considering the possibility his mother may not survive?" Of the issues now on the table, this seems to be the least controversial. Maybe it will be a good place to start.

Willa shakes her head in a way I have difficulty interpreting. "He is being stoic as usual and has been giving lip service to the fact that she has lived a good long life. In truth, I think he is already counting the money that he expects to inherit when she passes."

"He is her only surviving child." This does not surprise me.

"He's been riding roughshod over her for quite some time and making changes around here that she would never consent to had she known about them or if he'd sought her permission."

"Such as?" I ask.

Now Willa takes a long pull from her glass as the question sits between us. I get up and put another log on the fire and stir the fire making certain it catches and begins to burn. While my back is turned to her Willa says, "There are so many secrets in this family and I don't know who knows what. But given your contentious relationship with Pop I'm going to assume that whatever you already know or don't know matters less than how you will feel about what I have to say."

I continue to adjust the log with the old iron poker.

Willa continues, "Pop has been making unlicensed guns in the garage and selling them to preppers and this white militia he belongs to throughout the Adirondacks."

"Why would anyone up here need to buy an unlicensed gun? Every kid in the Town of Webb Union Free School is given a gun for his or her twelfth birthday."

"Everyone except you," my sister laughs.

"I didn't want one. I hate guns, ever since that kid in my class shot and killed his twin sister. Good God, we were only eleven years old. Sara was my friend and Sam was taken to juvie. They should have taken their parents to jail, too."

"So, you're not out supporting the NRA and revision of the open carry laws."

"No. Just no."

Again, the silence grows between us until a smile creeps across my sister's face. "You already knew, didn't you?"

I feel like that poor deer caught in the headlights. I think about denying it, but I know I'm already caught.

"You didn't seem surprised or ask any questions, when I told you about the unlicensed guns."

"Shit," I mutter under my breath.

"Pop has been going on and on about seeing your footprints in snow behind the garage, but in the end, I think you convinced him you were only looking for some snowshoes."

"Okay, well since I've been found out, I have a few questions of my own. How long has this been going on? Does Gram or Mom know what's happening? And how involved are Josiah and Lucas?"

"Pop's been involved with these *low lifes* off and on for at least the last decade, maybe even longer. Ever since the financial crash of 2008 and the election of Obama, he and his cronies have been looking for someone to blame their troubles on. He was just more secretive about it in the beginning. He just became more vocal when Trump was elected. Initially, Gram tried to be tolerant of his ranting, for he had been laid off and lost part of his retirement savings when the market went south. But as time went on, even she grew tired of the relentless diatribe. I don't know for certain, but she must have spoken to him as he's toned down the rhetoric, at least at home, and he started spending more and more time away from home. You remember those days, don't you?"

"Obama was elected when I was in high school. That's over ten years ago. I wasn't spending much time around here back then, either. All I wanted to do was get the heck out of here. So, I guess to answer your question, I don't remember much, except that I thought Pop was an asshole. But most of my friends felt that way about their parents back then. We were teenagers and they were forever getting in our way and trying to rein us in. I was all consumed with anything and everything that had to do with me, and paid very little attention to the whereabouts or opinions of my parents or grandparents."

"I guess all teenagers are self-absorbed. I know I was. Still that was when Pop got involved with the *brotherhood*. It was a time of the great gender divide. He has been keeping secrets from Gram and Mom, and me, too. It's only recently that he has had any use for Becca. It's as if the white bros have finally acknowledged that women might be of use to them in their white supremacy movement. The women involved seem to give them an air of legitimacy."

"As long as the women know their place," I grumble.

"You never did, and I don't either," Willa says as she refills both of our glasses.

"How has he been able to pull off a gun manufacturing operation and the building of a bunker, right here on the land that is still owned by Gram. She has always been abundantly clear about this being *her* land over the years."

"As in, 'This is my house and my land, and therefore my rules,'" Willa says as she shakes a finger at me while mimicking Gram's intonation perfectly.

"If I've heard that once I've heard it a thousand times."

"But Gram is ninety-one and has been getting out less and less over the last few years. She's been doing pretty well, but she hasn't been out surveying the land on her ATV like she used to, and certainly not this winter. She's not as steady on her feet as she once was, and frankly she's been afraid of slipping or falling on the ice."

"So, she doesn't know her only son is making and selling unregistered firearms in her garage or that he's built a bunker out on the north forty? She's not stupid, he couldn't have built that bunker without the use of some heavy-duty construction equipment."

"No, she's certainly not stupid, but she is ninety-one and Pop's always been pretty good at stretching the truth to suit his own purposes. He told her he's building us a shelter and storing food in case *the liberals* come for our guns, our food, and our lands. She's heard this kind of talk from Grand Pappa ever since he came over from Germany. So, she didn't question it."

"I guess people who've survived a world war have a real fear of something like that happening again. To me, it just seems so far-fetched and paranoid."

"I'm not sure it's paranoia, but I think it's Pop and the agenda of his white brethren that we need to be afraid of."

"So, Gram doesn't know?"

"I don't know who knows what. Mom has always been tight-lipped as she works her own gentle magic around this place. But I can tell you this, people don't confide in me, either. I think Pop and the boys are suspicious of Elias and because I'm his wife their suspicions extend to me."

"Well, since we're being honest. I'm suspicious of the whole lot of you. If you feel out of the loop and you live here, just imagine how I feel— like Alice in Wonderland and I've just fallen down the rabbit hole. This whole thing is so troubling and surreal. I don't know who to trust or who to fear." In spite of my best intentions, my eyes fill with tears.

"That's understandable," Willa says with a smile as she hands me a tissue from the box on the bedside stand. "Let's go slowly and I'll see if I can find a way to put you more at ease."

"Okay, but I have to ask you something." I take a deep breath, not certain how much of what I know that I really want to divulge to my sister. I, too, decide to go slow and proceed with caution. "I know that you have been on the *23 and Me* website."

My sister looks perplexed as thin worry lines appear across her furrowed brow. "And just how do you know that?"

"Every time someone signs in their account is flagged and the date becomes part of the public record."

"I see, so I guess there's little point in pleading ignorance and burying this all into the archives of ancient history."

"I'm afraid not. I only wish it was all ancient history but the facts remain, Becca is Mom and Grand Pappa's daughter. God only knows how that came to be, but for now that's beside the point. I'm afraid all hell will break loose when Pop learns the truth. I'm beginning to think that everything we've been asked to believe may be built on some pretty significant lies."

Willa turns her eyes away from me as she reaches for the wine bottle and refills our glasses.

"What do you know about Grand Pappa's other children? I always thought that Pop was an only child, but the information I've been able to gleam from *23 and Me*, leads me to believe that this is not true."

"All right, spill. Tell me what you know. There are already too many secrets in this family that put us all in a very precarious, if not downright dangerous situation. If you know something, you don't need to carry it all alone. Don't you think you could use an ally, if, and when all of this comes to light?" Willa says. The tears begin to stream down both of our faces as she reaches over and grabs a tissue, then she passes one to me.

And so, in the seclusion of the cabin under the influence of a couple of glasses of wine I confide in my older sister all that I know and all that I fear might be true and she listens as I pour my heart out to her.

We talk on into the night until the old Black Forest cuckoo clock on the wall chimes again, startling both of us. It's midnight. "Good God, doesn't that thing drive you crazy?" Willa asks. "I don't know how you can stand it."

"I only set it this afternoon, I get lonely over here all by myself. I thought the little bird might keep me company or at least grounded in the here and now."

"You do know how pathetic that sounds," Willa says with a laugh as she stands and hugs me. "I have to go. The girls will be getting up early for school with Becca. Next time, I'll tell you all about my worries and concerns about leaving my children with Becca and in the presence of all of these angry white men who come and go from here at all hours of the day and night. Did I mention my concern about the fact they're all carrying some kind of a firearm? Nothing like giving an angry man a gun to make you feel safe and secure, to say nothing of the stockpile in the old man's hideout. But that will have to wait for another day, I have to go."

I stand and help Willa into her coat. "I'm sorry, I'm afraid I've monopolized the whole evening," I shrug my shoulders in apology. "You have real worries. I'm sorry."

"Don't worry about that, Elias and I are on the same page and we have a plan. We just can't execute it yet. I'm just grateful to have you here keeping an eye on things. Let me know if you hear anything back from our aunties."

"Do you want me to text you or call?" I ask.

"I think it would be safest if you just send me a text. But don't be explicit. Just invite me to stop by for a coffee. I don't want any of our suspicions to fall into the wrong hands or even the prying eyes of my girls." Willa leans in to give me a hug.

I do feel better. Willa was right, it helps having someone to talk to.

Chapter 19

I climb into bed and my mind is racing, so much has happened in the last few days and none of it is good. Unable to slow my thinking down, the long litany of worries plays on and on in my head and when I get to the bottom of the list I start back over at the beginning until the wine I've had starts to work its magic and I drift off toward an unsettled sleep.

I wake in the early morning hours to the sound of voices outside of the garage. Good God who is here at this hour? Looking out the window, I see that something has triggered the flood lights. They glow brightly illuminating the entire area. Pop and Josiah are loading some guy's white pickup with wooden boxes, while he stands there with his hands in his jacket pockets supervising the operation. He must be the buyer. I'd like to get a look at him, but his back is to me. All I can see is that he wears a winter cap pulled down over his ears. The way the truck is parked I can't see the license plate either but the door of the truck has a logo of some kind. It looks like the same logo on the banner in Pop's man cave. It's on a black background bearing a red shield with a large medieval knight's helmet in profile. It's symbolic of the National Resistance Revival. Man, these guys are getting more and more brazen putting their business right out in the open. I'd think he'd be concerned about getting stopped by the police while transporting illegal weapons. It is then that he turns into the light, I can't say for sure but I think I know who he is. I shudder to think how far and wide the infiltration of this right-wing brotherhood and their compatriots might be.

There is no way I can sleep now. The implications are far too disturbing. My days and nights are running together with all the coming and going, this pervasive sense of impending doom, combined with my inability to sleep. I lift the electric kettle, it's still half full so I plug it in and wait for the water to boil. I hear the truck pull out of the driveway as the sound of squealing brakes pierces the silence of the early morning. I make myself a cup of ginger tea and sit at the little table near the window. It's chilly in here, but not as cold as it has been. Mom said it was supposed to get into the forties today. Icicles hang like prison bars over the windows and the faint sound of dripping water can be heard as I sit and sip my tea. It is the sound I associate with the beginning of the winter melt, which will be followed by the mud season. As I sit there lost in my thoughts, the flood lights go out.

Everyone must have gone back inside.

I am drawn back to the present moment. I open my computer and wait for it to boot up as I sit and take another sip of my tea.

I open up my browser and there on the Facebook icon is that little red box indicating that I have notifications. A chill runs down my spine when I think about all the friend requests I've sent out to members of the Proud Boys, and their wannabes, and lookalikes. I take a deep breath before I click on the app and it opens up. Yep, one hooligan after another wants to be my friend. I wander around on their pages trying to get a sense of who these people are and what they are up to. Most of it is despicable.

And then I stumble upon my sister Becca's photo with her long blonde hair and bright blue eyes. She is calling herself *Sister of the Revolution* and there she is liking, commenting, and reposting this bullshit. It makes my stomach turn.

The old phrase runs through my head— she drank the Kool-Aid. We studied Jim Jones and Jonestown Guyana in a psychology class I took where we learned about the power of propaganda and cults.

After spending some time poking around in the online lives of these neo-Nazis, I have concluded that Covid-19 is not the only virus infecting our country. The virus of hatred is every bit as dangerous and is carried and spread far and wide, even among those we would never suspect of such unbridled animosity. Those embracing this alt-right philosophy include fathers, sons, brothers, husbands, as well as doctors, lawyers, and engineers. The justification they espouse for their hatred runs both wide and deep.

I need to think about this before I say or do something I may regret. I promise myself that for now, I will just observe and learn. Too much is at stake and mistakes could be costly in terms of my own personal safety.

I close the Facebook app on my laptop. I joined Facebook back when I was in middle school and I used it to keep up with my friends, to find out what was going over the weekend, and to share photos when all cameras converted to digital. I thought it was fun and harmless. I no longer feel like that. The bigotry and hatred that is being posted here is like throwing gasoline on a match as these homegrown extremists openly advocate the use of unrestrained violence as a means to an end. And members of my own family appear to be committed to this vision of the future. The whole thing fills me with fear and trepidation. So now what?

I pace around the room, but the cabin is so small and there is nowhere to go to get out of my own way. It is still dark and has started to rain. Ugh. I feel like a captive with nowhere to go and no one to talk to. I return to my laptop and try to refocus my attention elsewhere.

With a mounting sense of apprehension, I enter my user name and password into my *23 and Me* account. Maybe one of my long-lost aunties will have written me back.

The icon with the little bell on the upper right-hand corner of the page has a little green circle at the top indicating that I have an unread message. I take a deep breath before clicking on it, I don't know if I can stomach anymore from my dysfunctional family. Good God it's not even daylight yet, and already I am overwhelmed with anxiety. I click on the icon anyway. How bad can it possibly be?

There is a letter addressed to me from Margrit Wolfram.

Dear Emma,

I must say that I am as surprised to learn of your existence, as no doubt, you are to learn of mine. Forgive me as I do not speak English, only German, which is my native tongue. I have asked my granddaughter, Winnifred, to help write this letter to you. Her English is much better than mine. So, we will try.

Like you, I did not know that my father, Winfield Graf, had any other children.

My father left our home in the town of Freising, outside of Munich, in 1942 to serve in the military. I was only seven years old at the time and we never heard from him again.

I grew up believing that my father was a war hero. I was just a child of ten, in the spring of 1945, when my mother and I learned that my father had been killed in action the previous year. My mother was given my father's Iron Cross for his meritorious service to the fatherland. Attached you can see a copy of a photo where my mother holds my father's iron cross with its oak leaves and crossed swords. The year 1944 is embossed on the bottom.

I click to open the attachment. Here is a photo of a pretty woman who looks to be in her thirties. She has her hair pulled back and wears a simple dark dress with a lace collar while holding the Iron Cross. She looks as if she has been crying.

I close the attachment and go back to the letter.

This military medal of honor was my mother's most prized possession, and at her request, she was buried with it in 1975. Although my parents never married, my mother considered my father to be her husband. He was her one true love. She never married and died alone when she was only fifty-seven years old.

And now, over seventy-five years since I last saw my father, I've learned that so much of what I once believed about him is based on lies. He was not killed in the service to his country, but instead he changed his name and immigrated to America. He never initiated any contact with my mother or with me, and he went on to have another family. This news is devastating to me as I have always believed he loved me and my mother. I am only glad that my mother never learned of his betrayal as she loved him dearly and mourned him all the days of her life.

In fact, my granddaughter, Winnifred, was named in the memory of my father.

Although all of this comes as a great shock to me, I do want to learn more about the man you know as Winfield Earl.

Most Sincerely Yours,
Margrit Wolfram

I read and then re-read the letter. My heart is breaking for this woman and her mother. How could my grandfather have just left his family behind and started a new life all the while allowing them to believe he died in battle? What kind of a heartless soul would be capable of such cruelty? Then I open the calculator app on my phone and I do the math. Margrit's mother was only 17 when her daughter was born. I enter the year of Grand Pappa's birth. He was also only 17 when Margrit was born. I guess it was young love.

But who did that Iron Cross belong to, for my grandfather clearly did not die in battle? Did he send it to his family when he planned his departure to America? Was he fleeing justice for something he did during the war? Or was this just a case of mistaken identity? Somehow, as much as I'd like to believe that, the theory just doesn't seem to fly given all the lies that have already been uncovered.

I pull up my profile page to recheck what I think I remember. Julia Jaeger was born in 1942 and Ruth David was born in 1945, yet Margrit Wolfram and her mother were informed of Grand Pappa's death in 1944 and Margrit was always led to believe that she was an only child. All of this inconsistency is perplexing and upsetting. Where is the truth in all of this?

Not for the first time do I think about the fact that one of my grandfather's daughters lives in Israel. I can't help but wonder if Ruth David is Jewish. I fear the reality of her conception may be even more horrific than my imagination can allow.

I check the message board, there is still no response from Ruth David. But it appears that she was on the web site yesterday, so she must have received my note. Maybe she doesn't want to talk to me. Given everything I've learned about my grandfather this week, I can't blame her. I'll let it sit for today, maybe she needs a little time to process all of this. I know I do.

Chapter 20

It's morning— overcast, gray, and raining. The snow is melting and is already starting to look dirty. This is the start of what is lovingly known as the mud season around here. In the years gone by anyone and everyone with the wherewithal to get out of this Adirondack town would be planning an escape to Florida, but not this year. Everything is shut down thanks to the pandemic and the wisdom of Governor Cuomo. Everyone is supposed to be sheltering at home. Emphasis is on the words *supposed to be.*

I've been working at home and have finished sewing the prototype of the silk negligee and robe I started when I was back in the city. I received an email this morning from my boss, the divine Miss Maria, and of course she wants it right now, if not sooner.

I'll need to take a trip into the post office and send it off to her by express mail. I wonder if anyone is going into town, maybe I can catch a ride or borrow a car.

I walk over to the house to ask.

I try the handle. Today the front door is unlocked. "Good Morning," I call as I walk inside.

"Hi honey, I'm in the kitchen," Mom calls back.

I pass my father's office, where the French doors are closed. I wave to him and he scowls. One look at his face and I know I have committed an egregious offense. Pop is on the phone in his office. I can hear his voice, loud and clear, even through his closed glass door. He glares at me and even without speaking the words I know what he is thinking, *Women and children should be seen and not heard.* He said this so many times when we were growing up, I can almost recreate his intonation. Anyway, I guess that means me on both accounts.

Mom is in the kitchen cleaning up the dishes from breakfast when I walk in.

"Good Morning, Emma. Would you like a cup of coffee?" she asks.

"No thanks," I say from behind my mask. "Any chance I can borrow the car, I need to go into town and send a package to my boss."

"Oh honey, I don't know. You haven't driven in almost ten years and the roads will still be icy this morning."

"Really Mom? I know how to drive."

"Why don't I take you. I need to get a few things at the grocery store. Do you need to go right away, or can I finish up the dishes first?"

"I can wait, no hurry."

"Do you really think it's necessary to wear that mask in the house?" she asks as she turns to look at me.

"Better safe than sorry," I say using words I have heard her say all my life. "There have been quite a few people coming and going from here the last few days."

"I thought the President said wearing a mask wasn't necessary and we should save the masks for the health care workers."

"I made a half a dozen or so from some scraps of fabric and a bit of elastic I found in the bottom of my sewing bag. So, I'm not taking any essential supplies from those who might need them. But if the health care workers are wearing them as protection to prevent the spread of infection, then I think it only makes sense that we should be wearing them too. Just my opinion. I have one for you if you want it."

"We'll see," she says as she turns back to the sink to finish washing up the dishes. "I'll just be another couple of minutes."

"Where are Becca and the girls?" I ask as I take a sponge from the sink, dip it into the hot soapy water, and start to wash down the sticky kitchen table.

"Becca has set up Tilly and Heidi downstairs for a lesson on American History," Mom says.

One of their books remains on the kitchen table. I pick it up to peruse it while Mom finishes the dishes. God help us. The title is— *Rush Revere and the American Revolution* written by that conservative talk radio pundit Rush Limbaugh. I can't stand that guy, he makes my blood boil. This would be laughable if it wasn't so freaking scary. I look again at the cover, there is a picture of Rush Limbaugh's face superimposed on a character I can only assume is supposed to be Paul Revere. And these folks complain about liberals wanting to rewrite history! I can only shake my head in disgust as I think about the propaganda they are filling my nieces' heads with. I turn the book over. There is a full body shot of the author, no doubt it has been *Photoshopped*, but there he is, good ole Rush himself along with a list of accolades for his book. Apparently, this book is a New York Times Bestseller and was the Winner of the 2014 Children's Choice Book Award. There's no accounting for taste.

"Okay, I'm ready to go," Mom says. "Just let me grab my purse and leave a note for your father so he'll know where I've gone."

We walk out to Mom's old sedan. Her car is a good ten years old, it's rusty and looks even older. It is no longer undercover since Pop has commandeered the garage for the armory. Mom starts the car, turns the defrost on high and hot as we both work to clear the ice from the windshield. Eventually the ice begins to melt and give way. The wipers move rapidly across the windshield covering both of us with slush. "Come on let's get in and warm up, it should all be cleared off in a minute or so."

She doesn't have to ask me twice, I'm freezing. There is something about that damp cold that chills me all the way down to the bone.

Mom backs the car up and turns it around.

I'm glad that Mom insisted on driving when we fishtail on the black ice as we pull onto Route 28. I reach behind me and fasten the seatbelt that someone has previously belted behind me to keep the annoying reminder bell from calling for compliance.

"You don't have to wear it, few people do up here," Mom says as I notice her seat belt is also already fastened behind her.

"If it's all the same to you, I think I'll wear it. I'd just as soon avoid a face plant into the windshield."

"Suit yourself, all I meant was the police never issue tickets for that kind of thing around here."

"Not if you're white," I say under my breath.

"That's hardly fair," Mom responds.

"I know, but there are no people of color who live here."

"What about Samuel Henderson and Jon Bodaway and their families?"

"Come on Mom, those folks are summer residents with big houses on Fourth Lake. This whole region has almost no racial or ethnic diversity, and the police are known to stop anyone who looks like they don't belong."

"I don't want to get in an argument with you this morning. I know it is true, but this little town has had more than its share of drug related crime and tragedy. Maybe the police are just being careful."

"They should be stopping the locals if they're looking for drugs."

"There are plenty of good hard-working people who live up here."

"I know that, and you are one of them," I say, wanting to change the subject. I reach over and give my mother a squeeze on her shoulder and she smiles.

"Sorry," I say mutter. "I don't know why I get so ornery." Once spoken this seems so disingenuous. I have my reasons, good reasons to be irritable and cantankerous, but I decide to let it go.

Mom swings into the parking lot of the post office and I hop out with my package. "Do you want me to wait for you?" she asks.

"No, I'll walk down to Di Orios when I've finished. I might want to pick up a couple of things from the grocery store, too."

"Okay, I'll see you there," Mom says.

I walk into the post office and there are three people in line ahead of me and two postal workers that I can see behind the counter. No one in the whole place is wearing a mask. All of a sudden, I feel very vulnerable as another person comes in and is encroaching on my personal space. I want to swat at him like a horse's tail does to an annoying fly that is somewhere it has no business being. Instead I clear my throat loudly, "Harrumph," hoping he will get the idea and back off.

Instead I hear him say, "Emma Earl, is that you?"

"Hi Jed," I say with very little enthusiasm.

"Ha ha, I hardly recognized you behind that mask. Are you planning to hold up the post office for their stamp money?" He laughs at his own little joke.

Too bad the mask does not cover my entire face as I roll my eyes at him. I can't help myself. I've been called out for this all my life. I don't intend to do it but it's some kind of an involuntary response to his idiocy. "Nope, just trying to do my part to stop the spread of this virus."

The guy in front of me turns around and sneers at me. "Are you Ed Earl's kid?" I can't help but notice that he wears the red Trump MAGA hat.

I nod.

"I thought you moved to New York," he says as he turns to look me over and shifts the packages in his arms.

"I do, or I did, up until a week or so ago when they determined I was a non-essential worker."

"Are you the one who infected your brother and grandmother?"

Now everyone is looking at me and you could hear a pin drop as I search for some kind of a response. I watch as people now decide to give me a wide berth as they back away from me as if I was a rabid rodent intent on biting them.

"They are both at Saint E's," I say. But I'm certain most of these people already know that as news of other people's business spreads like wildfire in this little town. Before I can tell them that I was *not* the one who infected them, the man in front of me has turned on me.

"You city folk need to stay the hell away from here. Aren't you supposed to be stayin' at home? What the hell do you think you are doin' comin' up here and infecting us. Because of people like you, that lefty liberal governor is closin' down the whole goddamn state, and we'll be goin' broke because of...," he sputters with anger as he struggles for a word, "vermin, like you."

He is so angry his face nearly matches the color of his red hat. Here we go *Makin' America Great Again* by calling other people names.

"Oh, come on now, Grady, there's no sense callin' this young lady names," Jed, the guy behind me, says.

For once I am speechless, and this yahoo comes to my defense and to protect my honor. Apparently, he doesn't think the label, *vermin*, applies to me. How comforting. A soundtrack filled with snarky comebacks plays on in my head. There are so many to choose from.

"Emma comes from a good family. You know the Earls. She's a local and the Earls have been part of this community for as long as I can remember. She's a good ole PLU," he says as he reaches out to put a hand on my shoulder. I cringe at the paternalistic gesture that implies I need his protection.

I turn and shrug my shoulder to remove his hand before asking, "What's a *PLU*?"

Again, he breaks into a big ole self-satisfied grin showing all his teeth, "Oh honey, you know, *people like us*."

I simply nod my head as I bite my tongue. I want to tell him that he mistakes me for someone else, for I am nothing like them. And I'm proud of that.

The guy in front of me has completed his business at the counter and now it is my turn. Just as I lay my package on the counter the guy in the red MAGA baseball cap heads out the door and yells back at me, "Go back where you came from and take that Chinee virus with you."

I shake my head and swallow hard not daring to speak and trying to keep from crying. After a moment I say, "Hello Sarah." Everyone knows Sarah as she has worked here for years.
"I need to send this overnight."

She looks at the package that is already sealed uptight and labelled. She picks it up and puts it on the scale. "Shouldn't you be in quarantine?" she says.

"I tested negative for the virus. My grandmother and my brother were not infected by me."

She gives me a loud, "Harrumph," then returns to weighing my package and calculating the postage. "That will be one hundred and thirty-two dollars."

"Yikes. I guess that will be okay. It will have to be." I hand her my company credit card.

She looks it over and says, "Fancy," as she reads the company name embossed on the front: *Le Fleur Lingerie.* Then she hands it back to me, "Just use the credit card terminal."

Once I've conducted my business, I can't get out of there fast enough. I wave at Jed who has been standing behind me. He's harmless and in the words of my mother, 'he means well.' Still I can't help but feel like *persona non grata* and that does not feel good.

Standing outside the post office, the cold damp air leaches into my bones and I shudder with a chill. I decide to walk down to the grocery store, maybe if I get moving I'll warm up. I've only gone a block or two when I see my mother driving in the opposite direction. I guess she's already finished her shopping. I turn to walk back to the post office when I see her drive right past it. Where is she going?

Old Forge is basically a one street town and small enough that all the shops and businesses are clustered within a few blocks. I continue up the street. Maybe she has gone to the hardware store. Are they considered an essential business?

I walk past a couple of restaurants and bars that are all closed up. Even the diner that always does a robust breakfast business is shuttered up tight. The hardware store appears to be open but Mom's car is not parked outside and the parking spaces are wide open. It's more than a little bit eerie how few people there are out and about this morning. Then I spot Mom's old blue Chevy Impala up the hill in the parking lot at Community Bank. I trudge up the hill past the knoll overlooking First Lake. It doesn't look like the ice will be going out anytime soon. By the time I reach her car I'm freezing and grateful to find the car unlocked. I guess I'd have been surprised if it wasn't. No one locks their cars around here and most people still leave their keys in the ignition, at least in the off season when it's just the locals up here. Clearly, Mom is the exception. I'd love to turn the heat on but she's taken the keys with her today.

What is she doing at Community Bank? Our family has always banked at the Adirondack Bank across the street. I wonder when they changed. I lower the visor and take a moment to look in the mirror intending to do something about my hair when I see in the mirror that Mom is sitting in a private office inside the bank. But who is she with? It looks like Mrs. MacLean, she's the banker and my childhood Girl Scout leader. Mom sits on the opposite side of the desk. What's going on?

I brush my hair and I'm trying to decide if it looks better if I just leave my ski cap on, when the car door opens. "Good gravy, Emma! You scared me half to death!" Mom says. She is trembling as if she has just seen a ghost.

"I'm sorry Mom." I giggle as she tries to regain her composure. "I didn't mean to frighten you. But I saw you drive past me when I was heading to the grocery store. Nearly everything in town is closed and I didn't want to wait outside."

"You gave me such a fright. I just wasn't expecting anyone to be in the car."

"It's only me."

"I know," she smiles and nods nervously as she takes a burgundy colored folder with the bank's logo on it and tucks it between her car seat and the door.

Is she trying to hide it from me?

183

"When did we start banking at Community Bank?" I ask as she pulls the car out of the parking lot and turns towards home.

"Emma, for the love of God girl. Can you please just leave it alone? Please stop asking so many questions! There are things happening here that you are better off not knowing. Can you just trust me on this?"

"Okay, Mom. Okay," I say as a tear slips down my cheek. My mom has always been my confidant and dearly beloved. It hurts my heart that she doesn't trust me to hold her secrets and her pain. "I trust you completely."

We drive on as we both weep as the silence between us grows, neither of us daring to try and find the words for what we are feeling.

Chapter 21

When we get home, I help Mom carry the groceries into the house and put them away. Before we are finished Pop comes into the kitchen and one look at his face tells us that something is wrong, very wrong.

"What is it Edward?" Mom says as she leads him by the hand and settles him into his chair at the head of the kitchen table.

"It's Mother," he says as tears fill his eyes. "She has left us." Mom and I reach for chairs so we, too, can sit with Pop.

"Glory Be," Mom says. In times of turmoil and stress she reverts to the Catholicism of her childhood. Tears fill her eyes and mine as well.

"I'm just so sad that none of us could be with her to hold her hand and comfort her in her passing." This doesn't come as a shock to any of us, and still that doesn't make her passing any easier. I walk to the bathroom to get the box of Kleenex. I know my father is usually embarrassed by any and all show of emotion and he would probably prefer to grieve in private. Still he seems to need to talk, so I return to the table in silence and hold space for him and my mother.

"That Chinee doctor called ten minutes ago and said the nurse found her. She passed on in her sleep. Just stopped breathin', that's what he said." Pop clears his throat, too choked up to continue.

"I'm so sorry Edward," Mom says as she lovingly lays her hand upon his arm.

"Maybe we should have agreed to put her on the ventilator. I was so sure she was going to pull out of it. She has always been so strong," Pop says out loud to no one in particular.

"I know Edward, we were all hoping she'd pull through, but she was ninety-one and none of us is promised forever," Mom says as she gently strokes her husband's arm.

I just nod and keep quiet.

"Now she has traveled on to be with her beloved Winfield." Mother hands my father a tissue from the box and he blows his nose loudly as I feel a crushing sensation in my chest as the reality sets in. Oh, how I will miss Gram. Thank God, Gram never knew the truth about her *beloved Winfield*. I find a bit of consolation in that, for it would have broken her heart and destroyed her memories of him. I dearly loved my grandmother but I also remember how dismissive she was of my mother and how many times she hurt Mom's feelings. Either Mom is a great actress or she has an overwhelming capacity to forgive both her mother-in-law and father-in-law.

Pop stands and shakes himself free of Mom's loving caress. "You'd better start calling the family and makin' the arrangements," he directs his demands to Mom as he turns to walk out of the room.

"Edward," Mom calls after him, "did you hear anything about Lucas and when he might be released."

He turns on my mother like a wild dog, "Do I have to do everything around here? I just lost my mother. He's been layin' around in that goddamn hospital long enough. Get him out of there before they kill him, too. Make the arrangements and get that boy home. I need some help around here."

Wow, if I didn't know better I'd think he was strung out on some kind of drugs.

Then he turns on me, "Don't you have something productive that you can be doing? Or are you just going to sit on your ass in my kitchen all day and eat my food?"

Good God, what is wrong with him. Maybe this is what a personality disorder looks like, complete with displaced anger. I shake my head as if I can simply shake off the nastiness that he has just been spewed out all over me.

Mom and I sit in silence until we hear the front door slam.

"Don't take it personally, Emma. You know how he is."

I take another tissue and wipe my eyes. "Can I help you with anything, Mom?" I ask.

"Not now dear. I have to make some phone calls and make the arrangements."

"I'd be happy to help you," I offer.

"No honey, there are some things I just have to do myself, and these are some of those."

"Okay, but if there's anything I can do, just ask."

I stand and give my mother a long hug before I head back to the cabin. I breathe a sigh of relief as I make my way down the path and back to the sanctuary of the cabin. It may be small, but I'm grateful to be out of harm's way— at least for now.

Chapter 22

I close the door behind me only to find that the fire has died out. I guess I've been away too long. The one room cabin is cold and gray and I debate starting another fire or just going back to bed and losing myself in my grief. This has been a helluva day and it's not even noon. Maybe I should see if I can find a ride back to the city, at least if I have to quarantine in my apartment I'll have Cassie for company.

I can't leave, not now anyway. I'll have to wait at least until we get Gram buried. I think about my grandmother and how tidy and industrious she was her entire life. She worked every day right up to the day she got sick. In honor of her memory, I decide to do what Gram would have done. I sweep the old ashes into the metal bucket and put them outside before laying a new fire in the fireplace.

I light the fire and it doesn't take long before the cabin is filled with a cheery glow of both golden light and a comforting warmth. I can almost feel Gram's approval and the warmth of her presence. I wash the few dishes that I'd left sitting in the sink, straighten my bedding, then take a dust cloth and give everything a light once over.

I put the kettle on and make myself a cup of herbal tea then take a seat in front of the fire taking some time to remember the love of my grandmother and indulge my grief. I don't know how long I sit there, but long enough for the logs to burn down. Pulling myself back to the needs of the day, I head out to the woodshed for another load of logs. It has started to drizzle and I am glad to go back inside.

My father's words resonate in my head, "Don't you have something productive to do."

Maybe I'd feel better if I did.

I open my computer and there on the *23 and Me* icon is a little green circle indicating I have a message. Oh God, do I really want to open this? I'm already feeling so battered and bruised by the drama and trauma of the day. A wiser woman would have let it go, but I cannot. I'm too curious. I click on it and it opens.

Dear Emma,
I am sorry it has taken me a few days to get back to you. It has come as a great surprise to me to learn that I have family living in the United States, but that is not the biggest surprise for me.

I was told that my parents met in Bergen-Belsen, a refugee camp for displaced persons, after the war, and that is where I was born in July of 1945. We lived there during my early childhood while awaiting transport to Palestine, now Israel. I have no memory of the refugee camp, I guess I was too young. That was the story I was told, my parents had a great love story, and that is the one I cling to and have so desperately wanted to believe.

My parents were Jewish and held in two different concentration camps during the war. Throughout the remainder of their lives, neither of them ever wanted to talk about the war, the memories were just too painful. They did not want the remainder of their lives to be marked by the terror and tragedy of what they had lived through, so they did not speak of it. My papa spent his life taking care of Mama and our family, we wanted for nothing.

But as I grew older I began to suspect that they were keeping something from me. I look nothing like my father as he was a small man, with dark hair and dark eyes and I am tall and blonde with light eyes, rather unlike my mother, or any of my younger siblings. When I was growing up in Israel the other children teased me and called me *shiksa*.

Mama and Papa were held in different camps. Papa was in Auschwitz and Mama was in Dachau, but I now know that I had to be conceived before Dachau was liberated. I love my father, and he loved me whether he was my biological father or not. It does not matter. He was the best and I was blessed to have such loving parents.

Both Mama and Papa are gone now and I am an old woman left with so many unanswered questions.

Perhaps you can help me find the answers I seek.

Best Wishes,
Ruth David

I read the letter again. What's a *shiksa*? I type it into the search engine.

Shiksa- is a derogatory term used by Jewish people for non-Jewish women.

That must have stung, especially for a young girl being raised by parents who were Holocaust survivors and immigrants to Palestine after the war. Kids can be so cruel to one another. I feel very uneasy as I think about investigating this any further. How is it that my grandfather, an SS officer during the war impregnated a Jewish woman who was being held in a concentration camp? I need to face the truth; this story cannot be anything but vile and sordid. I feel dirty and sullied just by association. What kind of a monster was he? And then before I can change my mind I do something that I have only contemplated heretofore. I pull up a website listing Nazi war criminals and type in my grandfather's German name, the name he was known by before he immigrated to the United States— Winfield Graf. My heart drops as I see his name and photograph on a chart of hundreds of people identified as Nazi War Criminals that are still unaccounted for and are still wanted for questioning.

Most of these people must have died by now as the war ended in 1945. How old do you have to be to be a war criminal? I'd say at least 20. That would make the youngest of these people about 95.

I return to the list.

I'd like to think that it is a mistake for there must be many people who have the same name, but that line of reasoning just doesn't fly as there is an uncanny resemblance between the young man in the photo and my handsome brother Josiah. My grandfather must have been in his early twenties when this photo was taken and Josiah is now at least a decade older. There is no denying the truth, this Winfield Graf is the same Winfield Earl, my paternal grandfather.

Unlike many of those convicted of war crimes and sentenced, there is no information here on what crimes and offenses my grandfather was involved in. For this I am grateful. This is more than enough information to fill me with horror and shame.

Just when I think I have seen all that I dare to look at, I Google the names of my long- lost aunts, Ruth David, Margrit Wolfram, and Julia Jaeger. I include birthdates and any information I have on their birthplaces or their current residences. All these women are older now and grew up long before the advent of the internet and the scope and pervasive claws of social media. Still there may be something out there. I look for their pictures.

Ruth David is the only one I find. The picture is an old one. It looks like it was taken when she was in her forties. She looks like Becca with her statuesque body and long blonde hair. But there is something about the way she tilts her head and smiles that looks so much like expressions I have seen in my father and my grandfather, and Becca, too.

As upsetting as this is for me, I can only imagine how truly disturbing it must be for Ruth David to learn who her father was. I can only surmise what he did to her mother, and to my mother, too.

Although my mother has admonished me, only this morning, for asking too many questions, it is time to bring some of this to the light of day. I'm not the only one who has questions and needs answers, there are at least three other women who have the right to know the truth about Winfield Graf or whatever he wanted to call himself. Bringing this out in the open may be critical to their understanding of their own life stories, as well as my own understanding. There are some secrets that cannot be held onto if there is ever going to be any healing.

Perhaps, today is not the day.

Today is the day of my beloved grandmother's passing, and we, as a family are grieving. Still I wonder, did she have any idea who or what her husband was?

From across the room I hear my phone buzz indicating I'm getting a text message. I drag my sorry ass out of the chair to see who else wants a piece of me. For the love of God, I haven't much more to give. The message is from Willa. All it says is—*coffee??*

I text her back. *Sure.*

I hear the buzz of her reply. *I'll be right over.*

Chapter 23

I close the cover on my computer as I try to decide how much of what I have just learned I want to share with my sister. Before I can even reset the table with clean coffee mugs there is a knock on the cabin door and Willa is walking in with Mom's old picnic basket hanging over her arm.

"You must have been pretty sure I'd be here," I say as I gesture towards the thermos and plate of oatmeal cookies she is pulling out of the basket.

"You know Mom, the coffee is always hot and no one ever goes hungry."

"Thanks Willa, the truth is I could use some company. Either that or I'm going to go back to bed and pull the covers up over my head."

"I know Emma, I'm sad too."

"Gram was a love. I'm going to miss her, too," Willa says as we both take a seat at the table.

"I don't know if I ever adequately thanked her for all she taught me. If she hadn't been so persnickety and fastidious about always doing things the right way, I never would have been hired on at Le Fleur Lingerie. I never would have gotten out of this God forsaken town."

A smirk crosses Willa's face, before she breaks into a full rip snorting laugh.

"I'm sorry Willa, I meant no offense. I didn't mean that it's a bad place for you or your family. You have the girls and Elias. This is a great place to raise kids. It's just that there is nothing and I mean nothing for me here."

"No offense taken. Although I question whether this is such a great place to raise my girls, unless I want to indoctrinate them in the same bigotry that we were subjected to." Willa is still laughing.

"Then what's so funny?" I ask as I pass my sister the coffee cups so she can fill them.

"I don't think there is another person of your entire generation that uses the word *persnickety*." Willa says as she spills the coffee on the old wooden table.

Now I'm laughing too. "But it's a pretty apt description of Gram, don't you think?"

"I couldn't come up with a better one if I tried." Willa says as she mops up the spilled coffee with a wet dish cloth before she hands my cup to me.

We both drink our coffee as Willa passes me the plate of cookies.

"Josiah just brought Lucas home from the hospital."

"How is he?" I ask.

"He looks like shit, if you ask me. He's lost a lot of weight and is still coughing. But the doctor assured Josiah that Lucas is no longer contagious."

"Poor guy, at least that's one good thing."

"Pop was planning on having Lucas to help him out. But he's in no condition to do any of that. In fact, he went directly to bed as soon as he got home and Pop is fit to be tied."

"What exactly did he want Lucas to do?"

"No one is saying, but I think Pop may have promised unmarked weapons that he has yet to manufacture and deliver."

"Sounds like Pop, overpromised and under-delivered."

"He started screaming at me, 'Get your goddamn husband over here. He's part of this family and it's high time he started pulling his weight around here.'"

"Oh God, does Elias know what's going on?" I ask.

"Don't worry about Elias, he knows enough."

I don't know what that means exactly, but I decide to let it go. "Is that what you wanted me to know? Is this why you wanted to have coffee?" I ask, "Because it seems like there is something more that you're not telling me."

"There is. How much do you want to know?"

"All of it. And none of it. Is there really any way to avoid the stink of this cesspool?"

"If the stink was the only problem, but this is downright dangerous."

"In for a penny, in for a pound. Isn't that what they say? Go ahead and spill." I say as my stomach heaves and I start to sweat. "Maybe I'd be better off if I just went to bed like Lucas. Can you wake me up when it's all over?"

"That's why I need to keep you in the loop, it's for your own safety."

"Okay, okay, okay, just tell me."

"Pop and his ill-begotten comrades are arming up for something. I don't know what it is but it sounds like it might be happening fairly soon or Pop would wait for Lucas to get better, and he won't or he can't. You've seen all those trucks coming and going from here at all hours. Even the local cops seem to be in on it."

"I thought I saw Barney Fife out here the other morning."

"Who?"

"You know, that new deputy, Bernie Finn. The locals call him *Barney Fife*, poor guy, couldn't think his way out of a paper bag let alone solve any real crime even if his life depended upon it."

Then the silence between us grows as we contemplate what this might mean until I can't keep quiet a moment longer.

"What am I supposed to do with this information?"

"Just keep your eyes and ears open for now. I'm guessing some of these guys will be kicking around the next day or two to offer condolences for Gram's passing."

"Have they decided when the funeral will be?" I ask.

"Pop wanted to have a big wake, church funeral, graveside burial service, and a luncheon. You know the kind the church ladies always put on. Gram must have made a covered dish for everyone who's ever been buried in the town cemetery. But Governor Cuomo has put the kibosh on that sort of thing because of Covid 19 and the possibility of spreading the infection. Needless to say, the governor is on Pop's shit list."

"As if Pop needed another reason to hate the man."

"Right."

"So, what are we doing?"

"The cremation will be done today and Reverend Winters has agreed to do a graveside burial service tomorrow morning at ten, just for the immediate family. However, that hasn't stopped Pop from inviting all of his buddies over to the house after the burial to raise a glass to the dearly departed."

"Do you think anybody is going to come, given Lucas is just out of the hospital and Gram died of a deadly, infectious disease?"

"You can't believe the ongoing chatter from these idiots and all of their conspiracy theories. The latest one is that Bill Gates is behind the pandemic."

"Bill Gates? As in the billionaire, computer genius, and philanthropist? That Bill Gates?"

"The same. The theory is that Bill Gates is behind the Covid-19 pandemic because he wants to get the world vaccinated so he can implant microchips into all those who get vaccinated. The theory goes that these tracking devices can and will be activated by 5-G cellular networks."

"What? What are these people smoking?"

"Beats me, still you won't see me getting in line for the vaccine should one become available," Willa says.

"Really?" I ask.

Before we can get any further, Willa's phone buzzes with an incoming text.

"I have to go back to the house," she says as she takes the rest of the oatmeal cookies off the plate and puts them on a napkin and starts to pack up the thermos into Mom's old picnic basket. "Elias is here and he's meeting with Pop and Josiah. I can't throw my husband into the lion's den without at least offering to run a bit of interference."

"I have some more unsettling info about our long-lost aunts, but it can wait. Go protect your husband."

"Okay, I'll see you tomorrow for the burial if I can't get back before then."

I nod, then Willa and I hug one another. "Be careful," I whisper in her ear.

"You too," she whispers back.

Chapter 24

I sit there in the drafty old cabin as the wind blows outside and the windows rattle and it begins to rain. There is something bone chilling about the rain and dampness of early spring. I throw another log on the fire, but I still don't feel warm. Fear and loneliness threaten to overwhelm me, something has to give. I can't just sit here and wait for my life and my family to unravel any further than it already has. I put on another sweater and my ski jacket before pulling on my boots, I'm going over to the main house. I want to know what's going on and I sure as hell am not going to learn what it is by staying over here.

When I walk in the aroma of roasting meats and baking bread fills the room. Mom must hear the door close as she calls out from the kitchen, "Who's here?"

"It's just me," I respond.

I follow my mother's voice to find her up to her elbows in soap suds and dirty dishes. "I'm just fixing a bit of food for the funeral luncheon tomorrow."

"So much for social distancing," I say as I look over the kitchen table which is already filled with homemade cookies, a couple of pies, and some rolls. "How many people are you expecting?" I ask.

"It's hard to say. You know your father, he may have invited the whole town for all I know."

"Do you think it's wise, given that we are in the middle of a global pandemic? To say nothing of the fact that Gram died of the virus and Lucas is still too ill to get out of bed?"

"I think your father and his associates are more concerned with people telling them what they can and cannot do and with the government trying to interfere with their freedom."

"His freedom and his right to pursue it will be greatly impacted if he should get ill," I say as I pick up a towel and begin to dry the dishes. "I'll be at the burial but I hope no one is offended if I chose to keep my distance."

"I wish I had that option," Mom says as the timer rings and she turns to pull another pie from the oven.

A thought rushes through my head as I think about how my father is putting everyone at risk, including my mother. "I think this is a really bad idea. Can't you talk to him?"

My mother turns to me as tears fill her eyes, "Emma, I have no influence over your father. I tried to speak to him after lunch and he will not hear of it. He is making a big deal of honoring your grandmother. But the truth is, now that she is gone and he is the heir to her estate he is feeling pretty full of himself. He plans to elicit some of the good old boys to help him make some changes around here, now that your grandmother isn't here to object."

"What kind of changes?"

"I'm not privy to any of that, but he has been on the phone and meeting with this one and that, planning and scheming ever since your grandmother took ill."

"Hmm." She may know more than she lets on. Mom's always been a wily one, never letting on as she listens in the background while going about her housework. She's already warned me about asking too many questions earlier today. I decide to take a different tack. "Unless you want all of Pop's pals hanging out here all tomorrow afternoon, perhaps you should stop cooking. Maybe if they get hungry they'll all go home."

Mom picks up the dish towel and starts to dry her hands. "I think you might be right." She smiles as she pours herself a cup of coffee and takes a seat beside me at the table. Just as I think she might be about to let me in on whatever secret she is holding on to, the front door opens and Elias, Willa's husband, saunters into the kitchen.

"Have either of you seen Willa," he asks.

"She said something about trying to get the girls some new books at the library," Mom says.

I remember the Rush Limbaugh book I'd seen sitting on the kitchen table earlier today and the fact my sister has gone in search of other books doesn't surprise me. "I thought all the libraries were closed due to Covid."

"Willa's dear friend is the head librarian and Linda has offered to bring some books out to the car," Mom says.

"I tried to call her but I couldn't reach her. Can you let her know that I need to run a couple of errands for Pop?" Elias says.

Both Mom and I nod. "Sure," I say. They live on the property and I can walk over once she gets home.

"I may stop and see a couple friends up in Lake Placid before I head back. Can you tell her that?" Elias says as he looks me straight in the eye.

"That's a long way to go," Mom says as she looks at her wristwatch. "It's already quarter to four and it may be getting dark and icy before too long."

Elias laughs, "Come now, I'm a grown man and I've been driving for decades on these mountain roads, even at night."

Mom laughs too. "I just meant that you'll not be back before dinner and you've already put in a full day's work doing Edward's bidding." And then her tone and demeanor turn more somber, "It's been a difficult day, with Grandmother passing over and the graveside burial tomorrow. I just don't know what could possibly be so important that you couldn't be home with your wife and children tonight."

"Will you be back tonight?" I ask, trying to figure out what to tell my sister.

"I expect to be. If not, I'll definitely be home in the morning and before the funeral. Tell Willa I'll call her from Lake Placid, but it's unlikely I'll have cell service between here and there."

Elias turns to leave and Mom calls after him, "Be careful."

A strange look passes in her eyes. She knows something and she's not letting on.

"The roads may be icy," she whispers under her breath as she takes her still full coffee cup to the sink to empty and wash.

"I'll go and wait for Willa and the girls to get home. I can see her driveway and the house better from the cabin," I say as I stand and go to get my coat and boots.

Mom just nods as she stands at the sink as the water runs, washing and washing that one coffee cup that has long since been washed clean.

Even before I pass by my father's office I can hear the voice of some political pundit masquerading as a journalist on Fox News. The door is part way open but Pop is not in there. I look for the remote so I can turn it off. There is Sean Hannity yammering on about how the Democrats and the media have overplayed the significance of the Coronavirus solely to "bludgeon President Trump with this new hoax." Good God, two members of my immediate family have been infected and one of them is dead. This is some hellava hoax Mr. Hannity.

While looking for the remote on Pop's paper laden desk, I uncover his calendar. There's a red pen stuck inside his planner marking his place.

Who still uses a paper calendar in this day and age? Doesn't he know he has one on his phone?

Curiosity gets the best of me and I flip it open. There in black ink he has written Dems Convention Miwakey on August 17, 18, 19, and 20. But it has been crossed out in red.

He's spelled Milwaukee wrong. His phone would have autocorrected that for him. I find the remote and go to turn off Fox News, when Tucker Carlson starts reporting how the Democrats have decided to hold a virtual convention and delegates will vote remotely given the fact that we are in a global pandemic. He scoffs and mocks the Democrats as August is a long way off and President Trump has just promised that we will all be back in church by Easter. That's less than two weeks away. Where are these people living in *Candyland?* They make my head hurt. I turn off the TV and head back to the cabin.

It's already dusk. The sun isn't due to set for another two hours but the cloud cover is dense tonight and it threatens to either rain or snow at any time. What little remains of the wet snow has already started to ice over and crunches beneath my boots. I decide against taking the sidewalk as I'm certain it will be slippery. Instead I take the well-trodden path weaving between a grove of evergreens and hard woods. I hope Elias will be safe, these mountain roads can be treacherous when they are icy. But something else is nagging at me and I can't quite put it all together when a group of snowmobilers emerge from the woods. They must be out for one last hurrah before the spring melt. I step beneath one of the old growth pines and wait for them to pass for fear these yahoos have been drinking and might inadvertently run me over.

They park out by the garage, which has become synonymous in my mind with *the armory*. The light is on, maybe Pop is out in his man cave conducting his nefarious business. This can't be good. In spite of the fact that I am freezing, I wait and watch as they enter the garage and return moments later each carrying what can only be some kind of a weapon. What is this the wild west complete with armed snowmobilers? I know that the state of New York is an open carry state, for handguns and rifles. But this is terrifying and doesn't make me feel the least bit safe and secure. These yahoos are under-educated and over-armed. This looks like a disaster just waiting to happen. What the hell are they planning to do?

When the last snowmobile pulls out into this rapidly descending gloom, I step from beneath the trees and continue on towards the cabin when I see the lights go on at Willa's. She and the girls must be back from town and the library. I walk past the cabin and go directly to my sister's, just as I promised Elias I would.

Chapter 25

I knock once and then just let myself in. Willa and the girls are still taking off their winter coats and boots in the mudroom.

"Hi Auntie Emma," the girls say in unison. I can't help but think that they may be the only ones who are happy to see me as I look at my sister's face.

"What's wrong?" I ask.

"I nearly hit some snowmobiler who was riding in the road and forgot to put his headlights on." She is visibly shaken. "The roads are covered with black ice and I nearly rolled the truck trying to avoid him." I know if her daughters weren't here she'd be letting loose with a string of profanity, but she's a mother and a very good one.

I unbutton my coat awaiting an invitation, but none is forthcoming. "Mind if I come in for a couple of minutes?" I ask.

"Please, sorry Emma. Come on in."

I hang my coat on a coat hook in the mudroom and step out of my boots.

"Girls, you just had a snack in town, so that should hold you for a little while. I need to talk with your auntie. You can go down stairs and read your new books. We'll have dinner in an hour when your daddy gets home."

The girls pout and fuss a little for they are not used to being dismissed, but when it becomes apparent that their mother has no intention of changing her mind they take their bookbags and head for the basement.

Willa calls after them, "And no TV, or you will lose your privileges for the rest of the week."

There is more grumbling from Heidi.

"Want a glass of wine?" my sister asks. "I think I could use a glass."

"Not tonight, something is up. I haven't figured out what it is, but I think I need to keep a clear head."

Willa leaves the wine bottle unopened as we both take a seat at her kitchen table.

"I was just at the house with Mom, she's cooking enough food to feed an army."

"Why?"

"For the post-funeral celebration Pop is planning," I say as my sister lowers her eyes and shakes her head in disbelief.

"I thought Reverend Winters agreed to a graveside service for immediate family only," she says.

"He did. But Pop has invited everyone back to the house after the interment of Gram's ashes."

"Did anyone tell that asshole that we are in the middle of a global pandemic? God Almighty what the hell is wrong with him?"

"You want the long list or just a short list?"

Willa smiles momentarily before she returns to the subject at hand, "I'm not going and neither are my girls. I'm not putting my family in harm's way, anymore that they already are. I can't take this Emma, I need to get us out of here. We're not safe, and neither are you." Willa gets up and goes to look out the window. "Where the hell is Elias. I thought he'd be home by now?"

"Oh sorry, that's what I came to tell you, Elias is off on an errand for Pop. He left about an hour ago. He said to tell you he would be back late or maybe tomorrow morning. He said, he'd be back in time for the funeral at ten."

"That doesn't sound like him. He's always here to put the kids to bed. It's his favorite time of day." My face must show my confusion. "He's a really good dad. He likes to read to the girls and talk to them about their days before they go to sleep." A tender look crosses my sister's face at the memory of her lumberjack of a husband tucking her daughters into bed.

"You're lucky, Willa. Elias is a good man."

"That he is," she says as she slowly nods in my direction.

"I remember Pop reading to us and kissing us good night, don't you?" I ask.

Then we both start laughing. "How about never," Willa guffaws. "What kind of an errand did Pop send my husband on? Did he say where he was going?"

"Just that he was running a couple of errands for Pop and that he was going to stop and see a couple of his old friends in Lake Placid. He didn't expect to have cell service between here and there, but he said he'd call you when he got there."

"Lake Placid? Are you sure?" Willa asks.

"I'm sure, why?"

"I don't think he knows anybody in Lake Placid, that's why." Willa stands and paces for a moment before she goes to check the landline to be certain she hasn't missed a call. "It's a little over two hours to Lake Placid, but that's when the roads are clear. He's going to have to drive slowly tonight. Still if he left an hour ago, maybe I'll hear from him fairly soon."

"I'd be surprised Willa, he said errands, as in more than one. I think he was going to do that, whatever that is, on his way to Lake Placid."

"Do you think he's running guns for Pop?" Willa asks as she takes a corkscrew from a kitchen drawer and opens the wine bottle.

"I don't know," I say honestly, "but what else would it be?"

Willa nods at me. "Want to change your mind?" she asks as she fills her own glass.

"Not really, this whole day has left me feeling more than a little queasy. Something is up but I can't quite put my finger on it."

We sit a moment in silence as Willa sips her wine and then she asks, "Want to have dinner with us?"

"Sure, can I read the girls a bedtime story when we're done?"

"That would be great, they love you."

I know this is a little overstated, Tilly loves me and Heidi is far more enamored with her Auntie Becca, but that's okay. I help my sister clean the vegetables and make a salad from the produce she has just brought home from the grocery store while she puts together a chicken casserole and gets it into the oven. We mostly work in silence as I know my sister is grieving the loss of our grandmother and now she is worried about her husband, too.

As we prepare dinner, another truck pulls into the driveway and Willa goes to the window to see if Elias might be home. "It's not him," she says, "just some guy lookin' to do a little business with our father."

"Did you see all those snowmobilers who were here just before you got home?"

"I passed a few on the road before that one reckless guy almost sent us off the road. Why?"

"I think they were all here buying guns from Pop, unless he's branching out and is now trafficking in narcotics, too. All I know for certain is that there are a lot of people coming and going from his illustrious *man cave* at all hours of the day and night and that traffic has been increasing at least since I got here a couple of weeks ago. Something is up but I can't figure out what they're doing."

"They're gun runners for some alt right cult, it's as simple as that."

"I don't think so." I let my words hang there for a moment.

"What do you think is going on?"

"They are arming up for something. There seems to be some kind of rush to get these guns into the hands of their comrades."

Willa laughs to break the tension. "Pop would lock you in the bunker if he heard you refer to these *good ole American patriots* as comrades, sounds down right socialist."

I laugh along. "I know what I'm talking about. There was something in Pop's planner regarding the Democratic National Convention in August and now that has been crossed out."

"What are you talking about? There is no way Pop would be going to any Democratic anything … "

And then it dawns on her, "Oh …"

"I think they *were* planning some kind of armed protest or something, but given the pandemic all plans for a Democratic Convention have been changed. It was on the news earlier today; the Democrats have decided on a virtual convention with the delegates voting electronically instead of in person."

"Oh, so now that their target has moved and they are all up in arms, so to speak, you think they will change the target. Am I reading this right?"

"I don't know. But maybe."

211

"Any idea what the new target might be or the time frame?"

"I have no idea."

"Where and when did you see Pop's planner?"

"I went in his office to turn off Fox News as it was blaring so loud it could wake the dead. His desk was a mess, as always. So, I was shuffling things around trying to find the remote control when I stumbled across his planner. There was a red pen inside and opened to August. The words *Democratic Convention* had been written in black ink and crossed out with red ink. He must have some inside information as the change of plans was only just announced today."

"Hmmm, where is Pop's planner right now?" Willa asks as she starts to pace again.

"I don't know, probably still buried under all the other crap on his desk. I put it back where I found it, after I located the remote."

"If they've gone to all this trouble to arm the rebels and stir up all this passion and discontent among these good ole boys, I have a hard time believing that they've cancelled their plans entirely. I'd place my money on the fact that they've only changed the venue now that their original plans have been foiled. This could explain why Pop has Elias out making deliveries in the middle of an ice storm. I bet they've moved the date up."

The timer on the stove buzzes and we both nearly jump out of our skin. "Let's get the girls fed and off to bed. I need to think. Maybe Elias will call in the meantime."

I set the table while Willa sends the girls to wash their hands. Both of my nieces are animated and chatting on and on about their trip to town.

"What books did you get at the library?" I ask the girls.

"I got *Harry Potter and the Philosopher's Stone,*" Heidi says as she beams with pride.

"Is that the first book in the series?" I ask as I try to remember.

"Yes."

"I read all of those books when I was growing up, I loved them," I say hoping my niece and I might find some common ground.

"Mom, wouldn't let me read them before now. She thought they were too dark and scary," Heidi laughs like this is the most ridiculous thing she has ever heard. "But I've read part of it already. My friend Ivy, you know— Rolfe's daughter, lent me her copy but I didn't get a chance to finish it before she took it back. She can be like that, she's an *Indian giver*."

I cringe at the racial slur. I wait a moment and decide to let my sister handle her impudent daughter.

"Heidi, we talked about name calling and using that specific term. It's inappropriate and offensive," Willa scolds.

"Whatever," Heidi laughs. "I'm just to the part where they've arrived at Hogwarts School of Witchcraft and Wizardry and everyone is being sorted into houses."

"I remember that, they have to wear the sorting hat," I laugh. "Which house would you like to be in?" I ask Heidi.

"Slytherin, for sure. I'd be with the cool kids, like Draco Malfoy. I'd never be housed with a loser like Ron Weasley." I nod my head indicating I've heard her. This is disturbing on so many levels. I remember enough about those books to know that Slytherin is where the evil malcontents are placed, but I rationalize that Heidi has only just started the series and doesn't know the characters yet or the implications of her choice.

"What are you reading, Tilly?"

Before Tilly can tell me about her new books, Heidi interrupts, "She can't really read. She only looks at the pictures. I was already reading chapter books when I was her age."

Tilly hangs her head and looks crestfallen. I ignore Heidi.

"I didn't learn to read until I was seven, maybe seven and a half, but your mama used to read to me until I learned how. Didn't you Willa?" Willa nods and smiles at Tilly. "Now I read all the time," I say, as I give Tilly a conspiratorial wink.

"I have a Winnie the Pooh book," Tilly says as a smile returns to her sweet little face. "It's not the Disney one like we already have, but this one has little pictures and lots of words."

"Maybe we can read it together after dinner," I suggest and Tilly smiles.

It's a nice diversion to find myself in the world of children while we eat our dinner. Willa's cheesy chicken casserole with bread stuffing is the quintessential comfort food on this dark and dismal night. Still every time another car or pickup pulls down the long driveway towards the main house, Willa gets up and goes to the window.

"Are you expecting someone Mama?" Heidi asks.

"Just your daddy. He's out running an errand for Grandpop and I was hoping he'd get back before his dinner got cold," Willa says as she shields her eyes to block the inside light and presses her face up to the frosted window pane.

"I thought you said he had gone to Lake Placid," Heidi says.

I wonder how she knows this. She was supposed to be downstairs reading. I need to be more careful as it appears that Heidi is up to her old tricks, eavesdropping on things that are none of her business.

Willa returns to the table and everyone is nearly finished with their dinner. "He told your Auntie Emma that he was going to Lake Placid. I just hoped that maybe he'd finished up early or decided not to go." Willa tries to rationalize her behavior. But the girls seem to be picking up on their mother's concern about their father's whereabouts.

Before the girls can launch into a long litany of questions, I suggest, "Why don't you girls head upstairs and have a bath, I'll help your Mom with the dishes and then read you a story before I head back to my cabin."

"I take showers and can read my own story," Heidi says with an unmistakable air of superiority.

"Fine. And don't forget to wash your hair. Great Grandma's funeral is tomorrow and I don't want you looking like nobody loves you."

"Fine," Heidi says as she marches up the stairs leaving her dirty dishes on the table.

"Auntie Emma, I still take baths and I'd love it if you would read me my story," Tilly says, her voice just above a whisper.

"Great, do you need me to run your bath?" I ask.

"Please," Tilly says. So, I follow her up the stairs and help her get ready for bed.

Chapter 26

When I come down from putting the girls to bed, I find a note on the kitchen table.

> I've gone over to the house to see Mom.
> Can you stay with the girls 'til I get back?
> Be back soon.
>
> —W

I take a seat at the kitchen table as I wonder what Willa might be up to. Another two cars pull up to the garage, one right after the other. So much for staying home and saving lives during this global pandemic. I peer out the window to see if I know who is out here on this cold and icy night. But both people are so bundled up against the weather it's hard to even guess their gender, let alone identify them. Still I'm pretty sure they are men, as all the others have been. As I'm busy scoping out Pop's customers through the kitchen window, the front door opens and Willa slips in.

"Good God woman, what are you doing skulking around like that? You scared the heck out of me."

With that Willa pulls Pop's planner from where she has hidden it inside of her coat. She beams with pride. "We need to look through this and put it back before he notices it is missing. He is up to something, I can feel it in my bones. I heard him leave and head over to the garage, I figured there was no time like the present. So, under the cover of darkness, I snuck into the house. Mom was in the kitchen, she's still cooking for the funeral luncheon and I snatched the planner from the chaos on his desk."

We sit at the kitchen table with the planner between us and Willa starts leafing through the pages. The red pen still marks the pages in August where Pop has crossed out the Democratic National Convention. We move on from there. There is nothing remarkable notated in the month of July. But the truth is that neither Willa nor I have any idea what we are even looking for.

We quickly riffle through the pages looking for something, anything that might give us a clue to what our father and his armed militia might be up to. Then there it is, in the same red ink. On April 1, 2020, Pop has written an address—138 Eagle St. Albany. And then below it in all caps he's written *NOMO COUMO*.

Willa and I sit in silence for a moment, before she flips to the back of Pop's planner where there are a couple dozen blank pages provided for note taking. Again, in the same red ink Pop has made a list under the title: April Fool's Day. His writing is barely legible and his spelling is atrocious. But we get the idea.

- Andrew Cuomo—Albany, NY
- Gina Raimondo—Providence, RI
- Phil Murphy—Trenton, NJ
- Gavin Newson—Sacramento, CA
- Ned Lamont—Hartford, CT
- Kate Brown—Salem, OR
- Tom Wolfe—Harrisburg, PA
- Gretchen Whitmer—Lansing, MI
- John Carney—Dover, DE

- Tim Waltz—St. Paul, MN

- Jay Inslee– Olympia, WA

"Why these people? Are these the governors? Are those the capitals? Are they all Democrats?"

Willa slowly nods her head as she tries to put it all together. "Yep, these are the Democratic governors who've insisted on a full-scale quarantine to prevent the spread of the virus. The ones who have openly criticized the President's handling of the crisis and haven't kowtowed or shown adequate gratitude to Trump."

"Gratitude for what? Failing to do his job and protect the American people." My sister doesn't respond so I continue to process this new information out loud. "What in the name of God has Pop gotten himself involved in. Looks like this is going to be a major cluster fuck, with lots of players and lots of moving parts."

"I have to get this back, before Pop notices that it's missing," Willa says as she goes to put the planner back in her coat."

"Wait a minute," I say as I pull out my cell phone. "We are going to need some evidence, or people will think we've lost our minds if we start making accusations and have nothing to back it up. Open up the months of April, and August, and the notes in the back, too."

Willa does as I request as I take pictures of the relevant pages on my cell phone. Just as I start to take the last photo, the outside lights are triggered by the motion detector and voices can be heard outside of the garage as Pop bids goodbye to his buddies.

"I'll go," I offer as I go to put on my boots.

"No," Willa says as she moves towards the door. She stands there a moment as a small puddle of melted snow drips onto the floor as she still has her coat and boots on. "Pop already knows you're one of those *liberals.*

I've been keeping below his radar for years. If he goes to look for his planner before I can put it back, he'll never suspect me."

Before I can offer any arguments, Willa is out the door and all I can do is wait.

The minutes hang like hours as I nervously await her return. I pace about the kitchen offering up prayers to whoever might be willing to listen and intervene on our behalf. The truth is Pop is not the only one in over his head, I'm terrified by the scope of all of this and I have no idea what we are going to do with this information. Gram is to be buried tomorrow and the next day is April first and that is when this whole thing is supposed to take place. I take a deep breath and pray for wisdom. If these yahoos are successful this could be a bloodbath. People will be hurt and others will go to prison.

Praise be, Willa is back in less than ten minutes. She is panting and out of breath as she enters the house. "Pop was in the bathroom when I got there. Mom and Becca were getting dinner on the table. Lucas is still in bed and Josiah is out running an errand for Pop. I told Mom I needed to borrow some printer paper, so she told me to help myself." Willa holds up a small stack of white paper. "I slipped the planner back where I'd found it, and no one is the wiser. Thank God."

"Willa, what are we going to do?" I ask as she takes her coat off and sits beside me.

She answers my question with one of her own. "Did Elias call?" she asks.

"No," I respond.

Willa looks at the clock on the wall. "It's seven thirty. He should be in Lake Placid by now. If that's really where he was going."

We sit in silence a moment as we both try to determine our next best move. Time is of the essence as these armed uprisings are planned for the day after tomorrow.

"What do they hope to accomplish? Is this some kind of coup d'état or insurrection on a state level?"

"It looks like it. They are now a well-armed militia, thanks to our father. These good ole boys are all about states' rights, when it serves their agenda."

"I don't think this is something we can take to the local police, that new deputy is in cahoots with these armed *patriots*. He was here early the other morning doing a bit of business with Pop. He even had the audacity to drive up here in his patrol car. And for all we know, Robo-Cop may be in on it, too. "

"There's something I haven't told you …"

"What?" I ask my sister, not certain I really want to know and I'm not certain she really wants to tell me either. But before she can tell me the old phone hanging on the kitchen wall starts ringing. Willa dashes from her seat at the table to answer it. She picks up the receiver before the second ring.

"Hello?"

I can only hear Willa's side of the conversation.

"Thank God, I've been so worried. Are you in Lake Placid?"

Thank God indeed. It's Elias. I step into the other room to give my sister a little privacy. Still her voice carries and I can hear almost every word she says. She isn't on the phone long before she joins me in the family room. She turns on the lamp as I have been sitting there in the dark.

"Emma, I have to go into town. I need to call Elias back."

I must have looked confused as Willa drops her voice to a whisper. "Elias is afraid Pop or someone in his organization may have tapped the phone. We can't be too careful now."

A shiver goes up my spine as the implications of all of this are mounting. I don't know what it means but I do know it isn't good.

"Is Elias in Lake Placid?" I ask tentatively. Willa shakes her head no, but does not speak.

"I need your phone. I need to send Elias those photos. Give me your password."

"Okay," I say as she hands me a pen and tears a sheet of paper from a notepad on the counter.

"Will you stay with the girls until I get back?"

"Of course."

"Thanks honey. Lock the door behind me. I'll be back as soon as I can and we'll talk then."

I want to press her for more information. She has taken my phone along with her own and is already putting on her coat and boots and before I know it she is heading out the door.

"I've got to go," she says and I can read the fear in her eyes. "I love you Emma."

"Love you, too. Please be careful."

She closes the door quietly, then I hear the engine of Willa's SUV start before she pulls out down the driveway. I watch through the kitchen window, in spite of the urgency of whatever it is she is up to, she drives very slowly and she hasn't turned on her headlights. It is clear to me she doesn't want to alert anyone to her leaving. Good thing Pop never got around to installing the motion detection lights over here.

Again, a shiver of fear runs through me as I go to the door and lock it, just as I've been instructed. Why does this feel so ominous? Perhaps because it is.

We are not one of those families where the words *I love you* flow freely or often. In fact, I can't remember the last time someone said they loved me, likewise I think the only time I have ever said such a thing was in response to some nameless, faceless boy in the heat of passion. Not because I loved him, but more because it was the expected response. I shake off the memory, it's irrelevant now.

Without my trusty cell phone, I feel at a loss at how to occupy myself as I worry and wait for my sister to return. I decide to lay a fire in the fireplace, it makes me feel useful. This may be a long night. The wood is dry and stacked on the hearth and it isn't long before there is a roaring fire filling the room with warmth and a golden glow.

I walk back into the kitchen and help myself to that glass of wine that Willa offered earlier. She is a girl after my own heart, she bought the good stuff, a Russian River Pinot Noir. There is something unseemly about drinking alone, but I rationalize, my grandmother died today, it is more than likely my grandfather was a Nazi war criminal, to say nothing of a philanderer and a rapist, and now my father is deeply involved in some kind of criminal conspiracy that is attempting to overthrow the government with an armed militia. To hell with any reproach I feel about the propriety of drinking alone, I top off my already hearty pour with a bit more wine.

I wait and worry, until nearly as silently as Willa left, I hear her key in the door.

She looks ashen and weary as she stands in the vestibule beneath the overhead lights. She leaves her coat and her boots and steps into an old pair of slippers she had left in the doorway. I meet her in the kitchen with her unfinished glass of wine. She looks at her glass and tops it off. Clearly, she needs this drink as much as I do.

"You've made a fire," she says as she takes a seat beside me on the couch and a slow smile of gratitude graces her weary face.

"We're drinking the good stuff," I say a bit apologetically.

"If not now, then when," she says as we touch our glasses together in some form of acknowledgement. But what we are acknowledging and drinking to, I do not know. The fire crackles as the logs begin to burn down and heat fills the room chasing away the chill.

"Did you get a hold of your husband?" I ask as the litany of questions form in my head and beg to be answered.

"I did. He said to thank you for having the presence of mind to photograph all those pages from Pop's planner."

"Where is he?"

"I think it is best if we don't talk about this, at least not now. Do you trust me Emma?"

"Of course," I say and I feel a flush of emotion come over me and I realize that I do trust my sister. Completely. "Absolutely. But do you trust Elias?" I ask my sister as I am not quite certain which side of all of this he is on.

She nods her head and closes her eyes as a tear slips down her face. "I'm afraid," she admits through a stifled sob. I take her hand as she weeps. "Things are going to get ugly."

I want to ask her all the questions that are begging to be answered, but I can't seem to find the words and I don't know if I really want the answers. All I know is that these men are armed and angry and that is a very dangerous combination.

"I think you should stay here tonight. The guest room is ready and waiting for you. Elias won't be back until morning. We will all go to the burial tomorrow, then you and I, and the girls will come back over here."

"No sense going to that *super spreader event* Pop is planning after the funeral. It's the perfect excuse to stay out of harm's way. Besides, I already told Mom I wasn't going to go. Reverend Winters wouldn't agree to do a funeral in the church, and only reluctantly agreed to a graveside service for the immediate family. The Governor has banned all gatherings of more than ten people. We don't need to make any additional excuses. We're in the midst of a global pandemic in case Pop has forgotten." I press my lips together to stop this nervous chatter as I am yammering on and on about things we've already discussed. I'm frightened, too.

"Oh, he hasn't forgotten. He just thinks it's a hoax perpetuated by the liberal media and designed to lead to the economic collapse of the country and particularly all the states governed by the left-wing radicals."

"He hasn't forgotten that this liberal hoax killed his own mother just this morning, has he?"

We sit in silence for a moment as I recall the *hit list* we found in our father's planner only an hour ago. Are they targeting the governors of those eleven states? Good God Almighty what are they planning to do? This thing is big and Pop is being played. He thinks he's a big man, but he is merely a cog in the wheel of something evil and treacherous.

Willa breaks the silence and my circuitous and fearful ruminations. "I think we should let this go for now. Remember what you said?"

"What? I've said a lot of things."

"You said, you trust me."

"I do," I say softly as I nod my head. I want to talk about this but clearly my sister has made some kind of promise to her husband. Clearly, they have a plan and I have no idea what that is or what part I will be asked to play in it. Perhaps, my role is to just get out of the way.

"Then let's get some sleep. Tomorrow will be here before we know it and God only knows how all of this will unfold."

We take our empty wine glasses back into the kitchen. I wait in silence as Willa washes them and puts them upside down on a clean towel to dry. Then she checks the lock on the door one more time before we head upstairs for bed.

Willa finds me a new toothbrush, a washcloth and towel, and one of her flannel nightgowns. "Sexy," I say as I hold it up to myself in the mirror.

She laughs, "Elias and I have been married for twelve years, we have two kids, and sometimes all I want at the end of the day is to be warm and to be left alone to sleep."

"When all this is over, I'm going to make you something sexy." I lean in and kiss her on the cheek.

"Won't Elias be surprised," she laughs as we head off to our own beds.

The house is quiet as I crawl beneath the covers. My mind will not rest as I toss and turn and try to figure out what is being planned. The outside lights go on. Someone or something has set off the motion detectors over by the man cave. I go to the windows and look out. To my great relief it is only a herd of deer grazing on the low-lying branches. I get back into the still warm bed and pull up the quilts as the list of questions runs on through my head. Where is Elias tonight that he couldn't get home to be with his wife and daughters on the day our grandmother has died? What is Elias up to? Is he working for Pop or against him? Who is he meeting with tonight? Clearly, Willa has agreed that she and I and their girls will not attend the post-funeral gathering. Something is afoot, this I know it like I know my own name. I feel a little cowardly, but also impotent to help in any meaningful way. Willa asked me, more than once to trust her. Perhaps this is the most important thing for me to do right now. Just don't mess things up.

Chapter 27

The first rays of the morning sun stream into the eastern facing window. It takes me a moment to figure out just where I am. I'm at Willa's. I shield my eyes with my forearm as the sun gleams off the icicles that hang from the eaves and cover the windows. The stand of hardwoods is still bare and it will be at least another month before they even begin to show any buds. The smell of coffee and bacon waft up from downstairs. I reach for my phone to check the time. It's still before seven. Bits and pieces of yesterday slowly invade my consciousness.

Elias must be home.

Gram is to be buried this morning.

And then what?

I look in the closet for a bathrobe, but there isn't one. This morning I'm glad for Willa's old flannel nightgown as I pull on the same wool socks I wore yesterday. Only two weeks ago I could have asked my grandmother to darn the toe, but now she's gone. My big toe threatens to push through the nearly thread bare toe of this hand knit sock. I guess I'll have to do that for myself. God knows Gram taught me well enough. I smile at the memory of sitting with her on winter evenings when I was growing up, both of us working through her mending basket. Gram was always checking my work and making me re-do anything that didn't quite measure up.

I hurry down to the kitchen hoping to catch Willa and Elias, before the girls get up. Maybe I can get some more information about what to expect today.

But it is not to be. All four of them have already gathered around the kitchen table for breakfast.

"Good morning, sleepyhead," Heidi calls to me before I reach the bottom step.

"Sleepyhead? It's not even seven o'clock," I protest as I step into the kitchen.

Willa smiles and hands me a cup of coffee. "You forget we country folk get up with the sun."

"Oh, I haven't forgotten, no one around here will let me," I say as I give Tilly's blonde hair an affectionate tousle. She looks up at me with her big blue eyes and gives me a smile that warms my heart. I might need to re-think my position on motherhood. But not today, today there are so many other things to concern myself with.

"Girls, you need to finish your breakfast and spend a little time with your studies before we go into town for Great Gramma's funeral. I've laid the clothes I want you to wear out on your beds," Willa says as her husband passes me a bowl heaping with steaming hot scrambled eggs.

"You better eat something Emma, you look like you're wasting away to nothing," Elias says as a look of concern passes across his face.

It is the first time that I've even considered how the stress of my homecoming might be wearing on me. "Thanks," I say as I help myself to the morning's offerings. There is so much I want to ask Elias, but now is not the time.

"Will you lovely ladies excuse me? I've been on the road since well before dawn and I could use a shower and a short nap before we meet with the good Reverend Winters. What time do you want to leave here, Willa?"

"I was thinking no later than 9:30. Does that work for you?"

"Sounds good."

"You'll ride out to the cemetery with us, won't you Emma?"

"Thanks, that would be great. I should head back to my cabin and see if I can pull together something to wear. I hadn't exactly packed with the intention of attending a graveside service at the end of March here in the north woods."

"The good news is the sun is out this morning and I'm fairly certain Reverend Winters is going to keep his prayers and comments brief. Still if you want to borrow anything of mine you are more than welcome to," Willa says.

"Thanks, let me see what I can pull together. Mind if I shower and use the bathroom before I head back to the cabin?"

"Go ahead. You can use the girls' bathroom, they both bathed last night."

I finish my breakfast, then rinse my plate. Standing beside me at the sink Willa whispers in my ear, "*This* is going to be okay."

"I just wish I knew what *this* is," I whisper back. My sister smiles at me with one of her closed lip smiles. Her message is clear, she has nothing else to say about the matter.

I head up the stairs and go directly into the girls' bathroom. I run the shower for a few minutes as I wait for it to get nice and hot before getting in. I should have thought about asking Willa for some shampoo and conditioner, but I suppose no one will care if my hair smells like a fruit salad. The only shampoo and conditioner here inside the tub and shower combo are something Willa has bought for her daughters.

231

As I stand beneath the flow of hot water and wash myself, I can't help but think about how far my father and his co-conspirators have fallen. At least from any sense of morality that I embrace. How is it that people can have such different ideas about what is *right* and what is *wrong*? And dear God, what will become of him if these people actually execute this ill-begotten plan of theirs? Are my brothers and Becca equally culpable?

I think my father is an arrogant, illiterate ass so much of the time. We rarely agree on anything, but he is still my father. How can I keep quiet when so much is at stake? And still I have given my word to Willa, and by proxy to her husband, Elias. I have promised to stay out of the way and allow *their* plan to unfold.

The temperature of the water goes from hot to cool very quickly, breaking through these fears of holy terror that will not let me be. I can't turn the water off fast enough and with a shiver, I step from the shower and wrap myself in the towel Willa had left out for me only last night.

If only I knew what they were planning, maybe then I could find some peace of mind. If I knew I was on the right side of this. There are no good solutions to any of this. We are caught choosing between competing loyalties and the lesser of two evils. Perhaps this is what is meant by an ethical dilemma.

I blow dry my hair and rub some baby lotion over my parched and flaky skin. Life in the north. I re-dress quickly in Willa's flannel nightgown, I'll just wear my old ski jacket over her nightie and run back to the cabin.

"Are you sure you don't want to borrow something," Willa asks as she sees me pulling on my boots and prepping for the walk back to my cabin.

"I'm good. It's not like we're heading to St. Patrick's Cathedral in Manhattan or for an audience with the Pope."

She laughs as I head out.

The sun is still out but it's cold as the breeze blows up the flannel nightgown and chills my bare legs. My cabin is unlocked, just as I had left it. The fire has long since gone out. I debate starting another as I have just showered and I don't really want to get soot on my hands. I find an old pair of garden gloves in the bushel basket beside the old pie safe. There is no way I can even begin to think about getting changed now, it's just too cold.

I pull on the gloves and start the fire. Then wrap myself in the old Hudson Bay blanket with its multicolored stripes and sit in the old hickory rocker near the fire while I wait for the room to warm up.

I check the time, it's already 8:30 and we will be leaving in an hour. It won't take me very long to dress, so I open up my laptop to see what is happening in the outside world.

My news feed is full of dire news of the pandemic, citing the number of new cases by country, state, and county followed by the number of people who have died. Another slew of articles feature photographs of those protesting the closing of all non-essential businesses, and the mandates to stay at home. There is even a video of an older woman screaming into the television news camera about her inability to get her hair colored and her urgent need for a pedicure. Poor dear, she does look like the wrath of God. Maybe a trip to the spa would help this poor deranged soul. God knows it couldn't hurt, *if only it was all about her,* as she so sadly believes.

I flip over to Facebook and sign in under my alias, *Quest18*. I look at my friends list. I have 22 new friends and almost as many new friend requests. All of this activity has taken place in the last day and a half. Nearly all of these people appear to men, or teenage boys. But then again, as I click on their profiles it is clear many are also using fictitious names and profile pictures. It's hard to know who of my new Facebook friends might be among the *real and true believers* and who might also be here just trying to gather information as I have been. The realization that I have stepped into something very, very dangerous causes me to shudder and for a moment I consider hitting the delete key and taking down my profile. But I pause a moment, before acting on my better instincts. I'm just too curious. I want to see if there is anything in my feed mentioning the armed militias heading to the state capitals tomorrow. I'd love to know what these people are planning. Willa and Elias seem to know, but they are not talking about it. My father, my brothers, and Becca and her boyfriend are up to something. I don't like being in the dark. One profile after another says 'follow me on *Tor.*'

Cassie told me to download *Tor* if I wanted to access the dark web, but I have not done that. I have been too afraid.

A horn blasts in the driveway. Oh shit. I look at my phone, it's only 9:20. We weren't supposed to leave here for another ten minutes and I'm not dressed yet. I close the cover of my computer and hasten to the bedroom. I pull on a pair of yoga pants and a black sweater. Not exactly appropriate for a funeral. There hanging in the armoire is a long black taffeta skirt. I don't know where this came from but I suspect my mother hung it here last night, just in case I needed something to wear. I pull it on over my yoga pants and then my skirt which is long enough and pretty much covers my snow boots. I cringe when I think about wearing my red puffy ski jacket with a taffeta skirt. It might work on the streets of SoHo, but not here and not today. Then I find Gram's old velvet cape that she has worn for Christmas Eve services for as long as I can remember. It, too, hangs in the armoire. I pull it on just as Willa pounds on the door to let me know again that everyone is waiting for me.

"Sorry, I thought you said 9:30," I say as I step outside closing the door behind me.

"My husband is impatient. He hates being late for anything." Willa slips her arm through mine as the sidewalk is still covered with ice. "You clean up pretty good little sister," Willa says.

"Leave it to Mom to be sure I have something appropriate to wear to church, or at least to this abbreviated graveside service," I say as I climb into the back seat of Elias' SUV.

"I think Gram would like it that you're wearing her velvet cape. It suits you," Willa says as I tuck the many yards of the luxurious fabric around myself being certain it is all inside before I close the car door.

"You look glamorous Aunt Emma," Heidi says, unable to keep the surprise from her voice while Tilly sits beside me petting the folds of velvet with her little fingers.

"Sorry I didn't get the car washed," Elias says. The car is covered with the lingering residue of road salt and sand, just like every other car that had been out on these icy mountain roads.

"You only got home this morning, dear, it's okay," Willa reassures him.

"I thought about going to the car wash this morning, but decided I needed the sleep more."

"In this weather? The locks would probably freeze and then we might've been stranded at the cemetery."

"Maybe that would be preferable," Elias mutters under his breath as he grips the steering wheel with both hands. Willa reaches out and puts her hand on her husband's thigh. No words are needed, this is a gesture of solidarity.

By the time we drive into town there are a few other cars already parked around the circular drive in the cemetery. A green canopy has been erected over the grave site. The canvas blows and flutters on this windy morning and I can't help but worry that the whole thing might become airborne before we get Gram's ashes safely interned in the earth beside Grand Pappa.

Reverend Winters, wears his mask as he makes his way over to my father's car. They exchange a few words and I see everyone begin to put their masks on. I'm very glad I made enough masks so at least everyone in the immediate family has one as it appears that Reverend Winters is insisting they be worn during the service. Willa passes out the ones I've made for her family, then I help the girls get theirs on.

"I like the one Tilly is wearing better, why does she get to wear the pink one. It matches my coat," Heidi complains and for once Tilly does not acquiesce to her older sister's demands. Heidi pouts, as she adjusts the black cotton mask so her nose is sticking out.

"That mask will not protect you or anyone else if you don't cover both your nose and your mouth," my sister says to her eldest daughter.

"I can't breathe with this thing on," Heidi grumbles.

"Come on now sweetheart, this will not last very long," Elias says as we all exit the car. Willa takes Tilly by the hand and Elias put his arm around Heidi as we trudge through the graveyard to our family plot.

Becca, Josiah, and Lucas are already standing beneath the tent when we arrive. Becca's nose is also free of the mask and she looks irritated that she has been asked to wear one. Lucas looks wan and grey in the morning light. I'm sure he would like nothing better than to go back to bed. I can't help but wonder if he is here of his own free will or if he's just doing what is expected of him in spite of his recent hospitalization. His mask is secured tightly around both his nose and mouth as he turns his head to cough into his elbow. His cough is both deep and rattling, and he appears to still be short of breath even once his coughing jag is under control.

Josiah extends his hand to Elias. They shake hands but no words are exchanged. I can't help but wonder if Josiah is just being friendly because he and Elias are brothers-in-law or is it because they are both Pop's errand boys. Or could it be something else?

Pop walks down the hill to the tent, even today he walks two steps in front of our mother. He's just as inconsiderate as always. Josiah goes to meet her and takes Mom by the arm. He escorts her beneath the tent where we all have gathered.

It is just about ten o'clock when a long line of cars, SUVs, and pickup trucks begin to arrive and park along the circular drive.

"Don't worry Rev, I told them they could come and pay their last respects as long as they didn't come down to the gravesite. They promised to stay up on the circular drive," Pop says in an effort to alleviate the minister's concerns.

The minister nods but looks displeased as he watches all these men dressed in their everyday work clothes, Carhart jackets and overalls, and more than a few of those guys are wearing those red ball caps. I don't need to be any closer to know their hats are embossed with the letters MAGA— these guys are Trumpers . They are hell bent on *Making America Great Again.*

The men stand beside their cars with their arms behind their backs. One man holds an American Flag as if my grandmother was some kind of war hero and they are the color guard. I spot the sheriff's SUV as it has the large blue and gold county logo on the door. I don't know if it is the sheriff or one of his deputies. But I do know this—they are all in on it, as thick as thieves.

It's hard to estimate how many people are here. It's mostly men, but there are also some women. No one wears a mask. There must be one hundred people, give or take. Did they even know my grandmother? Gram lived a quiet life, one centered around her family, her church, and her community. Who are these people?

The weather is starting to change and now a dark cloud covers the sun. The wind blows violently, and tree limbs crack and falls. One man plays the bagpipes and another one up there with the others in the circular drive, begins to sing *Amazing Grace*. He has a loud, deep, and resonant voice. It isn't long before everyone is joining in. The voices get carried by the wind, the tune is recognizable even if the words are carried away and lost to the wind. Everyone here knows the words, we have all sung this song so many times, and the sentiment stirs my heart.

I start to cry as Reverend Winters begins, "Dearly Beloved…"

Lost in my own grief and personal memories of my grandmother, I have no remembrance of anything the minister says until my father clears his throat loudly. Pop is getting choked up and visibly struggling not to display any emotion. He straightens his shoulders as he steps forward holding the antique wooden box embellished with a gilded bird which holds my grandmother's ashes. He reverently sets the box onto a wooden tray that will be lowered into her grave.

Once my father steps back, the minister continues. "Remember man that thou art dust and unto dust thou shall return."

And then a howling wind blows and the now darkened skies open up as if somehow my grandmother is expressing her displeasure about something.

We all bow our heads and say, "Amen," in unison. Then as if on cue we all turn and head back up the hill to our cars to avoid getting soaked in the freezing rain.

The procession of cars heads out of the cemetery and turns north on State Route 28 back to the family compound. We travel on in silence. Even my little nieces seem to understand that neither their parents nor I are in any mood to talk. I feel conflicted and confused as I had built up an image of these men, that my father and brothers have been helping to arm, as rough and coarse.

What was it that Hillary Clinton called them during her run for President against Donald Trump, 'a basket full of deplorables'? I think that is what she said. I remember being in full agreement with her at the time. But these people who came today, these men who carried the American Flag and stood at attention on this cold and blustery morning and sang *Amazing Grace* as a tribute to my grandmother, there was nothing *deplorable* here today. These people believe they are good Christians who are trying to honor my grandmother, my father, and my family. They believe they are performing a sacred duty, the moral obligation to honor and bury the dead, and to protect a way of life that they believe is at risk.

How is it that well-meaning people can look at the same problems and come to such different conclusions about how to rectify the wrongs?

Chapter 28

We pull into the driveway and there are already so many cars here. I see a cadre of church ladies carrying baskets and platters of food out the front door of the house and out into the woods. They are all lined up as if in a parade.

"Looks like the funeral repast your father has planned is going to be held in the bunker," Elias says as more and more cars and pickups pull in, they park bumper to bumper along the length of our long driveway. "If all the people at the cemetery come back to the house, there's no doubt the line of cars will be all the way out along Browns Tract Road as well."

"Can we go to the party, Daddy?" Tilly asks.

"No darling. There will be too many people there today and I don't want any of you getting sick. He looks about the car as if including me and Willa in this decree. Now head on inside and wash your hands. I bet your mama and Auntie Emma will be happy to make you something for lunch." The girls groan with disappointment. "Maybe you two would like to go downstairs and watch a couple of movies and have some popcorn this afternoon."

The girls erupt into cheers as their father brings their SUV to a stop in front of the house where we all disembark and go directly into the house. Clearly, Elias and Willa have well-choreographed every step of their plan.

"Go wash your hands and change your clothes," my sister calls after her daughters.

I start to head back to my cabin to change my clothes when Elias gives me a fleeting scowl and shakes his head ever so slightly. It's almost imperceptible, but I receive the message loud and clear—he does not want me to go back to the cabin.

"Emma come with me," Willa says. "I've got a new sweatshirt from the Old Forge Hardware Store and a pair of sweatpants you can borrow."

I change direction mid-stride and follow my sister and her husband back into their house. The girls can be heard giggling upstairs as they debate which movie to watch first. Once I'm inside, Elias turns and locks the door behind me.

Oh God, what is happening?

I follow Willa upstairs and see that she had already laid out a sweatshirt and a pair of sweatpants on the bed in the guestroom. She must have done this before we'd even left for the funeral. I change quickly, putting the old taffeta skirt and Gram's velvet cape on hangers in the closet. I'm still chilled from our brief outing at the cemetery, so I leave my yoga pants on as they can also function as long underwear as the weather has turned foul and I'm freezing. I head back downstairs to help my sister with the lunch as clearly this is all part of the plan.

Elias can be heard downstairs with the girls as he settles them in front of the television and they negotiate their selections on Netflix. In the kitchen, Willa silently makes a box of Kraft Macaroni and Cheese. I'm surprised as I've never known my sister to feed her girls anything like this before. My sister is in the running for *Mother of the Year,* selecting only organic this and organic that, and always only the best will do for her girls.

Next, she brings a two-liter bottle of Coca-Cola from deep within her pantry and pours two coffee cups full.

"Really?" I say as I can't believe my eyes when she reaches into the front pocket of the hoodie sweatshirt she wears and brings out a bottle of children's *Benadryl* and sets it on the kitchen counter. "What are you doing?"

"Benadryl is the active ingredient in Tylenol PM," she says as if this is the answer to the question I have just asked. "They don't need the Tylenol but I do need them to sleep. If I mix it in the Coke, I know they'll drink every last drop and they'll both be sound asleep in thirty minutes, maybe less." My sister takes out a measuring spoon and measures one and a half teaspoons into the blue mug and three teaspoons into the green one.

"I don't understand…" I say as I can't believe Willa is drugging her own daughters.

"I need my girls to sleep and stay asleep." Willa's voice starts to crack as she swallows hard before continuing. She whispers and her words come out in a rush as if time is of the essence. "I need to be certain they stay safe downstairs. I can't risk having them waking up. I fear what will go down here today. I won't put them in danger. If they witness any of this, they will be terrified at the very least."

I nod my head as if I understand. But I do not. I know my sister and she would never willingly put her children in *any* sort of danger. Perhaps this, too, is another one of those ethical dilemmas, where Willa has been forced to choose between the lesser of two evils.

She scoops the orange mac and cheese into two soup bowls then puts both bowls on a tray along with forks, napkins and the two coffee cups filled with the Benadryl-laced Coca-Cola. "Tilly gets the blue mug and Heidi gets the green one." Willa says this out loud as if she is reminding herself so she won't inadvertently mix them up. "See you in a minute." She picks up the tray and goes to join her husband and her children in the lower level.

I start the washing up as I wonder if I have enough time to run back to the cabin to grab my computer. Before I have finished the dishes, I see Elias has just come up the stairs. The voice of some Disney princess wafts up the stairs behind him when he turns and closes the door to the lower level. Then he turns the latch and locks his family in. "Willa will come up once the girls are asleep. It should only take twenty to thirty minutes. You'll need to unlock the door when you hear her knock. Then she will lock the girls back in." His words and his tone do not invite questions and I know I'm being asked to do as I'm told. His usual light-hearted demeanor is gone. I have never seen him look so serious.

I won't be going anywhere.

Elias takes the stairs two at a time toward the bedrooms and when returns to the kitchen a minute or two later he carries a backpack. Without a word to me, he heads to the mudroom as I watch him put on his coat and boots. He puts his right foot up on the bench to tie his boot when I see he has some kind of a leather holster and a gun strapped just above his ankle.

Against my better judgment I press him for some scrap of information. "Elias, please …" Is all that I can say, for I cannot even form a question.

"Emma…" the moment hangs there as Elias tries to decide what to say and I wait for some explanation. "We are on the right side of this issue. In time all will be revealed. Now stay inside and away from the windows. I'm trusting you to keep my family and yourself safe. Tell Willa and my girls I love them."

I am too choked up to speak. All I can do is nod my head.

"Lock the door behind me," Elias says as he steps outside and closes the door.

I do as I'm told. Once the door is locked, I fall to my knees, right there in the mudroom amongst the dirty boots, ski jackets, discarded hats, and mismatched mittens. I pray to the God of my childhood for his protection.

My prayers are borne out of fear, they are nebulous and unformed, as all I know is that we are in the midst of some serious shit. I have no idea what I need or how to obtain it.

Chapter 29

While still on my knees amidst the dishevelment of the mud room, I hear a soft knock on the interior door leading up from the lower level. I jump to my feet so Willa will not feel the need to knock again. I turn the latch and there in the shadows is my sister with her tear stained face.

I take one step back as she steps into the kitchen. She turns to re-lock the door behind her. I open my arms to embrace her as she trembles with fear.

Now it is my turn to try and to reassure my sister. It is her husband who is willingly stepping into harm's way because of some hare-brained scheme our ignorant father has brought him into.

"The girls are sound asleep," Willa says as she gives me another one of her close-lipped smiles.

I nod. "Do you want to talk about this?" I ask, hopeful that she might.

Willa just shakes her head no and the silence grows between us. At last she says, "I don't trust myself enough to know where to start or how much to divulge. I fear the more you know, the more dangerous it may be for you."

"Given that I have no idea what you are talking about, I'm hardly in a position to argue."

Willa nods her head. "How about I make us some lunch," she offers.

"Okay, but I think I'll pass on the Kraft Mac and Cheese."

"How about a Coke?" she says and we both laugh as I shake my head.

"I will have a cup of tea if you want to put the kettle on. Want me to make a fire?" I ask trying to think of something I might do to feel useful.

Willa nods and I head into the family room to lay the fire. There is a big picture window on the opposite wall that overlooks the woods to the north. The room is cold and I consider pulling the drapes. The sky is a steel gray and it is snowing again. The wind howls. I hear some of the ice laden branches from last night's ice storm are starting to crack and break. Then a branch falls with a crash in the yard around the house. I look up when something out in the woods catches my eye. I stand there, stone-still for another moment quite uncertain that I've seen anything at all. Then there it is again. Someone is moving through the woods, and then there is another, and another. They move through the shadows, nearly obscured by the blowing snow. They move from behind one tree to the next tree, all the while heading north towards *the bunker*. I have seen this kind of thing before, but where? Maybe in the movies or on TV. Then it dawns on me that they move like a SWAT team.

I hide for a moment behind the drapes as I try to still the panic and figure out what to do next.

I leave the fire unlit and go to join Willa in the kitchen.

Before I can tell Willa what I've just seen, there are three rapid knocks on the door to the mudroom. Willa and I stand stock still not knowing what to do next. Elias made it perfectly clear— we are to stay inside and not let anyone in.

"Girls, it's me. Please let me in."

It's Mom. Is she alone? There is an urgency in her voice and she sounds terrified. We take just a moment to look at one another, before we rush to the door. There is no way we are going to leave our mother outside when the whole property is being invaded and surrounded. But by whom?

I have no idea.

Willa quickly opens the door and grabs our mother by the arm and pulls her inside. Mom doesn't wear a coat and her long white hair is windswept and tangled. She looks a fright. I lock the door behind them. Mom takes off her boots, then goes directly to the living room without offering any explanation. She pulls the thick velvet drapes so they are completely closed over the picture window.

"Emma, could you get a fire going in the fireplace?" Mom asks. I go to complete the task I had set out to do only moments before.

The kettle whistles and Willa pours the boiling water into the teapot she had just prepared. She sets the steaming pot on the tray with the milk and sugar before adding another cup for our mother. "This may be a long afternoon…" Willa says as she carries the tea service into the family room.

Mom takes a seat on the couch in front of the fire that has only just begun to catch and burn. Mom is trembling. Is it the cold or fear? I do not know. The cold I can do something about. The fire catches quickly as the wood is dry and aged. I take the blanket from the back of the arm chair and wrap my mother in it. Today she looks so small and frail. She, too, is afraid.

In this moment, I know I must step into my own adulthood. It is my turn to protect my mother.

Willa sits on the ottoman in front of our mother and holds her hands while the Earl Grey steeps in the teapot beside her. The aroma of oil of bergamot mixes with the scent of burning ash from the fireplace contradicting the angst and anxiety that fill the room.

The silence is deafening and I feel like I'm the only one who does not know what is going on. When it is obvious that no one intends to tell me anything, I start to voice the questions I need answers to. "One of you needs to tell me what the hell is going on?"

They look at each other and neither of them speak.

"Okay, let's start with this: Who are those people sneaking through the woods? It looks like some kind of a SWAT team."

Mom and Willa exchange a look and I now know— our mother is in on this. I sit and wait as they try to decide who is going to tell me and how forthcoming they intend to be.

"You might as well tell me, because in a matter of minutes or hours or perhaps even days it is all going to come out. I would like to believe that you trust me with the truth rather than continue to treat me like a child."

Mom starts, "It is not that we don't trust you Emma." This is as much as she can say before we hear the sound of gunfire. There have been people hunting deer in these woods for as long as I can remember. There is no doubt in my mind that this is what I've heard and it is close, too close.

And then there is the distorted voice of some man speaking into a bullhorn. "This is the FBI…" he says as his voice is amplified to a shout.

"The FBI?" I say looking to my older sister and my mother for some kind of an explanation.

I stand and go to the window to look out when Willa shouts, "Emma sit down. This could be a bloodbath. Pop's militia is heavily armed. They've been moving much of their auxiliary armaments into the bunker over the last few days."

"And now they have enough food to hold out in there for days."

"Are the church ladies still out there?" I ask as the last time I saw them they were delivering the food.

Mom shrugs her shoulders indicating she doesn't know for certain.

I return to my chair in front of the fire. "Back up, why is the FBI involved?"

"Do you remember that list of governors you found in Pop's planner?" Willa asks.

I nod my head hoping she will continue. "The Feds are here because this scheme of theirs crosses state lines and jurisdictions. Pop and his cronies are part of a national white supremacist organization. Or more aptly put they're involved with a consortium of domestic terrorists."

None of this surprises me, given the snooping around I've been doing and what I've learned through my research on the internet. I nod my head encouraging one or both of them to continue.

Willa takes a deep breath and says, "They've been planning to kidnap all the governors who have openly criticized Donald Trump's handling of the pandemic, and then put them on trial in some kind of kangaroo court for being *un-American*."

"And just who is to be the judge and the jury? Who will decide what it means to be un-American? Hopefully, not our father. He couldn't even bother to get his lazy ass down to the high school to vote in the last umpteenth elections."

My mother looks like she might cry.

"Sorry Mom, but I have kept quiet for far too long as he has spread so much animosity and hatred for anyone and everyone who sees the world differently than he does. And now it has come to this. Now all the lies and bigotry have driven him and his fellow *patriots* to plan an attack on our democratically elected leaders. He has put our family, and innocent members of our church, and community at risk. For God's sake the FBI is here, armed, and raiding our home. Pop has gone too far. He and all of his hateful rhetoric has put us all at risk."

"Oh, my darling girl, you have nothing to apologize for. It is not that I don't agree with you, Emma. I'm the one who should be apologizing to you, both of you. For too long, far too long, I thought my best course of action was not to upset your father and just try to get along for the sake of the family." Now Mom is sobbing. Remorse and regret fill the space between us. Willa and I do our best to comfort our mother while offering quiet words of reassurance and something resembling forgiveness. Mom hasn't finished. She tries to catch her breath. "I've been too weak and too afraid of him to do what I've known was right. I should have left him long ago. I was just trying to protect my children and keep our family together."

Willa and I wrap our arms around our mother as her grief and regret threatens to overwhelm her, and us too.

The sound of police sirens can be heard in the distance and I wonder how many armed officers are coming up the road and who they are here to assist? Trump and the patriots have given lip-service to being pro-police. That doesn't mean that everyone who protests the policies of Donald Trump and the antics of the alt-right is anti-police, as the right has tried to paint the rest of us. I take a deep breath and try to remember that there was a time when the police were considered to be the *good guys,* at least by most people I know. I'm sure many of them are just that, if not most of them. A few trigger-happy racists have tainted the public's perception of everyone who wears the uniform and that seems grossly unfair.

The sirens are growing louder as the police cars get closer to our camp. They are coming here. Then ferociously barking dogs can be heard from the direction of the bunker and I wonder if the barking is from Bullet and Trigger or from some K-9 unit the police have brought with them.

Before I can even conjure up an image of the dogs, another round of gunfire rings out and almost simultaneously it is returned.

Mom stills. Then both she and Willa drop to their knees and start to pray. Willa prays for her husband and Mom for her children, as Josiah, Lucas, and Becca are out there somewhere. But do either of them pray for Pop? We sit in the silence, waiting and listening. But for what?

I'm too afraid to even imagine what might be happening just beyond our locked doors. Will this be another Waco, Texas? I saw that movie. Will this be a long drawn out stalemate or a bloodbath? Does my father play the role of David Koresh, the self-appointed messiah? Are my brothers and sister, my brother-in-law, the church ladies, and all of Pop's other followers destined to become cannon fodder for the Feds? I shudder when I contemplate my role in all of this. I should never have come home, I should have just stayed in the city and taken my chances with the virus.

I bury my head in my hands and I, too, begin to pray. Words elude me. What outcome am I even praying for? The only prayer I can come up with is-– please help us.

Again, there is the sound of rapid-fire gunfire and then the cries and howls of agony are carried on the winds.

Something has just happened.

Mom, Willa, and I sit as still as stones and listen, just listen.

Chapter 30

An alarm goes off on Willa's phone and we all startle. Then Willa gets to her feet.

"What?" I ask, clearly, she is distressed about something.

"I need to check on my girls. I need to be certain they're okay and still sleeping."

"How long do you expect them to sleep?"

"Somewhere between eight and twelve hours," she says. "Elias is going to call me if we need to evacuate and get them out of here."

"How the hell are we going to do that?" I ask.

"The girls may be too groggy to walk by themselves, or they might be totally out of it. You and I might need to carry them out and put them in the back of the SUV. I've already put some old quilts and pillows back there."

Mom just nods. Clearly, she has been privy to the plan, where I have not.

"Where will we go?" I ask hoping to be brought up to speed on the evacuation plan.

"We didn't get that far…" Willa's voice trails off for a moment as we consider where we might go, and where we might be safe. "We're just supposed to get away from here. I guess we'll figure that out if and when we need to."

Only hours ago, my sister asked me to trust her. Perhaps I had been naïve, too naïve, to believe that she and Elias had a plan. But a plan for what? Surely if an emergency evacuation was called for, then a destination or rendezvous point would have been part of a plan, at least any well-conceived plan.

My anxiety is mounting as I begin to pace and Willa disappears into the lower level.

To my great relief she returns momentarily. "They are still sound asleep and drooling on their pillows," she says with a smile. Just seeing them resting quietly seems to have eased her anxiety, at least for now. What would we have done in the midst of all this craziness if one of the girls was unwell due to the medication I helped their mother administer. I bow my head and say a prayer of thanks to whoever it is that might be capable of reading my thoughts. I would never forgive myself if something happened to either of the girls.

Willa looks again at her phone hoping for some word from her husband, but there is nothing. Willa paces between the living room and the kitchen, unable to settle. "I don't know how much longer I can take this. I feel like I've been left totally in the dark not knowing what is going on."

I want to say, *welcome to my world,* but instead, I say, "I'd rather be here in the dark, than out there with the rest of them. God only knows what kind of horror they are being subjected to." I regret speaking as soon as the words leave my mouth. I'd tried to put a positive spin on the waiting and not knowing and instead I stepped right into my mother and sister's anxiety and worry, only making things worse.

They both turn and look at me, straight-faced and solemn. But their collective gaze is like a laser and it burns right through me and fills me with regret. I have given voice to their fears.

Neither one says a word as I mutter, "Sorry," and drop my head in shame.

We do not have to wait long before Willa's phone starts to buzz indicating she has a text.

I check my own phone for the time, it's just after 3:00. This has already been a very long afternoon.

Again, Willa's phone dings indicating that she has another incoming text message. Collectively, we hold our breath as Willa reads her messages.

"They've evacuated the bunker and the FBI is making arrests. No fatalities or serious injuries. Elias will be over as soon as he can to give us the details."

"Thank God," I say, as both Mom and Willa nod their heads in agreement.

"Did he say anything about your father? Or Josiah, Lucas or Becca?" Mom pleads for some information.

"No. I'm sorry Mom. Just that there were no fatalities or serious injuries, I guess we can take some comfort in that…"

Mom closes her eyes and again nods her head to acknowledge the truth of Willa's words.

We sit there on the couch in silence, each of us trying to take in the news in our own way. I offer up a prayer of gratitude to the Almighty *that* … I am at a loss for words.

That what? No one died. Let's start with that.

An awareness begins to take root within me, although I grew up in a *Christian home* and we always went to church, I haven't been to church in a long time or really even prayed for years. I seem to have forgotten how. Yet in the midst of all this chaos and terror, in all of my ineptitude and helplessness, I find myself reaching out to the God of my childhood. Yet, somehow the rote prayers of my childhood don't seem to cover the drama and trauma in my family and certainly don't fit the situation I find myself in now.

And then it comes to me like a download, somewhere out of the ethers— maybe the prayers are different, but God is the same. Always present and always the same.

Willa is the first one to break the silence. As she gets to her feet. "Let us do what women have always done, during times of tragedy."

I look at her, perplexed as I have no idea what she is talking about. Mom gets to her feet and offers both of us a smile. Apparently, she knows what Willa is talking about, even if I do not.

"Cook," Willa says as she leads the way to the kitchen as Mom follows.

I stand and follow my mother and my sister into the kitchen. "Oh, what the hell," I mutter beneath my breath.

Willa is the first at the sink to wash her hands, while Mom and I wait our turn to do the same. The snow has slowed to light flurries and through the kitchen window we can see there is a big white truck parked beside the garage. The lights are on in the garage and Pop's man cave. Willa pulls a pair of binoculars from a drawer beside the sink.

"Most people keep their dish towels close at hand," I say and Willa laughs.

"I like to watch the birds at the feeder." She fabricates a little lie as her feeder is outside the other window by the kitchen table. She, too, has been keeping an eye on Pop and his associates. I decide to let it go.

The vehicle is painted with the letters ATF. They are big and bold, and I can see them from here without binoculars. "I can't read the rest of it."

"It says, United States Department of Justice. Explosive and Fire Investigation. National Response Team."

"Holy shit," I say.

"Shit is not holy," my mother and sister say in unison as they quote Gram. A laugh breaks the tension at least momentarily.

As we stand there and watch, we see teams of men and women dressed in dark clothing with the letters ATF emblazoned in gold letters on the back of their jackets. They are heading towards the backdoor of the garage. They carry out wooden boxes of what I can only assume are firearms and the equipment used in the manufacturing of those ghost guns. Others appear to be clearing out the office as they carry the desktop computer and an assortment of file boxes.

"Pop's in trouble," I say, stating the obvious.

"Trouble of his own making," Mom replies.

We all stand there glued to the window when at least ten large black and white vehicles back down the long driveway as they skillfully negotiate the snow-covered lane and all the cars and pickups already parked there. These big trucks effectively block anyone else from driving in or out. The last two vehicles park closest to the road— they are ambulances and the sirens are turned off but their emergency lights remain engaged.

They must have brought the injured out another way. Within fifteen minutes or so both ambulances turn their sirens on and pull out of the driveway. The closest hospital is in Utica and that's at least an hour's drive on a night like this.

Elias said there were no fatalities, but that doesn't mean someone might not make it to the hospital. It happens too often up here in the

Adirondacks. Usually it's a drunk snowmobiler traveling too fast on his sled and hits a tree. "I suppose if someone was badly hurt they would've airlifted them out of here and I haven't heard a helicopter," I say as the three of us peer out the kitchen window.

Willa's words resound in my head. Elias said, there were no serious injuries. But clearly something was serious enough for there are two ambulances en route to the hospital with both lights and sirens engaged.

It isn't long after the injured are evacuated that we hear angry voices peppered with profanity coming from the north woods. And then we see a group of people, there are somewhere between ten and fifteen of them, emerging from the woods. They're all dressed in their flannel shirts and jeans or Carhart's, just the typical north country attire. These are the locals, some are still wearing their red MAGA ball caps but they are not dressed for the weather.

"They must have left in a hurry, as no one is wearing a coat," Willa says as we take turns offering a commentary on what is obvious to us all. "Looks like they've been handcuffed," Willa says as she eyes them through her binoculars.

Sure enough.

For a moment, I wonder why they don't run. Most of these guys are hunters and have spent their whole lives in these woods tracking deer or whatever else might be in season. Then I understand their orderly compliance. Two people, each carrying some kind of assault rifle, walk directly behind them. They want to assure that no one tries to make a run for it. These two are dressed in all black, in what I can only describe as riot gear. They wear something that looks like a motorcycle or snowmobile helmet, complete with a face shield. The back of their jackets are emblazoned with the letters— FBI.

The locals are loaded into the waiting police vehicles at gunpoint. Those must be some kind of modern-day paddy wagon. Once the first vehicle is loaded and secured, the next group of handcuffed *patriots* emerge from the woods, also at gunpoint, and the loading is repeated.

"There in the third group of two, the one on the left, in the green flannel shirt and red hat— that's Becca's boyfriend, Rolfe," Willa says as she scopes things out with her binoculars.

"Good riddance to bad garbage," I say and then chastise myself for being snarky. But the truth is that's the way I feel. So much for the recent resurgence of my *Christian* love and compassion for others.

We stand there and watch as we try to identify some of the other men who are being detained and probably arrested until all ten vehicles are fully loaded and ready to go.

Mom starts to pace and goes to make coffee, then she pokes around Willa's pantry for something to bake. "Shall I make some brownies?" she asks.

She's nervous and resorts to old comfort measures. I, too, am filled with angst for we have yet to see Pop, or Elias, Becca, Josiah, or Lucas. I am filled with a sense of impending doom, for I can't help but wonder who was transported in those two ambulances.

Chapter 31

We don't need to wait long before we hear someone knocking at the door and Elias is calling to be let inside. "Willa, it's me. Unlock the door."

Willa bursts into tears as she runs to the mudroom to let her husband in. Mom and I turn away from the doorway to allow them a moment of privacy as Elias holds my sobbing sister in his big strong arms. He nearly carries her through the doorway and into the living room where he sets her, ever so gently, on the sofa in front of the fire. He looks a little bewildered, "Is everything okay here?"

I nod my head. "It is now. We've just been so worried, staying in here, not able to leave, and not knowing anything. We heard the gunshots and the sirens, and then we saw the ambulances and all the government trucks. We didn't know if anyone was hurt."

He nods his head and whispers sweetly to his crying wife, "It's all going to be okay." Willa continues to cry as she buries her head in her husband's shoulder, unable to catch her breath enough to speak.

I can't help but feel a little voyeuristic and intrusive on their tender reunion. However, since I am unable and unwilling to disappear, instead, I try to offer some relevant information to justify my presence. "The girls are still sleeping in the basement. Willa checked on them just a little while ago." As I say this I realize I really have no idea how long ago that was, everything came to a standstill as we waited and waited for some word about something, anything.

Mom stands in the doorway just waiting for someone to acknowledge her and address *her* concerns. When at last she can wait no longer she asks Elias, "Where are the others?" Her voice is just above a whisper and is barely audible above the sound of Willa's weeping.

Elias turns to Mom and me, then unwraps Willa's arms from around his neck before he gently settles his wife beside him on the sofa. Now her crying has become softer and her breathing eases.

I can't help but notice how Elias handles his wife. He is so gentle with her, it is as if Willa is a precious crystal vase, which he dare not risk breaking. Willa is blessed beyond measure to have found such a loving man. I think of my own father and how he treats my mother. The contrast is stark. No doubt my mother is equally aware of the difference.

"Pop was arrested and so was Becca."

"On dear God, no!" Mom cries out.

"They have been taken in by the FBI. They are being transported to the Ray Brook Federal Correctional Facility up near Saranac Lake."

Tears fall from my mother's eyes as she struggles to regain her composure. "Not Becca, she has been nothing but a pawn in this whole thing. This is all Edward's doing. Surely they can see that."

"They will have to go in front of the grand jury. The grand jury will decide if they have enough evidence to charge them and hold them."

"Charge them with what?" I ask.

"Illegal manufacturing of unregistered firearms, gun trafficking across state lines, as well as a long list of federal conspiracy charges," Elias says. His voice resonates with compassion for our mother as he tells her the truth and tries to help her see the reality of what they are facing.

"When will they be coming home?" Mom asks not quite grasping the seriousness of the situation and we can all hear the desperation in her voice.

"I'm sorry Magda. I guess that will depend on what the grand jury decides," Elias says.

"Oh Becca," my mother's cries turn into wails of grief and pain. "What about the boys?"

"Josiah and Lucas have also been taken up to Ray Brook and will be charged. They were little more than gun runners for Pop, maybe they'll be okay."

Mom continues to cry as Willa hands Mom a tissue. I try my best to comfort Mom as Elias explains what we might expect. "Becca's case is a little more complicated as she helped recruit some of the participants, organized the delivery of weapons, and was instrumental in setting things up for the April Fool's Day Rebellion over the internet. The FBI have some pretty solid evidence of her involvement in all eleven states for this April Fool's Day fiasco. She's just lucky Willa and Emma were able to figure out what they were planning before they were able to execute their ill-begotten plans. Had they been successful a lot of people could have been hurt and all of those involved would be looking at a long, and dare I say, well-deserved stint in the federal pen."

"Can you start at the beginning? I don't know about Willa or Mom, but I'm confused about how all of this went down and what role everyone played."

Elias looks at Willa before asking, "You haven't told them?"

"No. Of course not, you asked me not to."

Elias reaches over and hugs his wife. "You can trust this woman. She keeps her promises." He takes a deep breath and then begins, "I had no intention of getting involved in any of Pop's malfeasance no matter how much he tried to emasculate and berate me. So, last night when Pop sent me to deliver some guns in Long Lake and I told you I was going to Lake Placid…"

All three of us nod our heads confirming this is the story we'd been told.

"…well, I didn't go to Long Lake or to Lake Placid, instead I met with the FBI in Albany. While I was there I was able to make contact with Willa and she told me how you…" Elias turns his eyes towards me, "…and Willa had found Pop's planner and figured out what Pop and his co-conspirators were planning. I don't know if I would have been able to convince the feds if Emma hadn't had the forethought to photograph the pages of the planner and if Willa hadn't sent them to me in a text. Anyway, the guns I was supposed to deliver in Long Lake, I gave to the FBI and they were able to match the design and some fingerprints to other weapons that have already been used in other crimes that were committed up here in the Adirondacks. The combination of the guns and the photographs convinced them that Pop and all these other people were up to no good."

His words are gentle and almost childlike as he tries to spare Mom the scope and potential mayhem Pop and Becca were involved in.

I've been too long in this quagmire of uncertainty with no one to talk to and clarify anything. I have so many unanswered questions. I need answers. So, in spite of the voice within that calls for restraint, I blurt out a litany of questions. "What happened when you went out to the bunker? Where are the church ladies? How did the FBI get everyone to leave the bunker when all of the assholes… sorry Mom… were so heavily armed with military grade assault weapons? I was expecting a bloodbath…"

Mom's face is gray and she looks like she is going to throw up, so I decide I'd better shut up.

"One question at a time," Elias says as Mom starts to pant through her mouth. "Are you sure you want to hear all of this Magda?"

Mom nods her head, but does not speak.

"Okay. Pop stood at the entrance to the bunker and only allowed the men to enter. Lucas and some of his buddies took the food, so generously prepared for the funeral luncheon, from the church ladies while they were still outside the bunker door. Pop didn't let any of the women inside."

"Did he think they might be spies?" I ask incredulously, before I realize it could be true.

"If you can figure out what your father is thinking you've got better insight into all of this than I do. Good ole misogynistic Pop, thanked the ladies for the food right there in the middle of the snowstorm and then dismissed them. 'Thank you, ladies. Now, perhaps it would be best if you leave and leave the business of men to the men.' I have to say that most of these women looked just as happy to be heading for home. I think one of the agents must have been keeping an eye on things from somewhere in the woods as the FBI Critical Incident Response Group did not begin their operation or make their presence known until all the ladies had safely gone on their way."

Elias pauses and Mom mutters, "Thanks be to God."

I offer a silent response to my mother's prayer, *Amen, Amen, Amen* as I, too, have known these good women all my life.

"Upon arrival, all of the men were instructed to leave their coats and their guns in the lockers at the entrance of the bunker. It is part of their protocol and is common practice, no guns are allowed in the general meeting area. I guess Pop knows some of these guys can be a bunch of hotheads. And some of the others were not locals and had not been thoroughly vetted. As of late, Pop has been spouting off about his fear that they might be infiltrated by Antifa."

"What's Antifa?" Mom asks.

"Antifa is a left-wing group opposed to fascism and other alt-right extremism," Elias explains.

"Oh, I have heard your father talk about them, he made them sound as if they'd made a pact with the devil."

Elias lets Mom's comment sit for a moment without commenting before he returns to detailing what happened this afternoon. "While the *patriots* were busy filling their plates and eating, I went directly into the bathroom with my backpack. I waited there for what seemed like an eternity before I contacted one of the special agents via a text message. They'd installed a private FBI communication app on my phone last night when I was at their headquarters in Albany. I texted a single asterisk as instructed and that was the signal for someone to release the drone that delivered a canister of teargas down the exhaust pipe for the fireplace. While in the bathroom, I put on the FBI-issued gas mask and face shield that I was given last night. When I emerged from the bathroom I pulled the pin on the smoke bomb they'd given me then mayhem and chaos ensued. These federal agents are well-trained and single-minded. Their plan was perfectly executed, just like they assured me it would be."

Willa, Mom, and I just sit there. Not quite believing all we are hearing.

"How did they get everyone out?"

"As the men were crying and sputtering with anger, federal agents also equipped with gas masks and face shields entered through the back entrance and directed all the patriots outside and into the custody of the ATF and FBI."

"I didn't know there was a second entrance," Willa says.

"Neither did I, "Mom says.

"It was just rudimentary, on the northside of the mountain. Pop had planned to complete it with some of the inheritance he is expecting," Elias confirms. "Josiah said something about it to me while we were loading up the guns for delivery last night."

"Who was taken away by ambulance? What happened to all the others we saw loaded into the trucks?"

"One of our local cops, the guy they call Robo-Cop, was belligerent and pulled his service revolver once he got outside. Apparently, he had not put his weapon in the locker when the others did and no one checked him before he entered the main hall."

"Did he shoot someone?" Willa asked.

"He did." Elias nods his head solemnly.

"That was probably the gunshot we heard."

"You heard that? I guess you would. He started firing randomly into the crowd even though his vision was impaired by the teargas and the smoke bomb. He shot one of the other patriots in the leg. But it could have been worse, so much worse."

"Who was it?" Willa asks.

"Nobody I've ever seen before. Must have been one of the guys from out of the area. They took him to St. E's in Utica by ambulance and with a police escort. I'm sure he'll be charged, just like all the others.

"Anyway, one of the agents tackled Robo-Cop and took away his gun. Robo-Cop started yelling, 'Police brutality!' as he was lying there on the ice-covered snow being hand-cuffed. He didn't stop yelling until one of his fellow patriots told him to 'man up and quit being such a little bitch.' I saw the cop's face as they loaded him into the ambulance. He had a few abrasions on his face, probably from resisting arrest and being held face down on the ice-encrusted snow. I think he'll be okay."

"Do they know you were the informant?" Willa asks. I can see the worry cross her face, but Elias only shrugs.

"Where did they take everyone else?" I ask.

"Probably to the jail in Utica. They may have difficulty charging some of these guys because they were not caught in possession of their weapons. It may be difficult to say which of the unregistered weapons belongs to who."

"What a freakin' fiasco," I say, feeling quite certain that pretty much sums it up.

"No, not really," Elias says as he takes a deep breath before continuing. "The good news is that their plan to attack the other ten governors has also been foiled. The FBI is currently arresting these right-wing mobsters across the country who were also fully armed and intent on pulling off this criminal insurrection."

"I guess we have that to be thankful for," I say, but I don't really feel very thankful. Instead I feel rather sick to my stomach.

It is then that we hear a couple little voices calling and some knocking on the door from the lower level.

Elias and Willa jump to their feet and go to gather up their sleepy little daughters in their arms.

Chapter 32

Clearly Elias and Willa need to spend a little time with their daughters. "We should head back to the house," I say to Mom. "I can make a fire and maybe you'd like to have a nice hot bath or a nap. It's been a long and difficult day."

"It's been a long and difficult life," Mom mutters as she heads for the mudroom and pulls on her boots.

"Why don't we plan to have dinner together tonight? Maybe a late dinner after the girls have gone to bed," Willa suggests.

"There's a lot we still need to talk about that isn't appropriate for the children," Elias says.

"Dad-dy, I want...," Heidi starts to complain but she is still too sleepy to complete her thoughts as she slurs her words and drifts back toward sleep in her father's arms.

The two little girls still look pretty groggy snuggled up on the couch with their parents. "Maybe an early dinner, looks like the girls will be going to bed early," I say, trying to ascertain how much time we have.

"Why don't you come back at about 6:30?" Willa says.

"I could make dinner back at the house," Mom offers, calling in from the mudroom where she stands ready to go.

"No, Mom," both Willa and I say in unison. Mom has suffered through enough trauma for one day, her husband and three of her children have been taken into custody, the last thing she needs is the added burden of feeding the rest of her family.

I borrow an old jacket of Willa's and lace up my boots before Mom and I trudge through the newly fallen snow. Neither of us has much to say as we make our way out past the garage and back to the main house. The tire tracks from all of the police and ATF vehicles have been nearly obscured in the drifting snow. A long line of pickup trucks and SUVs that belong to recently arrested are still parked on the side of the driveway.

"Who needs to be notified to get these trucks removed?" I ask aloud, not expecting an answer from Mom. "If they're still here in the morning, perhaps I should call the sheriff."

But then the thought occurs to me, these men may be sending their friends or members of their family out here to collect their vehicles. Their car keys are either with them at the county jail in their pants pockets or they could still be in the coats they left behind when the tear gas and smoke bombs were deployed? My mind is racing as my imagination conjures up images of a second hoard of angry men descending on our land and seeking vigilante justice.

I don't want a confrontation with the friends or families of these incarcerated men. They could also be armed and intent on carrying out a vendetta against everyone they suspect of being involved.

Elias already indicated that he was pretty sure he'd been tagged as the FBI informant. He wasn't incarcerated with everyone else, and that is pretty strong evidence of his involvement with the FBI.

I've never kept my political leanings a secret either.

These thoughts invade my consciousness as one after another begins to take root.

We're still in danger.

Mom and I walk on in silence as I chose to keep my thoughts to myself. My mother has enough to worry about without me indulging my own fully fabricated paranoia.

We make our way up the snow-covered walk. There are footprints leading to the house. Others have been here, and not long ago.

I take a deep breath as I reach for the door handle. The door to the house is unlocked. I look at Mom who says, "I'm pretty sure I left it unlocked."

I push the door open and we walk in. When I flip the switch just inside the front door, it is obvious someone has searched the house. They must have been here while we were all over at Willa's. Pop's office has been cleared of all the dishevelment that usually covers his desk. A business card with the name and phone number of a special agent in the FBI agent has been left in its place.

I feel a sense of violation as it is clear someone has been going through the closets and the drawers in all the bedrooms. The bed linens have been removed and the mattress has been turned and searched in my parents' bedroom.

What more could they possibly need to find? They already have the guns, the three-D printer, and Pop's computer and files of invoices from his man cave. They must have found whatever it was they were looking for it as it appears that they have moved on. No effort has been made to set things to rights, they didn't even turn off the lights or bother to lock the doors.

I look out the window of my old bedroom, there are lights in the distance, out in the north woods. Perhaps they're out at the bunker now.

I help Mom straighten up her bedroom as we tidy up the drawers and re-make the bed. Mom works in silence as she so often does when she has something she doesn't want to talk about. I respect the silence and keep my thoughts to myself. Then we head into the family room and lay a fire in the fireplace and light it. Mom goes into the kitchen and puts the kettle on. Soon she brings us each a cup of tea and half of a sandwich. We eat in silence in front of the fire. Mom looks bone tired.

"Why don't you head off to bed and have a nap?"

Mom doesn't argue as I take her cup and plate from her. "I'll get the dishes." Mom nods and heads back towards her bedroom. "It's just after four and we don't need to be back at Willa's for a couple of hours. When would you like to get up?"

"Wake me in an hour, will you Emma?" Mom asks as she closes the door to her bedroom.

I sit in front of the fire as I hear her gently sobbing in her bedroom, but it isn't long before she has gone quiet and I hope, for her sake, that she has fallen asleep.

I take the dishes to the kitchen and go to call my sister on the landline. When I pick up the receiver the phone is beeping and the digital voice speaks, "You have three new messages. Enter your four-digit passcode to listen to your messages."

I don't know for certain what the passcode is, but I have a pretty good idea. Pop uses his birthdate for everything. I punch in the numbers and I'm not disappointed.

The first call is from Pop, "Magda, goddammit, pick up the goddamn phone. I need you to call John Quinn. I need an attorney. Tell him to get his ass up here to Ray Brook…" and then the line goes dead. The second and third calls follow in rapid succession. They, too, are from Pop as he reiterates his demands getting angrier with each call.

I thought people were only allowed one phone call when they'd been detained by the police, maybe that's only on TV.

There is nothing from Becca. I wonder who she called. Come to think of it, there is nothing from Josiah or Lucas either.

I go down the hall to peek in on Mom, she is fast asleep. I pull the blanket up and tuck it in around her shoulders. I decide not to wake her, Pop can just cool his heels and wait.

I think for a moment about calling John Quinn but decide against it. He has been our family attorney, not just Pop's. We need to think strategically. We don't want to limit our options by playing all our cards without thinking this through. This can wait until we reconvene at Willa and Elias' house later tonight.

I pick up the phone to call my sister. I have more immediate concerns like having the second string of angry white men arriving at our door and looking for car keys. Just as I'm about to hang up Elias answers on the sixth or seventh ring.

"Hello?"

"Elias, it's Emma. Am I disturbing you?" He sounds like I woke him up. He doesn't answer but kind of groans. I hear my sister whispering in the background.

"Call her back," she says, as it dawns on me that I might be disturbing an intimate moment.

I hasten through my concerns for fear he may hang up on me and get back to doing whatever it was they were doing. "Sorry to bother you, but I'm afraid that people might be coming by to pick up the trucks and SUVs that belong to the guys that were arrested. They are all still in the driveway."

"Lock your door. I'll take care of it," he says and hangs up without saying goodbye.

Well okay then.

I guess if everyone else is resting, then I will too. God knows I need it after the last two weeks and today in particular. I lay down on the couch in front of the fire and cover myself with the old afghan that Gram crocheted out of a soft ivory-colored wool. It feels like a tender embrace, this is my last conscious thought before I'm drifting towards dreamland.

I wake to the sound of the news. The TV must be on in Pop's office, it takes me a moment to figure out what is being said as I shake off the remnants of some convoluted dream. Only it wasn't a dream. Now some newscaster is talking, "… raids took place this afternoon across the country, where members of the National Resistance Revival, an extremist organization closely aligned politically with the radical right, had been planning an armed rebellion specifically targeting democratically elected governors in eleven different states."

I get up off the couch and go to turn off the television when I realize this television journalist is broadcasting just outside our front door. A van, with a WFXV logo on the side, is parked in the middle of the front lawn. Some glorified spot lights are illuminating the news guy and the entire front of our house. This is outrageous. I'm just about to pick up the phone to call the police when I see a squad car drive down the driveway with both the lights and the siren on. It is followed by another white truck with the words *Crime Scene Investigation* emblazoned on the side. It is under the glow of the spotlights that I see the yellow tape surrounding Pop's man cave. I've watched enough television to know this whole area must be considered a crime scene.

Did Elias see the TV news van or maybe the local police happened to see it on the news. Either way it looks like it's being handled as the spotlights have gone out and the television crew has started to pack up their equipment in preparation for departure.

I stand there in the dark looking out the window of Pop's office. I keep the lights off so I can see out but no one can see in. I hide in the shadows. I feel so ashamed of the spectacle and notoriety my father has brought down on our family. As I stand there behind the curtain I see one flatbed truck after another back down the driveway towards the house. A police officer gets out of his vehicle and starts directing the removal of all the cars parked along the side of the driveway. One vehicle after another is prepared to be hauled away and will probably be impounded. There are going to be some pretty angry people when they find out their cars and trucks have been towed away. There is little doubt in my mind that it's going to cost a fortune to get these vehicles released. These guys, or at least the ones from town, need their trucks to work and they don't have a lot of extra money just laying around, at least not for this kind of thing.

"Emma, what's going on?" Mom asks. She stands in the darkened doorway to Pop's office. I extend my hand to pull her beside me and back behind the curtain. We both stand there in the dark, neither of us speaking as we watch one vehicle after another being loaded onto the back of the flatbed. There are still so many more pickups and SUVs to be cleared, this could take all night.

Just as I'm about to tell Mom about the phone calls from Pop, there is a knock on the front door.

Chapter 33

Mom looks at me and all I can read is fear on her face. "I'll go," I say softly, as I gently move her from the doorway. "Wait for me in the kitchen and don't turn on the light," I whisper, as I don't want anyone else to know she is here. My mother is so used to taking orders from Pop and Gram that she simply does as she is told.

I wait until Mom disappears from view and is in the kitchen before going to answer the door. Before I can get there, whoever is outside raps again on the front door, this time more aggressively and calls out, "Open the door. This is the FBI." Trembling with fright, I turn on the porch light, and take a look through the peephole. There is a man dressed in the dark uniform of an FBI officer. I unlock the deadbolt and open the door.

"Emma Earl?" He asks, but this is not a question as clearly, he already knows who I am.

"Yes."

"I'm Special Agent Ferris with the FBI and I need you and your mother to come with me."

I am overwhelmed and my heart is racing. "This is a mistake," is all

I can think to say. "We've done nothing wrong, Officer." No sooner are the words out of my mouth than I'm certain I'm supposed to address him as Special Agent and not Officer.

"You are not under arrest and neither is your mother, we are just moving you and your family to a safe space."

"Oh. . . are Elias and Willa and their girls going too?" I ask, still standing there in the dark.

"Yes, miss. Get your mother. We need to hurry?"

"Are we in danger here?" I ask. I feel like an idiot, of course we're in danger or they wouldn't be moving us. He nods and a slow measured smile crosses his lips and for the first time it dawns on me how absolutely striking this man is. "Should we pack? How long will we be out of the house?"

He shakes his head no. I step to one side indicating he is welcome to wait inside.

"We have to go *now*," is all he says.

"Can I at least get my computer?" I ask.

"It has already been confiscated, Quest18. Our folks in the IT department will need to take a closer look."

"Oh my God, I made all that up. I was just trying to see what Pop and his armed militia were up to."

"We know. It's pretty obvious you're not an eighteen-year-old boy from Poughkeepsie." Again, this handsome man smiles at me and I can glimpse something soft and friendly beneath his tough guy exterior. "You should have it back in a day or two."

"Okay." I say, as if I have any say in any of this. "I'll go get my mom."

"Pack some night clothes and a toothbrush for both of you. We can get you anything else you might need later. We need to get out of here."

"Where are we going?"

"*Now*," is all he says. He will not be answering any more of my questions.

It's probably not wise to argue with any armed officer. Not that I've ever personally encountered an armed FBI agent before. I leave him standing in the foyer as I make my way into the kitchen to tell my mom what is going on. She grasps the nuance of the situation and says, "There is a clean nightgown in my dresser and the pink toothbrush in the bathroom is mine."

I head back down the hall to gather our things, I throw some clean underwear and another long sleeve cotton top into a canvas shopping bag along with her nightie and toothbrush. As I'm half way back down the hall it dawns on me that all my clean things are over in the cabin. Just in case this Special Agent decides not to let me retrieve my things from the cabin, I head back into my parents' room and throw some more of Mom's clothes into the bag for me. I find a new unopened toothbrush in the linen closet. I dilly dally trying to decide what else I might need while reflecting on the agent's demeanor and feel a sense of urgency. He doesn't think we're safe here.

Mom is already dressed and ready to go. She waits in silence by the door as I step into my boots and pull on my red ski jacket.

"Let's go," he says.

The three of us step outside where we find Willa, Elias and the girls in the back of big black GMC Yukon with darkened windows. Willa sits between her sleepy girls in the way back. Mom climbs into the middle seats next to Elias, leaving a space for me next to her.

Someone had the forethought to pack us some submarine sandwiches, chips and bottles of water which we eat and drink gratefully in the back of the SUV. I hadn't realized how hungry I was, it has been a long time since breakfast.

The plexiglass barrier separates us from Agent Ferris who drives us on through the darkness. He takes us down back roads that I was certain only the locals and some roving bands of deer knew about. It doesn't take long before it dawns on me that he is being careful we are not being followed. Everyone seemed to be lost in their own thoughts and the silence pervades the SUV allowing me ample time to review everything that had happened today. When I've been around that mulberry bush a few too many times I find my attention turning to the handsome man in the front. He does not speak unless spoken too, and no one is saying a word. Before slipping off to dreamland, I decided that Agent Ferris must be the strong and silent type. In the dark and the quiet I rest my head up against the window and doze off to sleep.

I don't know how long I was asleep but I wake myself up with the sound of my own laughter.

"What's so funny?" Willa asked.

"Nothing," I laugh, "Just a crazy dream." I decline to comment any further.

It's been so long since I'd been invited to spend the night with a handsome man, my imagination got the best of me. In my dream Agent Ferris invited me to an isolated camp in the woods for a romantic getaway, but as luck would have it, he also invited the rest of my family to join us. In my dream, I was dressed in my mother's floral flannel pajamas rather than one of my own beautiful designs. The irony of all of this just strikes me as funny.

Dreams are like that, besides the reality is that this man probably isn't any more interested in me than he would be in my mother's old PJs.

We drive on another hour or so until we have traveled even further into the hinterlands of the Adirondack Park. The park consists of over six million acres. It is equal in size to the state of Vermont. Much of the park is heavily forested and protected by the *Forever Wild* designation. If someone were looking to get lost, this would be a good place to do it.

I have no idea where we are now.

After thirty minutes more of driving, Special Agent Ferris pulls into an old camp with multiple outbuildings that probably were once used as bunk houses for the Boy Scouts or maybe some church groups. The light is on in the main building when we finally come to a stop. Everyone is exhausted after this long day. When Agent Ferris shows us to our quarters everyone goes willingly.

"We can talk some more in the morning," Elias says.

"Only after some strong coffee," Willa replies as we head off to one of two bunk houses. Willa and her family are in one, and Mom and I are in the other.

There is already a fire burning in the wood burning stove and the place smells slightly of smoke from other fires. Down sleeping bags have been rolled out on the upper and lower bunks. Mom and I take turns in the primitive washroom, at least this place has indoor plumbing. Dressed in my mother's night clothes, I climb into the sleeping bag on the top bunk as Mom is already tucked into the other.

"Good night, Emma," Mom says into the darkness.

"Good night, Mom," I respond. "Do you want to talk about any of this?"

"No, dear, not tonight," she says. I feel the bunk bed shift as she rolls over and starts to weep quietly into her pillow.

Through the dingy window beside my bed I can see another agent has joined Special Agent Ferris. Each of them appears to be stationed outside the bunk houses, just in case.

Just in case of what?

Chapter 34

To my great surprise, I slept well and only awoke when the sun came through the window. I look at my watch and it is only 6:40. The trees have not budded out yet. The window is dirty and that makes me fairly certain no one has used this camp since the last campers departed in the fall. Still I take the palm of my hand and rub the glass. There is a beautiful lake just down the hill and the sun on the water causes it to sparkle. Maybe we traveled south last night, as it must be warmer here than in Old Forge. The ice has already gone out of this lake. Either that or perhaps this lake just isn't as deep.

As I lay there looking out of the window and admiring the view, I hear my mother get up and go to use the washroom. She doesn't speak to me, maybe she thinks I'm still asleep.

When she returns she stops to put another log or two into the wood burning stove. "I see you're awake," she says to me as she makes her way back to her sleeping bag to warm up.

"Looks like a pretty day out there," I respond, as I climb down from the upper bunk to use the bathroom. "I could use some coffee, how about you?"

By the time I've been to the bathroom and have a long hot shower, Mom is dressed and sitting on the lower bunk and ready to go. "Sorry to keep you waiting but that shower felt so good. I'll get dressed and meet you over in the main building," I say, as I towel dry my hair with one of the rough, white, military grade towels someone has left out for us.

"If it's all the same to you, I think I'll wait until you're ready," Mom says. Given everything we've been through, her reluctance to go anywhere alone is understandable. Still I'm pretty sure I'd be unable to provide her or me very much protection.

I dress quickly in the clothes Willa loaned me, the same oversized sweatshirt and sweatpants I wore yesterday. I could fit two of me in this ensemble. I look like the Pillsbury Doughboy but at least I'm warm.

By the time we get over to the main lodge, everyone else is already there. Willa seems to have taken responsibility for cooking up the bacon and eggs, and the coffee is on. "Where did the food come from?" I ask, as I had expected cold cereal if anything at all.

"Agent Hank Holtz, this is Emma Earl and her mother, Mrs. Magda Earl."

He nods in our direction to acknowledge us. "I stopped at the grocery on my way here last night. I figured you'd all be hungry and in need of a little creature comfort after everything you'd been put through yesterday."

Tilly leaves her chair at the table to come and wrap her little arms around my legs. "Thank you, Agent Holtz," I say as I reach down to return my niece's embrace before she moves on to her grandmother.

"Why don't you have some breakfast then we'll talk about what's next," Agent Ferris says as he hands me a cup of coffee and another to my mother. Mine has both cream and sugar, just the way I like it, and I wonder how he knew. I take a sip and smile as I see my sister waving at me taking full credit. Of course. There I go fabricating stories to suit my personal agenda.

I take a seat next to Heidi who does not look up from her plate to acknowledge me or her grandmother. She pouts as she plays with the uneaten food on her plate and I wonder what she has been told.

Once we've all finished breakfast and I am well into my second cup of coffee, Agent Ferris suggests, "Why don't we reconvene in the great room in front of the fireplace in ten minutes. Does that work for everyone?"

Mom is already cleaning up the kitchen and Willa has taken her two daughters to another room where she will settle them in with an age-appropriate movie that should capture their attention, at least for a little while.

I offer to help my mother but she wordlessly shoos me away. So instead I take my coffee and find a seat in front of the large fieldstone fireplace.

Someone laid this fire a while ago and it is blazing brightly and warms the room. I settle in on the large upholstered couch. This couch has seen better days as I shift in my seat to get comfortable. Probably years of rambunctious children using it for a trampoline hasn't done much to prolong its longevity.

It isn't long before everyone is present including both FBI agents. Mom joins Elias, Willa, and me on the couch and the two agents are seated in chairs catty-corner to the fireplace.

"Where would you like to begin?" Agent Ferris asks.

I raise my hand, just like I'm back in school and this man is my teacher. Again, he smiles at me as he acknowledges my raised hand, "Emma."

"So much has happened and I need to tell someone, make that everyone, that just before we were hustled off to *Neverland,* Pop called and left three messages on the answering machine one right after the other."

"What did he want?" Mom asks.

"He wanted you to call John Quinn," I say, addressing my mother. "And he sounded really angry."

"Who's John Quinn?" Agent Ferris asks.

"He's the family attorney," Elias answers. "Your father is in big trouble and is going to need an attorney, but given the fact that Quinn is your family attorney, you may wish to retain him before your father does. Your grandmother's estate has not settled, and there may be other legal issues to be addressed, like what will happen to Josiah, Lucas, and Becca. They, too, may need representation and we don't want there to be any conflict of interest. Besides Pop is going to need a criminal defense attorney and Quinn is probably not the right person to handle his case." Elias takes a deep breath and sighs.

"That's what I was thinking," I say. "More or less," I add muttering under my breath. I feel a bit redeemed for not sharing this information any earlier.

"Hold on. It sounds like you've thought this through pretty thoroughly." Willa says as she takes a moment to catch up. "Anything else we might need to know?" She addresses her question to Elias but it is Mom who answers.

"I've already retained John," Mom says. Everyone in the room goes quiet and turns toward Mom.

"I gave him a retainer to represent me a couple of weeks ago."

A look of confusion passes between Willa, Elias, and I. Elias asks, "For what purpose, Magda?"

"Things have been getting crazier and crazier over the years, and even more so recently. I tried to hold this family together but I can't do it anymore. I've been making arrangements to leave and ask your father for a divorce. I had to save enough money before I could file.

"That's what I was doing at Community Bank the morning Gram died. I was moving some money around to cover the balance of my retainer so John Quinn could go ahead and have your father served with the divorce papers.

"The wheels are already in motion. I signed all the papers last week, but I decided to put everything on hold once your grandmother died.

"John Quinn is my attorney. Your father will need to find someone else."

"Wow, Mom…," is all I can think to say.

"Finally," Willa adds.

"I'm so proud of you, Mom, for getting out of that toxic situation," I say when the reality of what we've just learned begins to settle in.

"I should have done it years ago. Maybe if I had your brothers and sister wouldn't be in jail now," Mom says as she starts to cry again. "I've been paralyzed by fear for so long, I just didn't know where I'd live or how I'd ever be able to support myself. I finally decided it didn't matter, I'd find a way."

Willa and I embrace our mother while everyone else looks on. It doesn't take long for our stoic mother to dry her tears and regain her composure as she folds her hands in her lap.

"Wasn't John Quinn Gram's attorney, too? I'm pretty sure he was. I think he's the only lawyer in our one-horse town," Willa says.

We sit in silence as it begins to dawn on us how the whole estate, the houses, outbuildings, the bunker, and the thousands of acres of uncut timber that have been in Gram's family for hundreds of years, is yet to be settled. Everyone has always assumed it would all be left to her only son, our Pop. We have always been cash poor, but land rich. What will this mean if Mom goes through with the divorce?

"This can all wait a little while longer while we address some of the more immediate concerns," Agent Ferris says.

"And just what might those concerns be?" Willa asks as Elias reaches over for her hand.

"These people and their like-minded associates are dangerous. They know who you are and they are angry. If you return home, I'm not certain we can adequately protect you and keep you safe."

"Oh…" Willa says and the word just hangs there as the implications of all of this starts to dawn on us.

"Normally we would suggest some kind of long-term hiatus, somewhere no one knows you, until things settle down. However, much of the world has closed its borders to Americans given we are in the middle of a global pandemic," Agent Holtz informs us.

"Mexico is still open to Americans," Agent Ferris says. "Does anyone speak Spanish?"

"Poorly," I respond. "I took four years of Spanish in high school, but that was a few years ago, and I haven't spoken a word of it since."

"A few?" My sister laughs, "I don't think ten years qualifies as a few." I laugh too.

"What about my girls? They'll need to be in school," Willa says as she begins to see how this plan will impact her immediate family.

"They can go virtually, lots of kids are," Elias says and it becomes apparent that much of this has already been discussed with him.

Agent Ferris brings out his laptop and opens it up, "We can set you up with a home in Mexico, in a little mountain town until we're certain this has blown over and you are no longer in any danger. We will let you know the exact location once you are on your way. There are enough gringos and expats living there that you should be able to get along just fine."

"I thought Mexico is supposed to be dangerous," Elias says.

"Not as dangerous for you as staying here would be, besides *we* will keep you safe."

"Is this some kind of a witness protection program?" Elias asks.

"Yes, we may need your testimony, if they are charged and this should go to trial. But with all the evidence we've already obtained, it may not be necessary. Any attorney who does not advise your father or your siblings to plead to a lesser offense is not worth his or her salt," Special Agent Ferris elaborates. "The truth of the matter is the number of US citizens who think like your father is vast. They are organized, armed, and angry, and we don't know what they are capable of, and we don't want to take any chances. This will be temporary and for your protection."

Then he shows us the pictures of the town, the surrounding region, and the house. The house is stucco with a red tiled roof and has a large swimming pool in an enclosed courtyard that overlooks the ocean. "It has five bedrooms and each has its own en-suite bathroom. The town is really quite lovely."

"I'm in," I say without being asked. "My life is on pause now anyway and I've never been to Mexico. This place is gorgeous. When do we leave?" I ask.

"Easy there, Emma," Agent Ferris says with a smile.

"What about my children?" Mom says and starts to cry all over again.

"The wheels of justice are already in motion. They will all be going in front of the grand jury when it next convenes. They usually meet two or three times a month. However, I'm not certain how the pandemic will disrupt their schedule. The Department of Justice is attempting to set up video conferencing for grand jury proceedings but as far as I know that has only happened in a limited number of jurisdictions to date. This is likely to delay the prosecution. But there is nothing any of you can do about this now. We will keep you informed about the outcome of the grand jury investigation and the trial, if it comes to that. Once you have been moved to a safe location, Mrs. Earl, we will help you to reach out to your family," Agent Ferris says, his voice is calm and reassuring.

Mom nods indicating she has heard him.

"There are a few things that still need to be taken care of before any of you leave this safe haven. We need to contact John Quinn to make sure everything is tied up, as best as it can be, on this end."

"Is he coming here?" Willa asks. "I have no idea where we even are."

"It's better that way, safer for you. We will contact Quinn and set up a Zoom meeting. That probably won't happen until later today. One of our agents will be going to his office and filling him in on what he needs to know. He won't know where you are or where you are going. Before the meeting I will let you know what you can and cannot say to your attorney. Again, this is for your safety and protection. Do any of you have passports?" Agent Ferris asks.

We all shake our heads no.

"Not a problem, we can get them."

"We will need to give you new names to protect your identity. This won't be forever, but for now."

"How about Graf?" Willa suggests, "That was Grand Pappa's name before he came to the States and changed it to Earl."

"No," Mom and I say in unison. Mom turns her head to look at me, in this moment she knows. She knows that I know something. I can read it in her face.

Willa looks momentarily confused, but then it dawns on her why neither Mom nor I want to be known by this name. Everything associated with Winfield Graf is something neither of us is proud of or wants anything more to do with.

"How about Linden?" I suggest. My mother smiles at me.

"Yes, *Linden* like the linden tree and my maternal grandmother's maiden name," mom says.

"What do you think I've been doing over in the cabin every night all by myself? I've been researching our family tree." I chuckle and give the cute guy a smile. These two FBI guys know what else I've been researching. They have my computer. I continue anyway, "The linden tree is a sacred tree. It is a symbol of love, prosperity, fidelity, and friendship. I think it's about time we had a new symbol for our family, one that focuses on the good branches of our family tree, our strength and our resilience."

"I like it," Willa says. "I took Elias' name when we married. Will we need to change our name, too?" Willa asks.

"It is probably a good idea, at least for now."

"How about Matthews?" Elias says. "That was my maternal grandfather's name and he was, hands down, the best man I ever knew." Tears fill his eyes and Willa reaches over to comfort her husband.

She whispers to him, "And you are the best man I have ever known."

Willa's words hang heavy in the room and for a moment no one speaks. Mom and I silently acknowledge our own admiration for Elias. He is indeed a good man.

"Then it's settled, the surnames will be Linden and Matthews. We'll get going on securing the necessary documentation and travel documents," Agent Holtz says breaking the silence. "It looks like everything is settled, at least for now."

"Just one more thing, how will we pay for all of this?" my mother, always the practical one, asks.

"It will be covered by your tax dollars, with a thank you from a grateful nation. You folks are truly the *patriots* here. Don't let anyone tell you any differently. God only knows what terrible things could have happened if you hadn't been brave enough to step forward and put a stop to it," Agent Holtz says.

Then he and Agent Ferris approach each of us individually and one by one they shake our hands and offer us their thanks.

"Let's reconvene in a couple of hours. Try to make yourselves comfortable and if you need anything just let me know, I'll be happy to run out and try to find it for you. And I'll let you know once I've set up the meeting with your attorney," Agent Ferris says before we all retreat to try and process everything.

Maybe it was the early start or all of the stress of the last few weeks but I'm exhausted. I crawl off to find a blanket and someplace warm to take a nap.

Chapter 35

I have no idea how long I've been asleep before I'm woken by little Tilly whispering in my ear, "Mommy says we're going on an airplane."

I try to shake the last remnants of sleep from my head. "Really?" I say.

"Mommy says, you get to come too." She gives me a big smile. She has just shared her biggest and best secret with me and the joy and anticipation of this grand adventure fills her little face.

"That is so exciting. Do you know when we're leaving?" I ask.

"Right after we watch *The Lion King*," she says with delight, as if this day could not possibly get any better. I've got to hand it to my sister, she is doing a great job putting a positive spin on all of this and protecting her daughters' innocence. "Mommy says, you need to get up now. They need you for a meeting."

"Thanks, Lovie." I give my niece a little squeeze as I sit up and start to fold the blanket.

I have no idea what time it is. The cute FBI guy took all of our cell phones before we left the family compound. I wonder if we'll ever get them back. With all the safety precautions being implemented, I doubt it. I guess it wouldn't do any good to change our names and move us out of the country if we could still call our friends and post selfies on Facebook or Instagram. It's funny how little I care about any of that right now.

I wander into the main room, everyone else is already present, the fire blazes in the fieldstone fireplace, and someone has placed a laptop on a card table in front of the couch. I find my seat between my sister and my mother. "What's going on?" I ask.

"We're meeting with John Quinn. He should be joining us in a couple of minutes, one of our agents is with him now. He has been brought up to speed on what went down yesterday. He knows that you're all in protective custody and will be until we determine that the risk to your safety has passed. He will not ask where you are or where you are going, and you are not to offer that information to him or anyone else. Remember your safety depends on this." With this said, Agent Ferris reaches over and turns on the computer and John Quinn's face fills the screen.

"Hello Magda, Willa, Elias, and Emma. My goodness Emma it has been so long since I've seen you, probably since you were in high school."

"Hi John," my mother says. She appears to be more at ease with this man then the rest of us are.

"Let me begin by saying how sad I was to hear of Mrs. Earl's passing. I had the pleasure of seeing her a few months ago, I believe it was just after the first of the year when she stopped in. She was clear-minded and as spry as ever. My wife, Mary, joined us that day and can attest to her state of mind, as well."

Willa glances over at me. I'm sure she is thinking the same thing that I am, *what the hell is he going on about.* She turns her face back to the screen where John Quinn rambles on.

"I have spoken with Special Agent Bruce, with the FBI, and I understand there was quite a hullabaloo out at your place yesterday. Now I do not know the details, but I want you all to rest assured that I am your attorney, Magda. I, also, represent the estate of your mother-in-law, the late

Mrs. Katherine Earl, as well anyone in your family, who is present here today, as long as there are no conflicts of interest and everyone agrees."

Willa and Elias both nod their heads and I say, "That's fine with me." Although I have no idea why any one of us might need an attorney.

"Magda, would you like to meet with me privately to discuss…" the otherwise polished attorney appears to be at a loss for words.

"That won't be necessary, John, as I have already told Elias and my daughters of my intentions." She swallows as the words stick in her throat. She takes a drink of cold coffee left over from breakfast before trying to continue. "I've told my family that I've retained your legal services to represent me in my divorce. I am resolved to see this through. Anything you need to say to me, about how you intend to proceed, you can say in the presence of my daughters and my son-in-law." Willa and I reach out for our mother's hands attempting to offer her some comfort and reassurance.

"That is really all I need to know, Magda. All the preliminary paperwork has already been signed. I'll need to find out just where to have Edward served, but I'm sure one of these agents can help me with that."

Mom nods her head and gives my hand a squeeze. As always, Mom is putting on a brave face. This is difficult for her, but so was living with Pop for over thirty-five years. Things are going to get better for her, I just know it.

"I received a phone call from Edward earlier today, but I was out of the office when he called. He told Mary, he wanted to retain my services for the *difficulty* he finds himself in. Mary informed him, I no longer handle criminal defense and referred him to another lawyer over in Lake George. I have also heard from Becca and the boys, Josiah and Lucas. Their cases have also been referred out to capable and competent people."

"Do you think my children will be coming home?" Mom asks the same questions that she put to Agent Ferris earlier this morning.

"I really can't say Magda, we won't know anything at all until they have met with the grand jury and see what the charges are."

Mom nods her head and purses her lips together tightly, she was hoping for a different answer.

"Shall we move on?" John Quinn suggests. "I think it is time for the reading of Katherine Marian Earl's last will and testament."

Every one of us shifts slightly in their seat as I'm pretty sure we all know what to expect, Pop is the heir apparent. He was Gram's only child. I'm just a little surprised that John Quinn is going ahead with the reading of the will when Pop isn't even here. Maybe it's because he's locked up, and likely, will be for quite a while.

The camera shifts as Mr. Quinn reaches around behind him and brings forth a file folder from his credenza. As I said earlier, Mrs. Earl paid me a visit just after the first of the year, let's see it was on Monday, January 6th, 2020. My wife, Mary, was also in the meeting and Katherine Earl dictated a letter to all of you before making some changes in her last will and testament. At her request, I will read her signed letter to you indicating her wishes.

January 6, 2020

My Dearest Family,

If you are gathered together with our friend, John Quinn, then I have passed on and it is time for my day of reckoning. I will be the first to admit that I have made my share of mistakes in this life, in what I have done and in what I have failed to do, for this I ask your forgiveness. I hope in some small way, I can redeem myself in the decisions I have made in regards to this last will and testament.

First of all, to my son, Edward Winfield Earl, I love you. Please remember this. I want to offer you my most heartfelt apology, for I have failed to raise you to be a person of honor and integrity. I did not step up or step in often enough as you have followed too closely in your father's footsteps. You have come to believe that the rules of life do not apply to you, you have cast yourself as the victim in your own life, and have learned to fear and hate anyone and everyone who does not look or think as you do.

I think of all the times I took you to church, hoping that you would grow to be a person of integrity and humility, a good, kind, and honest man. But sadly, these characteristics do not apply to you and I am heartily sorry for failing you.

Your ill-founded beliefs reside in the fact that you believe you are better than everyone else, and therefore, entitled to that which you have not earned. It has not gone without notice that you have been spending my money as if it is your own, never asking for my permission.

I abhor your dishonesty as well as my own cowardice for not confronting you or your father while I was still alive. Still it is my last wish, that in my absence perhaps it is not too late, for you to learn to be a good man.

I know what you have been up to and you know I do not approve. You have assumed too much, I'm sure you remember me saying, *this is my land and therefore my rules.* Even though I am no longer in this world, I will be deciding what will become of my worldly possessions, my money, and my land.

Dearest Magda, I also need to ask your forgiveness for you are the backbone of our family and I have treated you unfairly. I know that your daughter, Becca, is also my husband's child. Winfield and I tried to have more children, for he was adamant that he wanted to have more sons to carry on his legacy, but Edward is our one and only child.

Winfield always had an eye for younger women and when I became too old to have another child I saw how he turned his attention toward you. I saw how you turned from him and shunned his affection, still it made me feel inadequate and unloved. I turned on you, when I should have turned against my husband.

I know you did not submit to him willingly, for one night in a state of intoxication, he told me how he took you against your will, how he hurt you, and how much pleasure he gained by being cruel to both of us.

I did not understand it then but have come to understand that this is what the German's refer to as schadenfreude— deriving pleasure from another person's pain. Winfield derived pleasure from hurting others: you, and me, and countless others whose names we do not know. I fear the person who he has hurt the most is Becca, as she is *so* much like him, and it will not serve her well. Is it in her biology or is she a victim of her environment? I cannot say. There has been so much that has gone unsaid, too many secrets, and too many lies. Please forgive me, Magda.

And if I can offer you one piece of advice from one woman to another. Leave my son, he doesn't deserve you. I wish I'd had the courage to leave his father. But I was afraid. Be brave, Magda.

Willa, Josiah, and Lucas, I love you all and I am certain you will grow into the people God intends for you to be.

Willa, you are blessed to have a good husband in Elias. I have seen the way he cares for you and how he listens to you and respects you. For the sake of my great granddaughters, please leave the area and get out from under Becca and your father's evil influence.

And so here it is, everything I own in this world is bequeathed to my granddaughter Emma Elizabeth Earl. You have proven yourself to be fair-minded and brave. I have seen you stand up to your father and make your own way in the world, never asking for anything. I know that you will be generous and take care of your mother, Willa, Josiah, and Lucas. I know you will see that all that we have worked for, over countless generations, will not be squandered but will become the seeds for new growth and opportunity for the generations to come.

There is all the land and all the buildings on it, but there are also investments which have been profitable. You may use the income derived from these investments in any way you deem appropriate, but you may not invade the principal. Remember to cover your needs, but manage your wants. You will have more than enough.

Your mother, and your sister, Willa, and her family are to be given a life estate on the land and allowed to reside in their current homes, rent free, as long as they so desire.

Josiah and Lucas will be allowed to continue harvesting the timber according to the sustainable forestry plan that was developed last year in conjunction with The New York State Department of Environmental Conservation. John Quinn has said documents. The land and all the timber on it are owned by the Earl Family Enterprises and will be under the control of Emma Earl. Josiah and Lucas Earl may be employed by the family business and will draw an equitable salary for their labor, if they so choose.

Josiah and Lucas, you have been too long under your father's control. You are both smart and hardworking, it is time to straighten up and fly right. Things will be different now. I trust that Emma will be just and fair with both of you.

Emma, you have a good eye for design, maybe it's time to open a design house under your own name. I know others thought you were wasting your time sitting at your grandmother's knee learning to sew, with all the stitching and re-stitching I insisted on until you got it right. I have seen how your father has mocked you and stepped on your dreams. I am sorry I did not save you from his cruelty, but you are strong-willed and capable. You always took the time to listen and learn from your old Gram and you have made me proud in so many ways. I love you dearly.

Becca and Edward will need to find their own way in the world, if you choose to help them, please, do not over indulge them. It is when we struggle that we learn the lessons we have been sent here to master.

If God is forgiving, and all that we've been promised comes to pass, I will see you on the other side.

All my love,
Katherine Marian Earl

We sit in silence as John Quinn closes up the document folder containing Gram's letter. Whoa.

I did not see this coming.

I don't think anyone else in the room did either.

It takes a moment before Willa breaks the silence, "Gram always said 'my land, my rules.' We should have known she would have the last word. I just assumed everything would be going to Pop."

"I think we all did," Mom says.

"I can't believe it," is all I can say.

"Did you know about Becca?" Mom asks, as if there is no one but our family in the room. Willa and I nod. Mom starts to cry. The FBI agents turn their heads to the floor.

"I only figured it out recently, when I got the results of the DNA testing," I say. I reach over for Mom's hand.

John Quinn clears his throat and we all turn back towards the computer. "Given that your father, brothers, and sister, Becca, are all named in the will, even if they are not beneficiaries, I will be heading up to Ray Brook Correctional Facility to see that they are given copies of Katherine's letter and her will so they will be informed of her wishes."

Agent Ferris directs his comments to John Quinn, "Any further communication you wish to have with any of *these* members of the Earl Family will need to go through one of our agents."

"I understand. Good thing your grandmother left you a forest rather than a dairy farm, Emma. It's a little more difficult to just pack up and leave a dairy farm."

Everyone laughs.

"Does anyone have any further questions for Mr. Quinn?" Agent Ferris asks.

"Can you give me some idea how much money Gram had invested?" I ask.

"Not including the value of the land, she was worth millions. I'll need to check with her financial planner to get you the exact figures. It may take a couple of days given so much is closed down due to the pandemic. Your grandmother lived through the depression and a world war, like many people of her generation she knew how to squeeze a dollar. She often did without, that's why you all will be well taken care of."

"We need to get going unless anyone else has any more questions for Mr. Quinn."

"Can you keep us posted on the grand jury findings in the cases against Pop, Becca, Lucas, and Josiah?" I ask.

"Of course, Emma."

"And can you appoint a caretaker for the property while we are away?"

"How about Brooker? He's as honest as the day is long," John Quinn suggests.

Elias nods his head. He agrees with Quinn's assessment.

"Good," I say. But I don't feel good. No, I feel edgy and bereaved. What am I to do with *this,* all of *this?*

"I'll be in touch. Safe travels everyone," our lawyer says and with that the computer screen goes dark.

Epilogue

Over a year has passed since we were escorted by a US Marshall through security in Mexico City and then onto our beautiful accommodations overlooking the Pacific Ocean. So much has happened in the last year as one country after another has closed their doors to Americans as the pandemic raged on in the United States and over 500,000 people in the United States died of the Covid-19 virus in less than a year.

My family watched the television in our beautiful casa, when on January 6, 2021 members of various factions of the alt-right stormed the capitol building in Washington, DC under the direction of then President Trump who claimed the Presidential election had been stolen from him. These right-wing mobsters espouse the same political philosophy and white-supremacist mindset as my father and his band of *patriots*. To my great personal relief there has been a change in leadership in the White House and despite all the lies, ultimately Joe Biden prevailed.

The United States is as divided now as it was when the south seceded from the union, only now the division is philosophical and not geographical. Even the US Senate is equally divided between the Democrats and the Republicans with each political party holding fifty seats. God knows how anything will ever be accomplished.

But from the television broadcasts and the international news I've been reading, it looks like there are people begging and pleading for a return to some middle ground where citizens can set aside their differences and try to work together to solve this dire situation we find ourselves in.

It is now mid-April 2021 and President Biden has been aggressively rolling out an immunization program. He is ahead of his targeted goals delineating the number of Americans to be vaccinated in his first 100 days in office. As of April 19, any US citizen who wants to be vaccinated will have the opportunity to do so.

It is interesting to me that one of the largest groups of holdouts, those actively campaigning against vaccination and are refusing to be immunized, are men who identify as rural, conservative, and gun rights activists. I can't help but wonder who is filling their heads with all of these conspiracy theories. They continue to be a threat to everyone, in one way or another.

Our handlers were able to obtain the vaccine for all of us, but only Mom and I chose to be immunized. Heidi and Tilly are not old enough, this I understand. But Willa and Elias are reluctant to be vaccinated. They are both smart, open-minded, and well read on a wide variety of issues. Their arguments against the vaccine are difficult to find fault with. They are fearful we do not have any good longitudinal data to indicate that these vaccines are safe. And this is true. Willa draws the comparison to herbicides and pesticides in our food and drinking water, for so long people told us not to worry about it and now we know differently. Elias doesn't trust the government to be honest with us. He can cite one example after another where the citizens have been lied to by their government, including the Tuskegee Study conducted in 1932 by the US Public Health Service and the ongoing betrayal of Native Americans in the confiscation of their lands and their right to self-determination. The issues are anything but simple. I try to refrain from judgement for I don't believe my sister and her husband are being paranoid, perhaps just cautious.

It is worthy to ponder how on some issues those on the far left and those on the far right have found somethings to agree on. Vaccination may be one, and the freedom to live as one chooses and to decide for oneself without governmental interference is clearly another.

Still I lost my beloved grandmother to the virus, so my decision to be immunized was personal. I got my vaccine, both doses. I feel good about my decision.

After another bloody week of gun violence and mass shootings in the United States, President Biden has vowed by use of an Executive Order to restrict weapons known as ghost guns, the kind of guns my father and brothers were manufacturing and distributing out of our garage.

My father and my sister went before the grand jury almost a year ago now and were charged with racketeering under the Federal RICO statutes. I have come to understand that RICO is the Racketeer Influenced and Corrupt Organization Act. It is the federal law to combat organized crime. My father and Becca were charged and convicted of selling assault weapons to convicted felons and drug users, and conspiring and threatening to commit multiple crimes of violence, specifically kidnapping of eleven duly elected governors. Upon advice of counsel, they both pled guilty and are serving time in the Federal Correctional Institution in Ray Brook, New York. Pop was sentenced to forty years and Becca to twenty. Perhaps Becca received a lighter sentence as her attorney argued that she was young and naïve and didn't have a good understanding of the serious nature of the crimes she was committing. I can't help but think she must have tossed her pretty blonde hair and acted the part of the ingénue. She must have played the role well as she is far from naïve or innocent. Perhaps both my father and my sister may be eligible for parole in a few years, if all goes well. If not, Pop will be over eighty and Becca will be forty-four by the time they are released. What a catastrophic waste of two lives and immeasurable human potential.

Josiah and Lucas were released last fall after they met with the grand jury. They argued that they were little more than mules, simply making deliveries as instructed. There currently are no federal laws against trafficking in firearms across state lines. It is not a criminal offense.

I'm relieved. I love my brothers and I know they are good men, but Pop was a force to be reckoned with and they didn't have the backbone to refuse to do his dirty work. Still, it seems wrong, just plain wrong, that our government can't protect us from the manufacture and distribution of illegal firearms. We can thank the NRA for that.

Neither of my brothers know exactly where we are, the FBI has insisted on that. Last I heard they had both gone out to California to look for work. Perhaps they will come back home once it is deemed that we can safely return.

Most of the men, who were arrested out in the bunker on that fateful day last March, were released and not arrested as they were not in possession of their weapons when they were detained. The weapons that were seized from Pop's man cave and the bunker were unmarked and without serial numbers so they couldn't be traced to any of the individuals involved. From what I understand from John Quinn, most of the good ole boys from our home town were happy to escape the consequences of their actions and have been keeping their heads down and their mouths closed, hoping everyone will just forget about it.

Robo-Cop, was transferred within the Sheriff's Department and is now on desk duty over in the town of Herkimer where he spends his days investigating online transactions for stolen merchandise.

It wasn't long after we arrived at our beautiful casa by the sea that a package arrived for me. It was a new computer with a note from Special Agent Ferris. He told me how this new computer had been specially encrypted so that I could begin to communicate with the outside world but no one would be able to find our location. I'm pretty dense when it comes to all this technology, so I just had to take his word for it. So far so good.

I've been in regular communication with each of my long-lost aunties and they have also been corresponding with one another. We've talked at length over Zoom about our lives and I've given them a thumbnail sketch of what has been going on with my immediate family. Individually and collectively, they have expressed so much compassion for all of us and the situation we find ourselves in. We've spent hours talking honestly about the prejudice and seeds of hatred that we've all been exposed to in one form or another, both the blatant and the less conspicuous, but every bit as pervasive. I am surprised to find that these women are not the least bit judgmental of me, my mother or my grandmother. Despite their reassurances, I still feel an overwhelming sense of shame for the sins and immoral transgressions of my grandfather and my father and all the pain their ideology and subsequent actions have caused. There have been too many secrets and too many lies, but the truth is that we are the innocents. I am trying to let go of the pain and the shame by bringing my awareness to these feelings whenever they start to creep in and overwhelm me. As my aunties have told me more than once, I didn't choose my father or grandfather any more than they did.

Still, by reason of our births, our parentage, and genetic link in some way we are a family. For that reason alone, all of these women want to meet us and each other, too. Once the international constraints of the pandemic are lifted, we are planning to gather together and meet one other.

I hope it will be soon as my aunts are getting on in years and I want to meet them. I think I'm going to like them. I think they'll like one another, too.

Mom's divorce will be finalized any day now. Given that Pop is likely to be incarcerated for the next forty years, he told John Quinn, "I have no need of a wife." He signed the papers.

Pop had a separate bank account where he'd been regularly making cash deposits from all the ill-gotten gains from the sale of his illegal firearms. All this money was seized by the Feds under the RICO act, leaving Pop pretty near penniless. He complained to John Quinn how his attorney has been hounding him for payment. But you can't get blood from a turnip, and he can't get a nickel out of Pop.

Elias has found work here in town as he plies his craft as a finish carpenter to some of the other beautiful homes up and down the Pacific coast. He has made friends with some of the local carpenters.

One night Elias invited some of his co-workers and their families over for dinner and a swim in the pool. Mom was in her glory having a house full of people to cook for. Elias raised his margarita to make a toast, "To these fine people from whom we have learned so much. These people are skilled craftsmen and women, who know how to make something beautiful out of nothing."

I don't know what we were all expecting. Maybe our expectations were tainted by the awful things former President Trump said about the Mexican people. This is how the seeds of hatred and distrust are sown. The people we have met are lovely, smart, hard-working, honest, and kind.

Heidi and Tilly were learning Spanish, given that we've been here over a year, they are now nearly fluent. Their little girlfriends come over to play nearly every afternoon, once they've finished their schoolwork. Tilly is as sweet as always, but Heidi is changing. She's no longer as insolent, overbearing, unkind, or rude. She's learning that those behaviors do not play well here.

I've been working on my new designs and Willa has helped me transfer them to some pattern-making software she found on the internet. Some of the local women, the mothers of Heidi and Tilly's little friends, brought beautiful fabrics from the market and have helped me put together the prototypes for my new collection. These women do beautiful handwork and are so industrious. They are happy for the work and Willa, Mom, and I are happy for their company and companionship.

When it's time to return to New York, I will have a complete collection of women's wear. It's hard to predict when we might be leaving, but given what Special Agent Ferris says and the rate at which people in the United States are getting vaccinated, I don't think it will be too much longer.

One last bit of news, Special Agent Ferris, sent me an email and has asked me out on a date. He wants me to join him for dinner when I get back to New York. He says he'll no longer be assigned to my case by then. So, he won't be breaking any rules and he wants me to call him James.

James is a little too by the book, for my taste. I've never been overly attracted to the law and order type. But I may make some allowances for Special Agent James Ferris. Did I mention he's very handsome? I hope he's up to the challenge of a strong-willed woman.

What did Gram use to say?

"Give it time ... in time all will be revealed."

ABOUT THE AUTHOR

Internationally acclaimed author Jeanne Selander Miller is the mother of two fully grown and fiercely independent adults. When not hopscotching across the planet, Jeanne may be found beachside in Vero Beach, Florida, in the Adirondack Mountains of New York, or in the quintessential New England town of Peterborough, New Hampshire. She enjoys long walks on the beach, swimming, bicycling, yoga, gardening, cooking, and reading. Although her writing is often thought provoking as she too struggles with the issues of the day, she also engages in general tom-foolery and has been known to wag her sassy tongue and offer an opinion about just about anything, even when it hasn't been asked for.

Made in the USA
Columbia, SC
11 October 2021

46556510R00193